The Bitch–Proof Suit

a novel

De-ann Black

Toffee
Apple

Toffee Apple Publishing

Published by Toffee Apple Publishing

The Bitch–Proof Suit

First edition 2010

ISBN-13: 978-1-908072-07-8

Toffee
Apple

Toffee Apple Publishing

For Sebastian

THE BITCH PROOF SUIT

Contents

Introduction

Manhattan, New York

Bitching can destroy you. It's a process of erosion. Once the rust sets in you can kiss your ass goodbye. I knew the business bitches were waiting for me but I wasn't going down without a fight.

It had been raining during the night in Manhattan and the hot, early morning sunlight glinted off the streets, bathing the city in a brand new glow. The air was fresh with the scent of potential. That's what I was hoping for too — a fresh start, a chance to work on the other side of the world for a few months, and I was going after it, no holds barred. This was my big chance to work in Dublin, and I had a few reasons for wanting to go back to the Irish city, including one who was tall, dark and heartbreakingly luscious.

I hurried along the busy street at eight in the morning. I was running a fraction late, but I was armed to the teeth with everything I needed to succeed including one thing in particular — my bitch–proof

1

suit. In the world of fashion marketing, I was about to put my suit to the ultimate test when I vied against a boardroom full of killer heeled, conniving business bitches to win the top job assignment — to head the coolhunting department in the company's new office in Dublin, and settle a few scores at the same time.

I've worked in fashion marketing for years. I'm known as a coolhunter or futurehunter — someone who susses out what's going to be the next big thing. Call it a faze, call it a fad, I call it being able to see the potential in something new that people will like. In my case it's fashion. But back to the suit . . .

My marketing experience helped me create the perfect suit. A lot of work had gone into honing the precise look, the design, the exact tone of charcoal gray for the jacket and skirt, teamed with an arctic white blouse that made the most of my blonde hair, which was styled to a mid nape length and gave just the right balance of fierce gorgeousness. It was a suit by no specific designer. I preferred to use bespoke tailors and have my clothes made with twice the precision at half the price. No labels, no trends, just sheer cutting edge class. I was never model material (unless prettyish, medium height, slender but shapely blondes ever became fashionable on the designer runways), but the suit upgraded what I had to work with.

You could cut through glass with the sharpness of the jacket. It was a classic, two button, single breasted design that could be dressed up or down for day or evening. The stitching and finish, from the length of the sleeves to the specific shoulder styling, was perfection personified. The suit skimmed the figure fluidly, rather than hugged it tight, and created a shield that deflected and defended the wearer from incoming insults. What was there to snipe about? Surely not the longer line jacket that flattered every ass from all angles, or the smooth lapels that emphasized the female form without brazenly shoving it in your face. The hem of the perfectly cut, A–line skirt sliced just below the knee with no trace of hemming, and of course, on the derriere there was no hint of visible panty line. We shouldn't even be thinking about VPL at this level. It just doesn't happen.

The anonymity of the suit and accessories was paramount. No specific designer was crucial. And I chose my shoes carefully. My shoes have great heels. I could run the length of Brooklyn Bridge in them and back at a pace that would make grown men crumble. Imagine court shoes of the third millennium. Futuristic, functional and fabulous. Beat that you bitches.

Several of us were vying for the prime opportunity to work in Dublin's design metropolis. Mega bucks, prestige and the power to influence the core of the fashion industry were at stake. So, as you can imagine, no one was going to take the challenge lightly.

The unspeakably glamorous and influential Verde Valmont (pronounced Verdi), had already set the wheels in motion. As one of the New York directors, she'd flown over to Dublin with her assistant, Emer, to secure the ideal offices and start scouting for potential trendsetting designers. Verde was known to her friends as Vee–Vee, so you didn't hear that name very often.

If I got the job, I'd be working with Verde, the epitome of a prize bitch, who gave a whole new meaning to the phrase, fiercely ambitious — seriously. When she'd been refused the backing of the company's board of directors for one of her projects, she threatened to jump out of the window of the boardroom unless they relented and gave her exactly what she asked for. They'd still refused. Big mistake — on their part . . .

I was there at the meeting that day, and had I not witnessed it for myself, I'd never have believed it. Verde, seething with rage, called their bluff. Taking everyone by surprise, she jumped from the fourth storey office window, but with it being spring, all the ad banners and canopies were out, and when she jumped, to spite them I may add, the canopies broke her fall and she landed with an undignified thud on the sidewalk below, and then got up and came back in with nothing more than a broken wrist. Whether she knew the banners would

4

break her fall, we'll never know, but the boardroom backed down and she got what she wanted. That was over a year ago, and by all accounts her wrist still cracked whenever she wrote a check. She wore expensive bracelets and bangles to disguise the slightly wonky wrist bone. They rattled whenever she moved and always reminded me of the ticking croc in Peter Pan.

Taking a few deep breaths of fresh air, I headed into the building. In the elevator I guessed who would be there. Company bigwig, Randolph, would be chairing the meeting, as always. Anyone who abbreviated his name to Randy immediately highlighted themselves as an outsider. He had about as much sex appeal as a concrete lamppost, and was just as gray, inflexible and toweringly tall as one. The only surprising thing about Randolph was his age. He was sixty, but he'd been a silver fox for over thirty years. Those who worked for his company were accustomed to his distinguished persona. He was rather like a statue that stands in pride of place for decades and never changes. Everyone thought he'd still be chairing meetings ad infinitum.

One of the main contenders for the job, and my official Manhattan based nemesis, Marina DeMar, would be throwing down the gauntlet for sure. Marina recently swore she had Irish blood in her veins from her great, great, great grandmother's side of the family and therefore she should go to Dublin. Go figure. It was a blatant lie of course. Last season she'd been of French Canadian descent. I seriously doubted Marina had any blood in her. She was frighteningly pale, wafer thin, and when the air conditioning was at its coldest, her blue veins looked like a road map. Okay, so she was an ex–model, but she still looked like death warmed up.

Then there was Azuree. Like the other harpies drenched in cookie cutter fashions, Azuree had a degree in superficiality, her only qualification for the job. The last time we'd gone after the same assignment, she'd won, and had stuck a diamond spangled finger up at me as she left the meeting and headed for Milan. I swear if you looked beneath the designer clothes that draped her fabulous figure, you'd find a ninety percent silicone label on her somewhere.

Not that I'm against giving nature a helping hand, but it's just not for me. And in a room with polished wood floors and nothing but original artwork and first edition books, it seemed I was the only one to get the irony of the plastic asses seated on the antique chairs.

Around fifteen faces that looked like they wanted to rip my throat out, verbally or otherwise, were waiting in the executive floor office. The sun threatened to burn a hole through the large expanse of glass, but it probably knew better. The temperature was warm, but the atmosphere was cold as steel.

Marina DeMar was glaring daggers at me. Her eyes were telling me I was late. My eyes were warning her to think twice about opening her plum lipstick mouth to even hint at it. The moment passed. I walked the length of the boardroom. Silence. Not one word, just vibes that were so strong you could've signaled by satellite on the seething energy. Another day in the life of an independent bitch slayer. By the way, my name's Blue (Bluebell) Byrne. Welcome to my world.

Chapter One

If Looks Could Kill

The meeting kicked off with Verde. Oh yes, she was still in Dublin, but she wasn't going to let the vast expanse of half the globe get in the way. Just typical. She was taking part in the meeting in Manhattan via webcam and her wide blue eyes watched me from the computer monitor as I approached my seat. Her disapproval of me was clear judging by the expression on her pursed pink lips that looked like a pussycat's ass. Like I cared.

'Hi, Bluebell,' she said, with all the false brightness of a fake diamond. 'Can I give you a brief personal message from Dublin . . .?'

I steeled myself for the flack. Whenever Verde called me Bluebell, it signaled an incoming dose of verbal vitriol. But I was feeling good. Give it your best shot I thought to myself. Unfortunately, her first strike was well below the belt. It hit me like a sucker punch.

'Morgan says hi,' she said, in her usual honeyed, husky tone, without letting her smile falter.

Ventriloquists had nothing on Verde. 'We had dinner *again* together last night and he sends his, eh . . . his regards.'

Yeah, right. Like hell he did. Men like Morgan Daire should come with a warning. Beware. This man will rip your heart out and feed it to the vultures if you're ever stupid enough to fall for his Irish charm, dimpled smile, sparkling eyes the color of green absinthe and silky dark hair that makes him look like a roguish pirate rather than one of the top movers and shakers in Dublin. Six years ago I'd made that mistake, believing he was *the one*. I'd spent a year working in Dublin, building contacts, making progress in my career, and I'd stupidly let my guard down and invited him into my life. The biggest mistake I'd ever made.

Morgan was sharp. A Machiavellian bastard to the core. He'd argued that I'd judged him too harshly, that I couldn't see the real man behind the scathing facade. It was business, it wasn't personal, he'd said. If there's one phrase that makes me want to spit fire it's that one. How if it involves me is it not personal?

He'd had the audacity to say he was actually being kind and that there was no place for me in Dublin or a future for us. He'd effectively jumped on me from a great height, crushing my career aspirations, hopes and dreams in one fell swoop. If that was him being kind, I was in for one hell of a fight when I went back to

9

confront him, to continue where I'd left off, to challenge him on his home turf.

He'd raged at me the night I finally found the courage to pack my bags and leave him, and Dublin, behind. 'You're nothing but a marketing mercenary, Blue,' he'd shouted as I ran across the Ha'penny Bridge over the city's River Liffey. 'Go on, run home to New York where you belong.'

And so I did. I threw my mobile phone into the Liffey, got in my hire car and drove to the airport. It had been a harsh goodbye.

Anyway . . .

I smiled calmly at Verde, as if taking the message at face value. Had she scored a point? She wasn't sure, and that was enough for me. I decided to chalk it up to yet another bad experience of being within ten feet of her, even if she was only on a computer monitor. And if anything, it made me a hundred times more determined to get this job, so in the oddest way, she'd done me a favor.

Indecision is something that really bugs Verde. I could see her flicking her blunt cut, glossy auburn hair in mild annoyance. After a few minutes of Randolph's introduction to the meeting, Verde had another run at me, just to be sure she'd put the knife in deep enough. I bet she wondered if I'd found someone else. Maybe Morgan Daire was indeed history and I didn't give a damn about him. Of course, this wasn't true. The hurt had mellowed, but it still bothered me when I thought about him, and how things could have been.

'You're looking . . .' Verde began, and then she couldn't find anything snide to say about my appearance. The bitch–proof suit was working. She didn't know what to pick on. Okay, so she could have said I looked tired (which I didn't, but that usually deflates most women's confidence), in need of a facial (ditto), or anything else, but when I wear this suit, it seems to disconcert those who'd like to undermine me. And the beauty of it is, they can't quite pinpoint why — the whole thing is subliminal. All that happens is that they get a feeling of not being able to dish out their usual spiteful comments. It has that effect. You see, no one knows this suit is designed to fight off bitchy attacks and protect the wearer from venomous remarks. It works ninety percent of the time, which is a huge bonus as far as I'm concerned. Anything to help water down the verbal poison gets my vote.

I'd never told anyone here about my suit. It was my secret. If I even hinted to Verde about its design, I could risk ruining its effectiveness. And I'd never do that. In fact, I have variations on its theme. You can't possibly wear the same look all the time. It's not a uniform. So I've also got a basic black and a classic plaid — and even a red hot scarlet version for specific

11

occasions. However, I have to say, the gray ensemble is the ultimate bitch–proof suit, and I really needed it for the meeting.

Verde's voice sliced through the air. 'We all know why we're here. Fashion is in a rut. Our clients are relying on us to find out where the industry's future lies. We've got to go beyond our usual coolhunting territory and scan the globe for the next big thing.'

I started to tune out. It was like listening to the commercials before watching a movie. I wished she'd just cut to the chase. We always heard the same old blurb about how the company was built on being one step ahead of the pack. How fashion trends were more difficult to pin down than a firefly. Firefly my ass. Each decade of the twentieth century, barring the nineties, had a very specific look. Now it was my job to find out what the future looked like. Some call it coolhunting. I call it futurehunting. I've got a degree in marketing, studied fashion and design, and I'd merged these skills to carve a niche for myself in Randolph's marketing company as a new futurehunter. I'd worked for him since I was twenty, and for the past eight years I'd been searching for what was hot and predicting what the market wanted. This information was filtered down to the fashion designers and peripheral industries. Sometimes they used the data, sometimes not, but it was exciting to be part of the process.

'Blue, we'll start by hearing your take on things,' Verde said briskly.

Here we go, I thought. But I was ready.

'We've got to look to the future,' I said, sitting where I was, and keeping my notes firmly closed.

'You're not suggesting some stupid spacey fashions,' Marina chipped in.

'Hardly,' I said. 'Silver suits and space age wear isn't where the future lies. I wouldn't want to hit the shops dressed in aluminum regardless of the labels.'

'Women need something new,' said Randolph. He spread his arms and glanced around the boardroom. 'We all want something new.'

'Exactly,' I said. 'No one in this company has found it yet. Not in New York or anywhere else. I reckon Dublin's pretty cool — a cosmopolitan city where innovative ideas are bubbling under the surface. I want to be the one to find them.'

Verde cleared her throat, for attention and effect. 'Perhaps it's escaped your notice, Bluebell, but I'm in Dublin right now, working on that precise thing.'

'And you've been there since when . . .?' I said.

'January.'

'This is what . . . the beginning of summer? I haven't read any of your reports on finding the niche of fashion gold we're searching for, Verde.' I was sailing very close to the wind with this one.

If looks could kill, I'd be toes up in the bone yard.

Marina decided to throw her opinion into the ring, which thankfully took the heat of me. 'It was agreed last year that Dublin was an untapped source of designer talent, of fresh creations, and that's why Verde spearheaded the new offices there. We just need the right coolhunter to track them down.' She took a deep breath. The bitch was biting to get out. 'I have to agree with Blue's snide conjecture that you've failed miserably and that someone else, someone younger, needs to go there to do the real job. While of course you continue to run the show in Dublin behind the scenes.'

Not only was Marina standing on thin ice, she was skating her way down the slippery slope to nowhere fast. We all knew Marina was Randolph's protégé but even he had his limits. It was one thing to insinuate, it was quite another to say she'd failed miserably and then add the killer twist — that Verde was way past her sell–by–date. Call me shallow, but inside I was cheering. I was mentally wearing a little ra–ra skirt and waving my cheerleading pom poms in the air. Marina was out of the contest.

A moment's lull, like an icy breeze, wafted through the boardroom then disappeared rather like Marina's career was destined to do.

Across the table, Azuree was flicking through her notes and getting set to argue why she should go to the

Emerald Isle. For entertainment value alone, I didn't want to miss it. Judging by the tired glaze behind her eyes, she'd had precious little sleep the previous night. If I knew Azuree, she'd been cramming for the meeting like it was a college exam. A sure sign of an amateur. If she didn't know her marketing statistics by now, she wasn't up to the task. No amount of meticulously applied under eye concealer could hide the fact that she was out of her league.

One by one the main contenders for the job bit the proverbial dust.

'Right!' Randolph finally announced. 'I've had enough of this farce.' He nodded to Verde who made no bid to disagree. Clearly she'd had enough too. The stress of listening to fifteen pitches for glory had actually taken the glow off her face and her blush was more pallor than perfect. Randolph put his hands on the table, fists clenched. 'Blue. You're going to Dublin.'

'Thank you,' I said, smiling.

'And remember,' Verde added, 'fuck this up and you're history.'

With this bolstering thought, the meeting was over.

As everyone poured out of the boardroom, Randolph took me aside. 'I want you to contact someone when you get to Dublin. He's set up an office in the city. Sears Pearson.'

'Sears?' I said, momentarily dropping my guard. I hadn't heard that name in a long time.

He handed me a business card with the contact details. 'Look him up. Find out what he's up to. He's always been a ruthless son of a bitch.'

I took the card.

'E–mail me the details, Blue. Don't go through Verde.'

I nodded. He didn't have to explain. Sears and Verde had a history, not of love but of war. I never knew what the scandal was, but suffice to say, Sears hated her more than most.

I slipped the card into my bag and walked away. Sears Pearson. It was like hearing about a ghost from the past. He'd been the only one to offer any sympathy when I'd been screwed over in Dublin by Morgan. At the time, Sears was working freelance for Randolph in the Manhattan office, but then he struck out on his own. Our paths hadn't crossed since then. If he was in Dublin, then we were right on the money. There must be new designs, styles and fabrics to be gleaned in Ireland. Sears was one of the best coolhunters in the business and made a small fortune out of predicting future markets. He also happened to be heart–meltingly gorgeous. Blonde, over six foot tall, with sculptured features, a honed physique and style of dress that could only be described as timeless. You could take Sears and put him straight into one of those movies where the hero strides across the desert, golden hair and sapphire blue eyes glinting in the sunlight.

I'd never thought of Sears as potential relationship material when I'd worked with him. I'd sort of put him in the untouchable category, like my best friend, Harry. Harry was sublime. Women adored him. He worked in the city doing stockbroker stuff. We'd been friends since college and shared an apartment in Manhattan. Harry had promised to look after things while I was away fighting the dragons in Dublin. I'd been friends with him for too long for it to be anything else but platonic. I guess that's how I'd always thought about Sears, or was it? There was no time to even think about that. Dublin was beckoning. I had to get my act together.

I walked out of the boardroom.

'Fuck you!' Marina whispered as we passed in the doorway. Her eyes were almost alight with the hatred she felt for me.

I paused, and looked right at her. I've been told that the coldness of my pale gray eyes is soul destroying. I held her gaze.

Within seconds she backed down, flicking her hair, glancing at my bitch–proof suit that in close up was every bit as intimidating as at a distance. What was she going to criticize? The color, cut and everything about it was a shield against the typical bitch. No holes in this outfit, real or otherwise. I didn't have to say anything. She stomped off, her killer heels sounding like an empty echo on the polished wooden floor.

Paper tiger were the words that brushed through my thoughts as I heard the last of her disappear into the elevator. A deep breath later, I took a call on my phone from Randolph's assistant confirming my flight schedule to the one place I swore I'd never go back to. Six years ago I'd left Dublin behind, sure that I'd never return. It had almost destroyed me once, but hell . . . I love a challenge!

Chapter Two

She Who Daire's Wins

That night, my plane flew over Dublin. The lights of the city glistened through the clear evening air, and far below I could see the River Liffey snaking through the city center like dark liquid glass. Numerous bridges spanned the river, lit up in a multi colored display of fantasy, and traffic poured through the streets in a constant stream of bright lights. I could feel the sense of excitement rising up to meet me. I'd almost forgotten how spectacular it was. And I couldn't help wondering if Morgan Daire even remembered how our lives used to be before the deceit and betrayal that sent me running back to New York.

The plane swept around towards the airport, and I saw the unmistakable silhouette of Dublin's medieval Christ Church Cathedral rising from the thousand–year–old city. It had been one of the last places I'd seen the night I'd left. Still casting an impressive dark shadow upon the landscape, it felt like I'd never been away.

Seeing the city again, I could hardly wait to get back. This was my chance to have another go at success here. I used to love Dublin's timeless mix of ancient and modern culture. The contrasts were amazing — there was everything from futuristic glass structures and modern sculptures, to narrow cobbled streets and cosmopolitan squares alive with people and music. Dublin was such a continental assortment of styles and fashion. The future had to be down there somewhere.

When the plane landed at the airport I phoned Verde's office, confirming I'd arrived in Dublin, and took a taxi into the heart of the city. It was nine in the evening, but Verde's world never slept. My call was transferred and picked up by her assistant, Emer. I could hear a party atmosphere in the background. Emer had my hotel booking all arranged. I was glad she'd chosen my hotel as she was the type of PA who could organize a full scale fashion trip to Europe in a couple of well placed phone calls. Emer also settled for nothing less than the best, so I was booked into one of the top hotels overlooking the River Liffey with a magnificent view of the city.

Verde came on the line. 'Hi Blue. Welcome back to Dublin.' She sounded almost genuine and upbeat. Had she been at the champagne?

'I'm throwing a party this evening,' she said. 'You simply have to be here. It's just two minutes walk from your hotel. Emer has left the details at the hotel reception. It's going to be wild. Dress to kill.'

I could tell from her tone that it wasn't a straightforward social invitation. Nothing was ever straightforward with Verde. It was a 'be there or you're dead in the water' type of invitation. I couldn't refuse. Even after a long haul flight I couldn't possibly rain check the party, which was no doubt a company promo disguised as a celebration — Verde's specialty. And there would be a theme. There was always a theme.

Settling in at the hotel, I kicked off my shoes and tore open the envelope Emer had left for me. I might have guessed what the theme would be — incognito. Verde had a fascination for mystery and secrets — and deceit. I liked a bit of mystery myself, in moderation of course, but my instincts warned me that there was an underlying reason why she'd chosen this. Perhaps she had a surprise for me. Let's see . . .? Could it possibly involve Morgan Daire? I sensed it would. How could Verde resist throwing a party to dangle Morgan in front of me and gloat at my reaction? Hmm. Dress to kill, she'd said. Well, she asked for it . . .

Although I'd wanted a shower, a latte and a time machine so that I could extend the half hour I had to get ready for the party, I settled for two out of the three. I showered first and then ordered a latte from room service. I'd really wanted to flake out on the bed, which was completely sumptuous, just like the entire room. It even had its own small balcony. I slid open the glass doors and stepped out to admire the view. It was the most perfect summer evening — warm without so much as a whisper of a breeze, and vibrating with potential. I sipped the latte, but it was the thought of the night ahead that lifted my energy, and I mentally prepared what I'd wear for maximum impact. No bitch–proof suit tonight. I was saving it for another day. Besides, there was more than one way to skin a cat.

I knew the venue well, which was a distinct advantage. I'd had dinner and drinks there a few times with Morgan in what seemed like another life. I know you can't change the past, but you can change how you feel about it. I wasn't sure how I'd feel when I saw Morgan again. I imagined it would feel like that empty zone where there's nothing left to say, nothing to make it right. Or just sheer rage. Either option wouldn't be pretty, but I'd geared myself up to handle it — and hide it. After all, the theme was incognito.

Okay, so I wasn't going in disguise, but I had a trick up the sleeve of my sheer silver jacket. It was an ace card that I could only play once. I was banking on Morgan being there. I could almost taste the set up. Fine, I'd play along. Verde was a master of manipulation, but I was betting that Morgan Daire was playing in a league he just wasn't ready for.

The evening air felt warm against my skin as I walked the short distance from my hotel to the venue. There were lots of people about, and I paused for a moment to look at the reflections of the nightlife sparkling on the surface of the Liffey. It was good to be back.

Taking a steadying breath, I approached the entrance to the party. Through the glass doors I saw that it was busy with hundreds of people. Two doormen in evening suits welcomed me in, and I noted that my name was near the top of the guest list. The sounds of laughter, lively music, and the buzz that only Dublin can stir up pulled me in. I glanced around and up towards the second floor balcony where gilded lights hung down from an impossibly high ceiling. The decor was a heady mix of the Far East with velvet seats, cushions and exotic palms with subtle touches of Irish hospitality. I had to admit, it looked fantastic, and although I knew I was here to play Verde's contrived game, I couldn't help feeling like I really wanted to have fun. It arrived sooner than I'd imagined.

'Blue! Hi! Isn't this fabulous,' Verde said, homing in on me. She was head to toe in her ubiquitous black separates and had a cocktail glass in her carefully manicured hand. I didn't hear her wrist crack as she sipped her drink, but she was wearing gold bracelets to camouflage the damage. 'We've even got our very own cocktail,' she said, giving me no time to respond. 'It's a Dublin Manhattan Gold — you simply have to try a sip.'

As if on cue, a waiter offered me a glass of the amber liquid. I tasted it. 'It's delicious,' I said, smiling, and without a hint of a lie. Perhaps it was the lack of sleep, food or both, but this thing had a real kick in it and the effect was . . . rather good.

'I had it specially created. It's an intriguing mix of Irish whiskey, rum, triple sec and sweet vermouth — with just a hint of mystery,' she said in a confiding tone. 'Perfect for women like us, Blue.'

'Whatever it is, it tastes good,' I said, feeling that momentary conflict of extreme emotions whenever I encountered Verde having not met her for a while. At one end of the scale, I despised her two faced bitching, and at the other I felt almost sad that we weren't friends. To outsiders we appeared to be on close terms and she almost managed to fool me a few times when her ingenuous smile led me to believe that deep down she really liked me.

'I do love your hair,' she said. 'I don't think I've ever seen you wear it like that before. I hardly recognized you.'

'I felt like doing something different with it.'

She nodded approvingly. 'You should wear it in a chignon more often. Blondes can look so sophisticated with an up do, don't you think. And I adore the firefly.' She was referring to the sparkling clasp in my hair. It was an antique, and the wings were studded with diamante. Although not expensive, to me it was priceless, a sort of lucky charm I'd had for years.

'Wherever did you get that cocktail dress?' she asked, suddenly stepping back to admire my outfit.

'Oh this is just something I brought over with me. I keep it for special occasions.' It wasn't a lie, but it wasn't the full story either. When I'd been packing my bags for the trip, I'd come across some amazing clothes I hadn't worn since Dublin. In fact, this is where I'd originally bought them. I'd taken them back home with me to New York. They were too beautiful to throw away, but the memories were too raw to wear them again — until now. They'd been perfectly wrapped in the finest tissue paper and hidden in my wardrobe all this time. Without a second's thought, I'd added them to my luggage. Tonight I'd worn this particular dress for a very special reason. Morgan was in for a surprise.

'Fabulous, really fabulous,' said Verde. She linked her arm through mine. 'We should go and join the others.'

Within the sea of faces I didn't recognize anyone, and then, from the second floor balcony, I saw Morgan, or rather, I saw his reaction when he saw me. The fun was about to begin.

Verde and I made our way up the stairs. This was it. No turning back.

'Morgan's been so looking forward to seeing you again,' said Verde.

I shot her a glance.

She squeezed my arm tight and pulled me closer to her. 'Seriously,' she emphasized, her blue eyes unflinching.

I smiled. 'You know I don't believe a word you're saying.'

'Oh but you will. Morgan's got secrets — and I know them all,' she whispered.

He was standing at the top of the stairs, his intense green eyes reflecting that I'd chosen the right outfit. Like a ghost from the past, I was back to haunt the present. I was wearing the same sheer silver and black silk dress and jacket I'd worn the last time Morgan and I were ever together. I'd even worn my hair in the same way.

'Doesn't Blue look divine,' said Verde, depositing me right in front of him. At well over six feet tall he towered above both of us, and was a vision of brooding darkness in a well cut black suit and deep emerald shirt.

'Like a familiar stranger,' he murmured. The resonance of his rich tone sounded clear above the bustling noise of the party.

Hearing his seductive Dublin accent again almost took my breath away. Luckily, I could see he wasn't coping very well with meeting me again. The muscles in his jaw were tightening and I sensed that his instincts had hit him like a hammer striking glass. I'd just shattered whatever he'd been anticipating. I'd done my best to step back in time as if the past six years were but a moment away. I hadn't needed that time machine after all.

Unfortunately, I'd put so much thought into creating an effect on him, that I hadn't prepared myself for the effect he'd have on me. I'd thought I could walk right up to him, but it wasn't that simple. Outwardly I gave the impression of being ultra cool and confident, but inside I was a wreck. Okay, so I'd definitely rattled Morgan, but I felt myself being crushed just seeing him again. His hair was even sexier than before, with a few dark strands falling over his forehead, emphasizing his deep, green gaze. His face was more sculptured, and although his lips bore no hint of a smile, the dimples in his cheeks were a permanent feature of his inherent charm.

'Blue's going to be working with me for the next few months,' Verde said. 'She's heading up the coolhunting office. It's going to be fun.'

'Good luck,' Morgan said, meaning anything but that. It was a Dublin thing to wish someone good luck in an undertone that really meant — yeah right, no chance.

'I take it you think I've a snowball's chance in a furnace of finding success here this time,' I said bluntly, using one of his favorite expressions.

Morgan blinked. 'Clearly you've become more fiercely ambitious than Vee–Vee, so I withdraw any insinuations. I'm sure you'll be a wild success.'

My blood was burning. How dare he! But I didn't want to rise to the bait, which was obviously what he wanted.

'I'll take that as a compliment,' I said, smiling defiantly.

Suddenly, a man stepped from the crowd and swept me off my feet — literally. I gave a scream of surprise, and then laughed as I realized it was Murphy, one of the closest friends I'd had in Dublin. He was an incorrigible rogue of a man in his mid thirties who was highly influential in the city. Last time I'd seen him, he was being lauded as the next big name in the designer industry. He placed me down, kissed my hand and gave me a warm hug. I'd never been so pleased to have an

Irish welcome. I swear Morgan's eyes turned a deeper shade of green.

'Murphy!' I squealed, 'It's great to see you again.'

Verde glanced between us. She hadn't anticipated that I'd know anyone at the party, especially someone like Murphy who was an immensely popular designer on the fashion scene. Lean and lithe with wild auburn hair and a week's worth of stubble on his chin, he looked like the epitome of artistic cool. Often described as a modern classic talent, it was a label that suited him as perfectly as his elaborately designed cream shirt.

Murphy held me at arms length. 'Blue Byrne! You look great. What's it been, five, six years now? You don't look any different.'

'That's because she's wearing the same dress she wore the night she ran away,' Morgan said. He didn't even attempt to disguise the bitterness in his tone.

'I'm surprised you remember, considering what a bastard you were to her before,' Murphy snapped in his lilting, Dublin accent.

There was an explosive silence, but inside I was cheering. Murphy had said exactly what I'd love to have told Morgan.

'Were you anything more than an ingratiating arsehole, we'd settle this outside,' Morgan growled at Murphy, then walked away to the bar.

Murphy shrugged off the insult and focused his attention on me. 'How long are you going to be in Dublin?'

'Four months,' I said.

'Brilliant!'

An announcement on the P.A. system interrupted our conversation. 'I'd like to ask everyone to raise their glasses and drink a toast to Murphy. Congratulations on your new fashion collection.'

Someone beckoned Murphy over to a raised platform. Apparently this was just one of several events to publicize his autumn/winter collection.

Murphy glanced at Verde and then at Morgan who was watching us like a hawk from the bar. 'These people don't even like you,' Murphy said to me. 'Come on over here with me. We've got a lot to catch up on.' He took hold of my hand and led me away.

Verde called after me. 'Work starts tomorrow at eight, Bluebell. Don't be late.'

I turned and nodded, as Murphy pulled me into the hub of the crowd.

I couldn't have asked for a better slingshot into the local fashion scene. The evening was abuzz with the party spirit and everyone wanted to know who the woman was on Murphy's arm. And it was me. He'd hardly let go of me. By the end of the night I had about ten different business cards in my handbag to kick start my networking with the movers and shakers.

I finally persuaded Murphy to untether me so I could go to the ladies room. Verde walked in behind me. She'd obviously been watching and waiting for her moment. The lack of my bitch–proof suit was about to be put to the test.

'Congratulations Blue. Round one to you,' she said, fixing her hair in the mirror and then enveloping both of us in a bubble of expensive perfume as she spritzed it on lavishly. 'Morgan has already left fuming.'

Maybe it was the cocktails, but she seemed happy her plan hadn't worked.

'Is there something going on between you and Morgan I should know about?' I said.

'Oh there's definitely something going on between Morgan and me — but you really shouldn't know about it,' she said cryptically.

'A secret, is it?'

'Absolutely,' she said in a conspiratorial voice, drifting back into the party crowd.

I let her go. If there's one thing I'd learned from experience, it was that getting a secret out of Verde was the human equivalent of prying open Fort Knox. The only way to get the information was to find a key. You'd never force it out of her.

'What are your plans for accommodation?' Murphy asked at the end of the evening as we walked back to my hotel. He'd insisted on seeing me there safely.

'I'm going to live out of a suitcase for a couple of weeks, just to see how things settle at work, and then look for an apartment to rent.'

'I've got friends in the property market. Let me know and I'll help you arrange something.'

'Thanks.'

At that moment, Morgan's sleek black car revved up and parked opposite the hotel.

'Call me paranoid, but I think we're being watched,' Murphy said, with a twinkle of humor in his mischievous hazel eyes.

Wickedly, Murphy and I both smiled across at Morgan and waved. He drove off at speed.

'Arrogant arsehole,' Murphy muttered, and then took my arm, linked it with his, and walked me into the hotel. He kissed my hand flamboyantly, with charm and wit, and bid me goodnight.

It was something else I'd forgotten about Dublin — the almost chivalrous hand kissing and old fashioned gestures. I remembered I'd even had men kneel down and kiss my Italian suede boots, making me feel like a damsel from another era. To find such gestures, whether or not they were frivolous tongue in cheek and part of the Irish charm, was like finding a diamond in the rough. In today's world of slick bastards and commitment phobic guys, it was refreshingly heartfelt.

Harry phoned the hotel minutes after I got up to my room.

'How did things go with the wicked witch?' he asked, using his favorite nickname for Verde.

'She set me up.'

'Still as predictable as ever, huh?'

'She threw a party, and spun a web for me while she was at it.'

'I take it Morgan was there.'

I sighed wearily.

'Okay, what happened?'

'Verde invited him to the party. I knew she would, so I was ready.'

'How did you feel seeing him again? Had he got fat, gone to seed, lost some of that legendary Irish charm you said he had?'

'No, he's even more handsome and as darkly charming as ever. I felt completely distraught. You know that time we went to the funfair? How you practically forced me on to that stomach churning roller coaster?'

Harry laughed. 'And when you got off, you looked like you'd been through a wind tunnel at speed.'

'Well that's how I felt when I saw him again,' I paused. 'I'm so angry. I thought I could handle it, but I messed it up big style.'

'What have you been drinking?'

'Who said I'd been drinking?' I said, and then hiccuped

'Oh it was just a wild guess.'

'Cocktails. Dublin Manhattan Golds to be precise. And they're good.'

'Too good by the sounds of it.'

'Don't worry, you know the cocktail lifestyle isn't my scene. I just needed to let my hair down a little.'

I glanced in the mirror. Strands of hair were dangling down from my carefully sculptured chignon. I'd been dancing the night away with Murphy's crowd. Dubliners certainly knew how to party. I looked like a wild woman, and unclasped the firefly to let my hair tumble free.

'So what's on the agenda tomorrow? Is Verde still running the show over there?'

'Pretty much, but I'm going to have my own office and I'll be heading the actual futurehunting,' I explained, recounting the details Emer had left for me. 'Despite everything, I'm looking forward to it. I met Murphy at the party. He's a fashion designer I used to know, and we've arranged to meet up. He's promised to give me the lowdown on what's happening on the design front in Dublin. We're having breakfast in one of my favorite places tomorrow. It's a traditional Irish cafe. I used to go there all the time. They serve the most delicious Dublin breakfasts.'

'You're making me jealous already.'

'Scrumptious, freshly baked soda bread and pancakes served with —'

'Your ass will get fat.'

'It will not.'

'It will, you're ass will triple like an overdone soufflé.'

I laughed. 'I lost weight the last time I was here. A diet of heartbreak, stress and harassment works for me,' I said, half joking. 'If anyone's going to get fat it's you because I won't be there to make sure you eat properly.'

We both laughed. Harry was a stickler for eating right and had membership of two gyms. He didn't have an ounce of fat on him.

'What time is it in Manhattan?' I asked, suddenly feeling a twinge of homesickness.

'Time you got some sleep. I'll bet Verde's going to be cracking the whip bright and early tomorrow.'

He was right, of course, as usual.

'Okay,' I said. 'Be good. Don't do anything I wouldn't do.'

'As if,' he said. I could hear the smile in his voice. 'And remember — don't let the Irish charmer get to you.'

'Never,' I assured him, hoping this was true.

Chapter Three

Secrets and Spite

'Verde says Morgan's got secrets. Have you any idea what they are?' I said to Murphy, and then munched into a freshly baked peach croissant. We were having breakfast in a cafe that was a heartbeat away from the River Liffey's boardwalk. It was one of those clear summer mornings, and we were sitting outside, shaded from the bright sunlight by a cool, green canopy.

Murphy poured us another cup of traditional Irish breakfast tea.

'She could be talking shite,' he said, stirring two generous spoonfuls of sugar into his tea.

'No, she's up to something. I can sense it.' I glanced across the river at the second storey windows of the office complex in the area known as Temple Bar where I'd be working with Verde. No lights, no movement, no one was in yet.

'When is she ever not up to something?' he said. 'The woman's a magnet for trouble — and so I may add are you.'

I blinked at him.

'Oh don't go looking like I've insulted you. You know fine what I'm saying. Morgan Daire and you were the fiasco of the moment the last time you were in Dublin. And with the raucous gossip and scandal–mongering that goes on here, believe me that takes some doing.'

'I don't often go looking for trouble,' I said in my defense. I was careful not to say I *never* went looking for trouble because that would've been a blatant lie. I was playing with fire just being back in Dublin near Morgan again.

Murphy viewed me with friendly suspicion. 'So why are you here?'

'To futurehunt. I'm heading up the marketing side of the new offices Verde set up —'

'No, why are you *really* here?'

'I'm here to find new fashion trends —'

'Listen,' he said, 'this is me you're talking to. Ditch the business spiel. Maybe you *are* here to find the latest designs, and probably to get one over on Verde, but that's not your only reason, is it? I'm guessing you're here to rake over the old coals, to settle a score with Morgan and lay some ghosts to rest. Don't tell me you're not bothered about what that cheating bastard did to you.'

He was right. Damn him! Morgan had been a tough businessman. Among other things, he owned several fashion boutiques, and although he didn't design any of the clothes, he had the best people working for him to keep him at the front of the trendsetters. Unfortunately fate played a cruel joke on me, and I became romantically involved with the one man who ended up being my main rival. Morgan's people were confident they'd discovered the next big thing in women's evening wear, but I'd already confided in him one night what I thought the market would want. And he stole my ideas. He denied it, but I didn't believe him. Then of course he'd added insult to injury by saying I was better off running back to New York where I belonged. If only I'd stayed and fought him. I really wish I had.

Murphy bit into a slice of buttered soda bread, and then sat back and gestured that he was waiting on the lowdown.

I sighed reluctantly. 'Well of course it bothers me, it's always bothered me. It's bothered me for six years. There, I've admitted it! Okay?'

He nodded. 'Okay, so what's your game plan?'

'I don't have one.'

He cupped his hand and held it up to his ear. 'I'm sorry, I didn't quite catch that. It sounded like you said you didn't have a plan.'

I took a sip of tea. 'I just want . . . I want Morgan to admit that he was wrong. He couldn't stand that I was his equal, that I was as good a futurehunter as any of the people he had working for him.'

'Is that all?' Murphy said sarcastically.

'Pretty much.' I ate the last bite of my croissant.

'I'll ask around, see what's happening on the gossip front,' he said. 'If he's been up to no good I'll soon find out about it.'

'Maybe Morgan's involved with Verde?' I said reluctantly. 'She told me they'd been having dinner together — and he calls her Vee–Vee.'

'I'm no expert on Morgan Daire's love life, but he's never struck me as being a rampant womanizer.' Murphy paused and considered. 'Though I've never thought of Verde as a woman. She's more like a cross between a heartless android and a cobra.'

'You always did make me smile,' I said.

He smiled back at me and leaned closer across the table. 'What we need is information,' he said, sounding as if we were planning some wild conspiracy.

I nodded. 'I'd love to know about the skeletons hanging in Verde's designer wardrobe.'

'I'm sure if we peeled back the layers of lies and two faced manipulation, we'd find that she's fueled by money, power or spite.' He paused. 'I can find out a bit about Morgan's financial situation, nothing illegal you understand, but we'll need someone who's brilliant at maths and understands the stock market to analyze the information. Number crunching was never my thing.'

'Harry!'

Murphy frowned.

'He's a friend of mine. We share an apartment in New York,' I said.

Murphy's eyebrows raised as his imagination ran riot.

'No, we're just friends. Harry's . . . well, Harry . . . and he's the best number cruncher I know.'

Murphy nodded and smiled. 'Great, we have a plan.'

'Now all we need is the luck of the devil,' I said.

Murphy winked at me. 'No, just the luck of the Irish.'

A light suddenly lit up Verde's office. Murphy noticed it too. I checked the time on the cafe clock. Two minutes to eight. I was late.

'It's showtime,' Murphy announced, his voice filled with a humorous lilt.

I picked up my laptop computer. 'I have to run.'

'Love the suit by the way,' he said, giving me a wink.

'Thanks, Murphy. I'll call you later.' I kissed him on the cheek, and made a dash for the Ha'penny Bridge, a pedestrian only bridge, and one of Dublin's famous historic landmarks. I hurried like mad and when I was halfway across, it dawned on me that here I was again, running across the footbridge, only I was heading in the opposite direction this time. It felt like events had gone full circle, and I was getting nearer to unraveling the past.

I arrived in the office complex only a fraction late. And yes, I was wearing my bitch–proof suit — the gray one, for maximum effect. My futuristic court shoes had added to my swift pace. See, I could've run the length of Brooklyn Bridge after all. The shoes had even navigated the cobbled street in front of the office building in Temple Bar, Dublin's cultural quarter.

Verde had leased out four offices within the complex. Temple Bar was renowned as one of the most popular 'party areas' of the city, filled with wonderful restaurants, bars, shops and nightclubs. It was right in the hub of things and there was a real buzz of excitement there — perfect for any futurehunter with an eye for people watching. The streets were narrow, cobbled and steeped in medieval architecture, but the atmosphere was that of a cosmopolitan city on the cutting edge of fashion. During the day it was bustling with shoppers, and in the evening the nightlife ranged from funky to fabulous.

I went into the complex. Verde had an office to herself, and the others were commandeered by her assistant, Emer, who was the first to greet me. I'd met her before in Manhattan.

Although Emer was Irish, she'd worked for Verde in New York for two years. By all accounts this was a record. Most of Verde's personal assistants lasted two days max.

'Verde's spitting fire,' Emer said dryly. 'I'd have an elaborate excuse if I were you.'

'Thanks,' I whispered.

Verde's office had a view of the river — and I could see the cafe I'd just had breakfast at. It was a fair distance across, but I wondered if she'd been watching Murphy and me. I'd read once that a hawk can spot its prey at quite a distance. And Verde had a distinct hawkish glint in her eyes this morning.

'I hear you went back to your hotel last night with Murphy,' she began. 'Please don't let any nocturnal shenanigans interfere with your work schedule.'

I let out the loudest guffaw, which was so unlike me. I never do things like that but hearing a diva like Verde Valmont say 'nocturnal shenanigans' made me want to roll around laughing. The Dublin jargon was getting to her.

'I'm thrilled you find your tardiness amusing, Bluebell,' she said, looking me up and down.

I paused, waiting for any bitchy comments.

Nope, the suit was working yet again.

She shuffled a pile of papers on her desk. 'You're in the office through there.' She pointed a finger with a beautifully manicured green nail at an office across the hallway. Oh yes, I thought, Dublin was definitely getting to her.

My office was basic but it had potential. From my window I could look down on the street and watch the world go by. For most people, this would be considered slacking on the job, but for a futurehunter searching for new trends in clothing it was a virtual goldmine.

I was gazing at the view and familiarizing myself with my surroundings when I heard Morgan's voice.

'So this is where all the action takes place, Vee–Vee. I always wondered what the control center for Randolph's business looked like.'

'Morgan!' Verde said, sounding thrilled. 'What a lovely surprise. Come in. Would you like a latte?' Her voice trailed off as the door to her office closed behind him. It was a strain to eavesdrop, but I managed it. Okay, so I was loitering near the hall. Come on, wouldn't you?

Morgan had turned down the offer of a coffee, thank goodness, because Emer would've been sent to get it and I'd have got caught listening.

Verde chattered about the usual stuff, how good it was to see him, he got the brief tour of her office and what she was doing, yadda, yadda. Obviously he'd really taken her by surprise. Finally the polite chit chat got interesting — and I had to run for cover.

'Is Blue working from here too?' he asked, sounding nonchalant, but I knew that double edged tone of his. He was fishing for information.

'Bluebell's right through there,' Verde said, sounding a little deflated. 'Blue!' she called through to me. 'Morgan's here.'

I dashed to my desk, opened up my laptop and pretended to check my e–mail. There was a mail from Harry, but I didn't dare open it in case Morgan saw what it said. Verde had eyes like a hawk, but she was short sighted in comparison to Morgan. He could glance at a room and tell you the ballpark price of the fixtures, fittings and people who were in it. No one could sum up consumerism quite like him. He missed nothing. And judging by the subject heading of Harry's mail — *is your ass getting fat yet?* — I didn't want him prying.

I turned the laptop screen towards the window, and looked up to find Morgan standing in the doorway watching me. His tall, broad shouldered stature seemed to fill it. He was wearing a black shirt and dark trousers that screamed casual but rich.

I hoped my bitch–proof suit would hold up to his scrutinizing gaze.

'Quite the chameleon, aren't you,' he said.

I blinked. 'Whatever do you mean?' I knew fine what he meant. Last night I'd been dressed as the old me, and now I was the woman I'd become.

'You look every inch the business woman,' he said. 'Except . . .'

Inside my stomach gave a jolt. 'What?' Had he sussed out the secrets of my suit? If anyone on the planet was savvy enough, it was him.

'I can't quite figure it out . . . it's like . . .' he seemed lost for words. This was a first!

I walked towards him, suddenly feeling a surge of confidence. I could see his eyes flick from my white blouse, gray jacket, gray skirt, black shoes, taking in every detail, calculating the finish and cut of the fabric. I sensed he was trying to figure out who'd designed the outfit and was coming up blank. If his brain had been a computer at that moment, he'd have had to re–boot.

'Like what?' I said, forcing the issue. In the quirkiest way I wanted his thoughts on it. It shouldn't have mattered to me, but it did. Morgan always had all the right answers, but I was wearing the fashionable equivalent of a conundrum.

'Your clothes look perfect but I get the feeling . . .' he shrugged those broad shoulders of his. 'I can't quite put my finger on it.'

Yes! I know it was shallow of me, but this made my day.

'I don't recognize the designer,' he said, circling me like a predatory tiger. 'A new talent in New York?'

I smiled sweetly. 'You could say that.'

'Ah here you are, Morgan,' Verde said, curtailing our conversation. 'Come and have a look at the marketing plans for the summer fashion event. I need you to approve the press release.' She turned and presented me with a copy. 'Morgan's holding a fabulous extravaganza at the marina in Dun Laoghaire. *Everyone's* going to be there.'

Dun Laoghaire (which the press release helpfully told me was pronounced Dun Leary) was renowned as Dublin's Riviera. The marina was set beside the Irish Sea and there were palm trees and lush green headlands, giving a continental feel to the town. Morgan had taken me there a few times. It was a short drive south, down the coast from the city. He owned a mansion there. A castellated mansion to be precise. Very exclusive.

'We're organizing a spectacular yachting event, speedboat race, and fashion show,' Verde said, sounding like a line from her own press release. 'It's going to be totally glamorous.'

Before I could glean any further details, Verde wafted out of my office, still chattering away to Morgan who was following in her perfumed wake.

I glanced at the press release. One name jumped out at me — Sears Pearson. He was competing in the yacht race. This I had to see! If Sears hadn't gone into business, he could've been a top yachtsman. He went sailing off the coast of New York and had offered to take me out once, but I'd refused, mainly because I never quite knew where I stood with Sears. Putting him in the untouchable category worked well for me.

I was searching for the business card Randolph had given me, the one with Sears' contact details, when Morgan stepped back into the doorway of my office. 'See you later,' he said, and then looked at me with secretly amusing curiosity. 'And your arse doesn't look big to me.'

What?

Morgan hurried away.

What the . . . and then it dawned on me. Harry's e–mail. He'd seen it! Damn! Damn! Damn! I snapped the laptop shut, and that's when I saw the note on my desk — the only piece of paper on the empty surface. I picked it up and read it.

Meet me in half an hour at the money tree. It was signed, *Morgan.*

The money tree! I'd forgotten all about that. It was a metal, tree like sculpture that stood near one of the banks on Dame Street. Morgan and I used to meet there, and this was his nickname for it. He thought it was strangely romantic, and so did I at the time. But to meet him there after all these years seemed heartbreaking. Why couldn't he have said meet me outside Trinity College, the cathedral, Dublin Castle, even the Ha'penny Bridge, anywhere but there. Even after all this time the memories were still raw, and it seemed like I was living in a weird reality where I could see the happiness of the past and the emptiness of the future like parallel worlds.

I decided, fuck him, I'm not going. Meet him there? He could kiss my ass! And then I reconsidered. If I could actually go there, then I really had put the past behind me. I figured it would be horribly good for me — if I survived with my soul intact.

Temple Bar was living up to its reputation as one of the trendiest areas in the city. I'd already been distracted by a selection of gorgeous scarves and accessories hanging in one of the shops, and there was a new jewelry exhibition in an art gallery that I aimed to see later.

I paused outside one of the cafes which was minutes away from the tree sculpture and checked my reflection in the window. Although Morgan had already seen me and my bitch–proof suit, I was feeling nervous and excited. It was the thought of going back to our special meeting place that was twisting my insides like a pretzel.

I glanced at the time on my watch, but it thought it was night time in New York and wasn't functioning very well. I was functioning only mildly better — but at least I was having a good hair day. I'd washed my hair early in the morning, and the local water had a wonderful effect on the condition. I looked particularly blonde, but not in a trashy way. Deep down I'm a dark blonde with potential to brighten to a pale gold during the summer months. But I mainly rely on a glistening blonde colorant that my hairdresser mixes to perfection in four delicious shades of highlights that transform me into a Viking bombshell (okay, so the New York version of it). Champagne, arctic cognac, beige truffle and crème de parfait was the magic blend. A potent blonde concoction that always sounded good enough to drink. Maybe Verde could use it as inspiration for a cocktail.

I hurried on up to the money tree, but there was no sign of Morgan. Good. I wanted a moment to compose myself. It really did feel strange standing there again. I looked around me. Dame Street was one of the main thoroughfares in the city, and it was busy with the rush of traffic and shoppers.

Because I was feeling nervous, I jumped when my phone rang. It was Murphy.

'Verde was right. Morgan does have secrets,' he said, his voice full of excitement. 'I've been talking to one of my most reliable gossip–mongers and they've told me everything.'

'Tell me,' I said, 'I'm meeting up with him.'

'No way, I want to see your face when I tell you,' he said. 'I've got to have some fun. One secret in particular — it's a corker!'

'At least give me a hint,' I said urgently, while keeping a lookout for Morgan in the crowd.

'We'll have dinner tonight and I'll explain everything,' Murphy promised.

'Can't you just tell me one of his secrets —?'

'Am I late?' Morgan said over my shoulder.

'Okay,' I said into my phone, trying to sound businesslike. 'I'll get back to you about that later. Sounds intriguing.'

Morgan's gorgeous green eyes viewed me with vague suspicion. 'It certainly does . . .'

Chapter Four

Head for the Malls

'Don't hang up!' Murphy shouted down the phone. 'Morgan's there, isn't he?'

'Oh yes,' I said, smiling tightly.

'Does he suspect you were talking about him?'

'Absolutely.'

'Then whatever you do, don't hang up,' Murphy insisted. 'If you do, he'll know you're lying through your teeth. This early on in the game you can't afford to let that toe rag score a single point.'

'Okay,' I agreed, pressing the phone firmly to my ear so there was no chance of Morgan overhearing the merest whisper from my partner in gossiping crime. I just knew I shouldn't have worn earrings today but if you're going to have a gold hallmark impression scrunched into your earlobe at least it's better to have a classic twenty–four carat one.

'We've got to throw some doubt into the mix,' Murphy said in a voice that made me believe he was a master at it. 'So let's chat for a minute as if we're not a pair of scandal–mongering gossips.'

The way he said it made me smile and for a moment I saw a flicker of doubt in Morgan's deep gaze. He'd been certain that I was talking about him and his secrets but now he wasn't so sure. Yes! I could feel my guilty syndrome wafting away in the light summer breeze and the triumphant swoosh as the ball landed back in my court.

'Bring a copy of the new designs and we'll discuss them over dinner tonight,' I said, hinting to Murphy that I would have dinner with him.

'Eight o'clock. Our favorite restaurant. The one where you categorically denied falling down the stairs tipsy on too much champagne and flashing your frillies to all and sundry. My treat.'

'I'll be there. Looking forward to it,' I confirmed brightly.

'Quite the socialite,' Morgan snapped at me. 'You don't waste any time getting back into the life here do you?'

I smiled sweetly and continued my conversation with Murphy. 'See you at eight. And if you have those financial figures, bring them with you.'

'I've got some of them, enough for your number cruncher friend to work on.'

'Great. I'll tell Harry.'

'Is Morgan's blood boiling yet?' Murphy asked.

I shot a cool gray glance up at Morgan. 'Oh definitely.'

Murphy laughed like a demon and even with the phone glued to my ear Morgan overheard him and began pacing like an agitated panther.

'Want to add the killer crunch?'

'You know me,' I said, not quite realizing that Murphy was indeed going for the jugular with his next suggestion.

'Repeat after me . . . sounds great, Sears, and it'll be so good to see you again.'

I almost gasped. Sears? As in Pearson? I could feel my sorry ass sprouting chicken feathers. The warring vibes between Sears Pearson and Verde was nothing in comparison to the ferocious bitterness between Sears and Morgan. When I'd run back to Manhattan and Sears had been a shoulder to cry on, he'd made a few phone calls to contacts in the fashion industry that hit Morgan where it hurt most — in the wallet. I never found out exactly what Sears did but even Verde had grudgingly admitted that Sears had effectively hung Morgan's financial laundry out in the wind to twist. It had been a big power play by Sears. Morgan hadn't forgotten it and he could hold a grudge for years.

'Hurry up and say it,' Murphy urged me.

And so I did. I even said it with a trill in my voice. 'Sounds great, Sears, and it'll be so good to see you again.'

Kapow! It hit Morgan like a heavyweight fist right in his ego. I gave him five seconds before he stomped off. Okay, two seconds. One for the penny to drop that I'd been talking to Sears Pearson and the other one for his rage to kick in.

'I'll talk to you another time,' Morgan growled at me. 'When you can fit me into your busy, bloody high life schedule!' He stomped off, the muscles in his broad back taut with rage underneath his black shirt.

'Has he fucked off?' Murphy asked hopefully.

'With smoke pouring from his ears. We've definitely thrown him a curve ball.'

'Never let a man catch you gossiping behind his back,' Murphy advised sagely, 'especially an egotistical swine like Morgan Daire.'

'Never,' I assured him, with every intention of keeping my word, and suddenly feeling better about standing beside the money tree with its memories cast in metal.

'I'll see you tonight, Blue.'

'I'll be there, but tell me just one of his secrets, even a hint of scandal–mongering.'

'Okay, just one secret . . .'

I held my breath.

'Sears Pearson is looking for you.'

Maybe I needed a latte but I couldn't immediately see the connection. 'What's that got to do with Morgan?'

'Morgan's already warned Sears to stay away from you. Sears saw you leave the party last night with a tall, dark, handsome hunk — that would be me,' Murphy added before I had a chance to unintentionally insult him by denying any such thing. 'And he saw Morgan sulking nearby in his car and went over for an unfriendly chat —'

'Sears had the guts to approach Morgan?'

'Apparently the two of them almost came to blows.'

'There was a fight?' I shrieked and then noticed a few passers by eyeing me with suspicion, so I walked away from the money tree and headed for the nearby shoppers paradise, otherwise known as Grafton Street, that's simply loaded with all the top brands.

'No fisticuffs but very close,' Murphy said. 'Not sure who my money would've been on. Morgan's Irish temper versus Sears' New York savvy. I'd have paid for a front row seat to see that skirmish. Anyway, I've got to dash. See you tonight, Blue. Oh and wear something devastating.'

Devastating? I'd need to give that some thought later. Hopefully I'd packed *devastating* along with *trouble making* (the one hit wonder I'd worn last night), and a *doozie* I was saving for extreme emergencies. Flaunting my booty isn't my style, especially as there's precious little about my ass that's worth showcasing in public, but sometimes you've got to go for the hard sell particularly in the fashion business where your butt can literally be on the line.

I walked on. At the corner of Dame Street I suddenly felt the rush of energy and heard the buzz of the crowds in Grafton Street, but my mind was still visualizing Morgan and Sears having a set–to. I wasn't sure who my money would've been on either. Probably me — and not because I've dabbled in martial arts, but because I hate it when men like Morgan take it upon themselves to veto who can and cannot contact me. How dare he! I'd have pounced on him (and not in a sexy way) claws flailing. Jet lag and six years of heartache and wanting to get even is a powerful cocktail. Yes the smart money would've been on me.

When I say I've dabbled in martial arts that's exactly what I mean, thus the claws flailing rather than any slick kicks right in his family jewels. I've been to various kickboxing and jiu–jitsu classes on and off for years. Nothing serious. The only black belt I've got is in shopping.

Speaking of which, Grafton Street was just as fabulous as I remembered, maybe even better. The sunshine had brought people out in their droves and the majority looked like they'd made an effort to appear trendy. Or colorful. Or both.

The whole street was pedestrianized. It was bordered by narrow side streets and flower sellers whose extensive floral displays filled the air with a heady fragrance. It was like an aromatherapy treat for shoppers. In the past I'd walked by and breathed in the exhilarating scents and it had always given me the boost I'd needed to continue shop trekking — every futurehunter's forte. The streets were where the real trends emerged.

I gazed around me, almost motionless as the crowds flowed by, the sights and sounds familiar as ever. I'd hardly been in Dublin a day and yet here I was, standing in the hub of the city again, as if time had simply folded over like the single page of a favorite book. I was back as if I'd never been away. And I was glad. I was so glad. And I was hopeful for the first time in a long while. Hopeful of what? I didn't know. Just the sense you get when life feels brighter.

'Flowers, dearie? Would you like some fresh flowers?' one of the sellers said, smiling at me.

I blinked. 'Eh, yes, I would,' I said to her, almost dazzled by the vast selection of scents and colors.

'What kind would you like?' she asked.

I couldn't even begin to decide. 'What would you recommend?'

She held up two beautiful bunches of vibrant colored flowers. One was yellow with a rich brown center and lush greenery. 'These are a bit special.'

I leaned close. 'They smell of chocolate!'

She smiled broadly. 'They're chocolate daisies. Don't know if you've got them in New York.'

New York? 'Is it that obvious?' I said. Okay, so she knew I had an American accent but she'd nailed me right.

'Thousands of tourists come past here every year,' she explained. 'You get to recognize the main regions. And you look like you're a New York . . .'

Her words trailed off and I saw her eyeing my suit. She didn't know what to call me. A diva? Fashionista? Career woman?

I took the daisies. Anything that combined flowers and chocolate got my vote. Then I looked at the other bunch of flowers — deep burgundy, violet and velvety purple flowers with cool green foliage. I'd noticed that quite a few people were wearing these muted burgundy and plum tones, either as tops or accessories, which struck me as unusual because these colors are associated with the autumn rather than the summer. Was I seeing a future trend?

'These are very popular,' the woman said, noticing my interest.

'More of an autumn selection I'd have thought?' I said, fishing for an insight.

'Not this year,' she said. 'People seem to have a fad for deep purple flowers. They're even wearing dark purples. See?' She pointed to someone walking past whose handbag was the color of mulled wine. And so were her tights, worn with pumps, a long line plum colored t–shirt and short skirt. Quirky but it worked.

I took both bunches of flowers. A treat for me and work combined.

Before she handed the two bunches over, the seller added a couple of reddish purple flowers that looked like long tassels with a texture like chenille and multicolored greenery. 'For luck,' she said.

'The colors are beautiful,' I said. 'What are they?'

'Amaranth flowers. Love–lies–bleeding. They're everlasting. The color never fades.'

'Love–lies–bleeding,' I murmured.

'For love that's wounded but has never really died.'

She looked right at me as she said this and for a moment I had the strangest feeling she could see right through me. I remembered that the Dublin streets had quite a few fortune tellers and I'd often been tempted to cross their palms with silver. However I was never sure whether I really believed in horoscopes and fortunes, or perhaps I was worried I'd believe too deeply, especially if they were accurate in their reading.

I paid for the flowers and went to walk away. Then I stopped. 'I have to ask,' I said boldly. 'Was there some reason for giving me Amaranth? Is there something about me, something you see or sense?'

'It's the weirdest thing,' she said thoughtfully, quite happy to answer, but clearly unable to explain what it was. 'You look . . .' She shrugged. 'I can't quite fathom it to tell you the truth. I pride myself on being able to sum up a person in the blink of an eye, but with you . . .' She shrugged again, and smiled. 'Maybe you've got too many men in your life.'

'Excuse me?' I said. 'I've got too many men in my life?' I didn't have any men in my life. None, zilch, nadda. Except for Harry, who was a friend, and Murphy ditto . . . and Morgan but he didn't count because he'd been out of my life for so long . . . and I supposed if I really thought about it there was Sears . . . but no one special, no man who was my man.

'What makes you think I've got too many men in my life?' My senses were jangled and I announced it too loud. The disapproving glare I received from a woman walking past screamed — floozie! Then her busybody eyes caught the full impact of my bitch–proof suit and as if someone had flicked a switch, a glazed expression of

61

non comprehension replaced the steely eyed glare. Did I look like a floozie? Not in this damn suit!

The flower seller regained my full attention. 'Men cause confusion in the best of us,' she said, as if I should know what she was getting at. In a way I did and in another way I totally didn't. Jeez! I wished I'd bought the freesias and been done with it!

I walked away, feeling anxious, looking at the love–lies–bleeding and torturing myself with thoughts of how my relationship with Morgan had been summed up by a total stranger selling flowers!

What had Morgan wanted anyway? I'd been too busy scoring points against him at the money tree to hear what the hell he'd wanted. Murphy had a lot to answer for.

I needed a latte and headed to St Stephen's Green shopping center at the top of Grafton Street. The center was a stylish glass atrium filled with shops, restaurants and cafes where I planned to succumb to a coffee and a slice of chocolate cake. Damn those yummy smelling daisies!

Harry's e–mail wafted into my thoughts along with the delicious scent of freshly made coffee as I took the escalator from the ground floor to the self service, cosmopolitan style cafe. Would my ass get fat from eating scrumptious chocolate gateau? Would it expand like a soufflé? My ass, not the cake. I doubted it. I probably wouldn't tell him anyway, and I definitely wouldn't tell him that I was about to attempt making my specialty cappulatte, as he jokingly called it, from the self service coffee and tea counter. As its name suggests, it's a cross between a cappuccino and a latte — with sprinkles, created through sheer serendipity at a coffee house in Manhattan where subsequently the welcome mat had been whipped out from under me. A serendipity sounds better than confessing that pressing the right buttons on self service gadgets usually results in disaster for me and the machine. It's just one of those things. Like the umbrella in the rain thing but don't get me started on that one.

The fact that a five–year–old kid can press the right buttons on the orange juicer and I can't handle an equivalent set up without causing a mess and a fuss was severely disheartening. Until you've been visually scolded by a little kid for making a frothy mess of your espresso in public, you've never truly been dissed.

Before I had time to cause a shaving cream style froth fest, my phone rang. It was the office in Temple Bar. I assumed it would be Verde cracking the whip, but I was wrong.

'Hello, Blue, it's Emer. Just a quick warning. Sears Pearson's hunting for you.'

I'm sure she hadn't deliberately intended causing my stomach to do a triple somersault. Emer was oddly straightforward. Possibly that's why she'd survived working for so long as Verde's PA. If both of them had been twisted it wouldn't have been efficient for business. So if Emer said Sears was hunting for me that's exactly what he was doing.

'Luckily I took the call,' Emer said. 'If Verde had picked up, well . . .'

We both knew that encounter would have caused a shit storm of trouble. Frankly, Sears had taken a chance calling the office. Verde would've gone into meltdown. They hadn't spoken since their so–called battle royale, the nitty–gritty details of which I'd yet to glean.

'If I were you,' Emer advised, without me having said a word, 'I'd head for the malls. He knows you're out and about in the city center. Blend, Blue, blend.'

I heard Verde's voice perk up in the background, followed by some mumbling and accusations and then Emer said to me. 'The Internet connection in your office has been fixed, Blue. Everything's working fine now. Okay, byeee.' And she was gone.

I glanced furtively around me suddenly feeling like I was being watched, which was crazy, but crazy sometimes works for me. Now it was true that I was going to contact Sears anyway. Randolph wanted to know what he was up to, and I was keen to see Sears again. After all, we'd been good friends before he'd left

Randolph's company and we'd never officially been rivals. Had we? I searched my memory for any shred of evidence that would prove otherwise. No. He was one of the best coolhunters in the business and I was . . . well, I was doing very well thank you. The rumor that Sears had been pissed with me at New Year when I beat him to one particularly lucrative deal was probably a big fat lie.

Chapter Five

Bar Brawling and Atrocious Lies

Big fat lies aside I still felt I was being watched. I picked up a patisserie menu and tried to trick myself into concentrating on the cake selection rather than escalate the sense of paranoia. Of course I wasn't being spied on. Hmm, chocca mocha cake with fresh cream? Now there's a distraction for you. But not enough to stop me wondering about Sears and giving a furtive glance around me every few seconds.

So how would a hunter like Sears figure out where I was? This was a big city. Okay, so it wasn't *that* big. You could walk from one side of the city center to the other in half an hour especially in these shoes. If I wasn't in the office, at my hotel (first place he'd have checked), I'd have to be out and about reacquainting myself with the main shopping areas. Yes, he knows me that well. Or he did. Considering there are two main shopping hubs, Grafton Street area and Henry Street area, each on either side of the river Liffey, I'd be scouting around in one of those. But which one? Probably the one on the same side as the Temple Bar office, to begin with anyway. So that would put me slam dunk in the Grafton Street cache. If I'd decided to take a coffee break, he could narrow it down to St Stephen's Green shopping center — shops, eateries, ladies loos. Which means I would be standing right here in full view of anyone coming up either escalator and —

Jeez! Was that him? Mr stunningly handsome blonde man was looking over here. No, no, no, I didn't want him to see me. This wasn't how I pictured meeting him again. Not with two bunches of flowers and a yummy cake menu in my paws. This was not cool.

I immediately took Emer's advice. The blending part. Shielding my face with the chocolate daisies I zipped towards the nearest clothes boutique. Was that him? How could I not remember what he looked like? Had time been inordinately kind to him? Morgan had weathered the clock superbly. Time had even improved him and I hadn't thought that would've been possible, or fair. Morgan was good looking enough without it honing him to new heights of irresistibility. What were the odds of Sears still being a complete hunk who could make women do a double take as he sauntered past them? Cream linen shirt sleeves were rolled up casually to reveal lightly tanned, whipcord forearms and he had a physique that was in the vein of a classic movie star.

Everything about him was casual but refined and set him apart from the crowd. His hair was short at the sides and longer on top and more golden blonde than mine. I was almost envious because his was completely natural. And he looked like money. He'd that steam cleaned look to him that you only get from wearing crisp linen shirts and neutral colors and fabrics that smack of sheer quality. This was Sears all right.

Life could be so cruel. To me, not him. He looked like he'd been living the life of Riley while I'd drawn the short straw and been lumbered with the strife of Riley.

I peered out from between a clothes rack absolutely undeterred by the strange looks I was getting from the boutique sales staff. The survival techniques were kicking in fast. I was searching for the quickest route out while keeping a watchful eye on Sears. He was scoping around the cafe to see where I'd gone.

Sears was a hunter in the truest sense. I was more a hunter by default. If he sensed it was me hiding behind a bunch of chocolate daisies in the middle of Dublin then he really hadn't lost his knack for finding a new niche in a haystack of fashion banality.

'Where's the stairs to the main exit?' I whispered desperately to the sales girls.

'Body swerving an ex–boyfriend, huh?' one of them surmised.

I smiled anxiously and nodded. 'Something like that.' I indicated towards Sears. 'Blonde guy.'

'Can I have him?' the other one said, giving a cheeky wink.

'Gift wrapped,' I said.

'What's wrong with him?' the first girl asked. 'I mean, he looks luscious.'

'He's a ruthless son of a bitch,' I said, repeating Randolph's recent description of him.

Their glowing admiration for him faded, and while one of them distracted him by pretending she was sure she'd met him in a nightclub, the other showed me the racing line out of the shopping center that led to Grafton Street.

The great thing about being brand new to a city is the fleeting anonymity of it. The last time I'd lived here that aspect of merging totally into the crowd of complete strangers ended after about two weeks. By then I'd made numerous acquaintances and in a compact city like Dublin whose main thoroughfares criss crossed the Liffey via the O'Connell road bridge and the Ha'penny Bridge, it was astonishingly easy to come across familiar faces. I'd enjoyed being virtually invisible and was sorry when it ended. But here I was again, an unknown, at least until the pattern repeated itself.

Taking a deep breath I took full advantage of being anonymous, and keeping a tight grip on my flowers, I made a run for it down Grafton Street.

Putting as much distance between myself and Sears worked for me. I didn't care what people thought as I dashed past them. You could get away with things like that in Dublin whereas in Manhattan the cops would've cornered you thinking you were a thief. Here you got the benefit of the doubt. Even the look the flower seller lady gave me as I whizzed by was mildly accepting of my bizarre behavior.

I skidded to a halt near the bottom of the street, and took a sharp left up a cobbled alley, and then ran back to the office in Temple Bar which took less than five minutes at the rate I was going. Who needed to go to the gym to get in shape? It was barely lunchtime and I'd already had two mad dashes on the strength of a peach croissant.

Emer looked guilty when I walked in. She'd blabbed. I knew it. She'd told Verde that Sears had phoned.

'I couldn't help it,' Emer said. 'Barefaced lying isn't my forte.'

Had there been more time I'd have debated that whopper but I truly couldn't be fussed. And I didn't blame her. Verde could've wheedled a confession out of hardened criminals. Sometimes I thought her skills were wasted in the cut throat world of fashion marketing. Then again . . .

'Verde wants to see you in her office as soon as you come in,' Emer said in a warning tone.

I smoothed down the skirt of my suit and steeled myself for the flack.

'Ask her yourself, Randolph,' Verde said as I walked into her office.

The silver fox was peering at me from Manhattan via the webcam on Verde's computer screen.

'Randolph's having a deaf day,' Verde whispered to me.

'What was that?' he asked sharply.

Verde smiled directly at the screen. 'I said here's Blue.'

Randolph nodded. He was indeed having a deaf day. For years I'd thought it was a wily ruse to catch people off guard when they were talking about him. However, having seen him nearly hit by a taxi as it approached him from the rear, I realized he did have bad hear days brought on by excessive stress. I'm surprised when working with Verde he wasn't perpetually deaf.

'Have you been eating chocolate?' Verde snapped at me.

'No,' I said firmly.

Wide blue eyes accused me of lying.

'It's the flowers. They're chocolate daisies.' I tried to explain, but the smirk on her glossy lips showed she didn't believe a word of it.

'I'll buy you a bar of chocolate, okay?' I said in exasperation.

The air froze. 'Do I look like I eat fuckin' candy? Do I?'

Judging by her scrawny chicken neck that would be a no.

Verde continued her sugar crazed tirade. 'I'm not like you, Bluebell. My metabolism isn't fucked to Kansas.'

Whatever that meant I pretty much assumed it wasn't a compliment.

'Who's in Kansas?' Randolph piped up.

Verde took a deep breath and regained her plastic grin. 'I was just explaining to Blue about the purpose of this meeting.'

'Sears is screwing us over and we've got to close him down,' Randolph recapped succinctly. 'There's a lot of money at stake, Blue. We can't afford to let Sears secure the main coolhunting leads, not this time. This is a mega bucks crisis. Go get 'em, Blue. I've e-mailed the details to Verde. Forget anything I said in Manhattan. I need you and Verde to work together on this.'

'Okay, so what you're basically saying is that Sears has beaten us to the finishing line,' I said, swallowing the urge to blame Verde for not moving fast enough. She'd been here since January. What the hell had she achieved except a fetching shade of green fingernails?

'No!' Randolph's voice boomed out at me. 'What I'm saying is — nail him. Get the information off him. Lie, cheat, steal it from him. Whatever it takes.'

Verde speared me with a direct stare. 'Someone's going to have to be the bait.'

Was that someone going to be me? All's fair in love and futurehunting, but I draw the line at some things.

'One of *us*,' Verde emphasized to me, 'is going to have to be the bait.'

I truly thought she was meaning me but no, she figured she was the one with the booty to entice Sears. Good luck with that. When it came to women Sears set the bar high. The only asset Verde had that would make Sears' heart race was the hatred he harbored for her.

'But he loathes you,' I dared to say. Mega bucks crisis warranted I speak up.

'Love and hate are simply flip sides of the same coin,' she said, flicking her auburn hair. 'Deep down he has feelings for me. I know he has.'

I didn't doubt it. Deep, deep down he'd have loved to kick her scrawny ass. But who knows. Verde was full of weird surprises.

'What if Sears doesn't take the bait?' I ventured to ask.

'Then Sears can stick his sorry ass down the crapper for all I care,' Verde shouted.

The office had a cold resonance that emphasized the spite in her snippy tone.

For a moment we both looked at each other.

'Isn't the crapper where a guy is likely to stick his ass?' I said, wondering where the hell else he'd put it.

The pink, shiny lips curved into a smile. 'Sears can stick his *head* down the crapper is what I meant to say.'

And then we both laughed.

'It's been a very confusing day,' Verde said, sighing.

'Tell me about it.'

Verde hooked her expensive silk jacket from the back of her chair. 'Let's get out of here.'

Randolph was still on screen as Verde sashayed past the computer. She smiled sweetly and mouthed silently, 'Fuck you Randolph.' And with a wave of her hand we were gone.

Casting a glance over my shoulder I saw Randolph shuffling his notes, and he seemed quite the thing that the meeting was over.

Verde put her designer sunglasses on as we stepped out into the sunlight.

'Where are we going?' I said, feeling less invisible as she took hold of my arm to help steady her when navigating the cobblestones in five inch heels.

I felt like we looked totally out of situ — a couple of chic Manhattan divas in the wrong zone.

'There's a bar just over there,' she said. 'It's downstairs.'

The bar was a richly decorative haven of calm away from the hectic buzz of the day. Lit with a mellow glow, it was mildly busy so we opted for a private alcove with plush sofas and seated ourselves there. A waiter approached.

'Two Irish martinis,' Verde said.

For a second I thought she'd ordered for both of us, and then I realized my mistake. 'I'll have a glass of red wine.'

The waiter nodded and hurried away.

Verde spread her arms out across the back of the sofa, took her sunglasses off and sighed long and hard. 'What a shit storm we're in.'

She seemed tired.

'What's your plan with Sears?' I said.

'A ton of under eye concealer to hide the effects of only three hours sleep,' she said, 'and calling a truce with him.'

'Think he'll go for it?'

She shrugged. 'Sears and I go back a long way.'

'What happened?'

'What didn't happen,' she said. 'Sears used to like me until I became ambitious and Randolph promoted me over him.'

'Is that why Sears quit the company?'

'Yes. He couldn't handle the competition. Oh and I know what you're thinking, Blue. Why would Randolph promote me when Sears is clearly one of the hottest coolhunters in New York?'

That's exactly what I was thinking. 'Sears never told me why he left. I assumed it was a business move. He was ready to go out on his own.'

Verde shook her head. 'Sears would've stayed with Randolph's company, but he couldn't accept working under me, and I'd been busy *working* under Randolph.' She gave a suggestive wink.

'You slept with the silver fox!' I couldn't hide my surprise. This was a new low, even for Verde.

'Don't let the wily fox's gray hair fool you. That guy can go like a loco.' She smiled to herself. 'Of course it soon fizzled out, especially when his wife found out.'

'Randolph's got a wife?' Where had I been? Why didn't I know about these gems?

Verde waved a dismissive hand in the air. 'She's perpetually in Honolulu these days.'

'So what about Sears?' I really wanted to ask if there was any other reason he hated her like poison.

'Sleeping with Randolph to beat him to the promotion was it,' she said. 'I didn't sleep with Sears if that's what you're wondering. Thought about it though.' She hesitated and then added. 'Why are all the good looking guys complete shits?'

The waiter approached with our drinks, walking into the full force of Verde's remark. She didn't bat an eyelid, but the martini glasses rattled on the tray he was carrying.

He put the drinks down. 'Two Irish martinis,' he said, 'and a glass of house wine.'

Verde's wrist cracked as she signed the tab.

He walked away.

'Don't say you hadn't thought of Sears like that,' Verde continued. 'The guy's a heart crusher. Have you seen him lately?'

I told her about my sprint down Grafton Street. Why not? We were having one of those rare moments when she was recognizably human.

She almost choked on her martini. 'Seriously, Blue, I'd love to have seen Sears' face. No wonder Morgan says there's no one quite like you.'

I wasn't buying it.

'Oh come on, you know he's tortured by what happened between the two of you.'

'I wish!' I said.

She downed the first martini. 'We've got to stick together, Blue. I know you think I'm a total bitch, and sometimes I am, and maybe I need to be in this business, but if we don't stand up against Sears then Randolph's company's going to take a major financial blow.'

'You set me up last night at the party with Morgan,' I said.

'I did,' she confessed boldly. 'But you beat him good. And me.'

'Why are you okay with that?' I demanded. 'Don't you care? I thought you were involved with Morgan. Having dinner with him *again*,' I said, mimicking her.

She leaned forward. 'I'll tell you something. Morgan's not what you think he is. At least with Sears what you see is what you get.'

Fort Knox was opening its doors. I was just about to pry it open further when a man approached our table. He was quite good looking and spoke with a local accent.

'Would you ladies like to join me and my friends for a drink?' he offered, dark eyes shining in the overhead light. His friends were two other guys on the opposite side of the bar. They were looking over at us.

'No thanks,' Verde said. 'We're out of your league.'

The insult ricocheted off his broad chest.

He leaned down and spoke to me. 'Is your mam always this friendly?'

He'd gone for the double whammy. Verde had a pet hate of arrogant guys approaching her in the first instance. She said it made her feel like cheap trash. Then he'd doubled his score by calling her my mother. This was not going to end well.

Verde kicked him on the shin, her heel connecting right on the bone. He yelled and jumped back. No major damage had been done, except to his ego.

'Get the hell away from us!' she snarled at him, as only Verde could.

The man lumbered forward and for a second I thought he was going to slap her in the face. Despite our differences I couldn't let that happen and instinctively got up from the sofa and stepped in front of him, preventing him having a go at her, verbal or otherwise. Unfortunately I was still holding a glass of red wine. I hadn't even had a sip, and in the melee, the entire contents were spilled down the front of my gray bitch–proof suit.

'Fuck! Fuck! Fuck!' I screamed, or words to that effect. My suit was ruined!

Bar staff and a member of security came rushing over just in time to see Verde take a wild punch at the guy's chin.

With me trying to wipe off the wine that was running down my clothes and Verde on the verge of boxing the guy, we were asked to leave the premises before they called the Gardai (the Dublin police).

We left. Verde put her sunglasses on. I wished I could've borrowed them and disappeared into the shadows, but there was no hope of that in the bright midday sunlight. She took my arm again to navigate the cobbles and we headed back to the office.

Of all the people going past, who would've thought it had been us, two New York fashionistas, who'd been thrown out of a Dublin bar for fighting.

'I look nowhere near old enough to be your mother,' Verde commented as we walked along.

'The man was an asshole,' I assured her.

She glanced at her reflection in a shop window. 'I don't look old at all.'

'Definitely not,' I agreed, 'although . . .'

She stopped dead. 'What?'

I wondered whether to tell her or not and then decided — what the heck. 'It's just your styling, it's sort of stuck in an eighties time warp.' There I'd said it. I'd wanted to say it for a long time. Verde's clothes and hair made her years older than she really was, or less young than she could've been. Either way, they were adding years to her.

'There's nothing eighties about my style,' she said, not very convincingly.

'It's quite a glamorous look,' I said, 'but ever so slightly dated. Those shoulder pads for instance are passé.'

'What shoulder pads?' she said.

I jabbed a finger into where I thought the padding was and found it was all her. On her bony frame her shoulder muscles were out of proportion even though she probably had a knack for arm wresting.

'Power yoga,' she said by way of explanation. 'Ten times a week.'

'I'd cut back if I were you,' I advised. 'Unless you're thinking of running off and joining the circus.'

She gazed again at her reflection in a shop window. 'So you think I could peel back the years?'

'Absolutely. A makeover would do you the world of good.'

'Okay,' she agreed. 'We'll do it this afternoon. If I've got to shake my booty for Sears tonight I may as well do it with a new makeover.'

'We . . .?'

'We'll have a girls' afternoon. I know you're pretty much as good as you're going to get, but at least have a mani and a pedi.'

'I hate people jabbing at my nails,' I said.

'Then have your hair done. I know this great salon in Dublin . . .'

My heart sank. Verde's idea of a great hair salon had never come close to mine. She had a favorite in Manhattan that I avoided at all costs. The hairdressers wore head to toe black, they had the palest complexions, and their hair was dyed stark blonde or raven black to within an inch of its life. It was like walking into the village of the damned.

By the time we got to the office I'd agreed to go along for the makeover. Somehow it was less exhausting when Verde was a bitch. I just wasn't used to dealing with Vee–Vee.

An argumentative vibe met us as we walked in. Emer was haranguing someone on the phone. Her Irish accent always became more pronounced when she was irate. 'I can assure you that Verde Valmont was not involved in any bar brawl. Such accusations are nothing more than atrocious lies, do you hear me? Atrocious lies I'm telling you!'

Then Emer saw us standing there with wine spilled down my suit and Verde's cheeks still flushed with rage. 'So you can get lost!' she snapped at the caller and banged the phone down. She railed on us. 'I can't believe it.' She came over for a closer look. 'The pair of you brawling like cheap floozies!'

I think it was the expression on my face that made her shut up. Deep down, I was pissed off. Really pissed off. My suit was ruined and I'd a girlie afternoon planned with Vee–Vee.

'Awe, Blue, look at your beautiful suit,' Emer sympathized. 'Want me to skoosh it down with soda water?'

I shook my head. 'It's a total right off.'

Emer nodded. 'Red wine's a bastard to get out.' She paused. 'It is wine, isn't it? It's not —'

'No one got hurt,' Verde assured her.

While Verde told Emer the gory details of the bar fiasco, I thought about my suit. One day in Dublin and my ultimate secret weapon was ruined. Okay, so I'd brought the black one, the red and the plaid suit with me, but I really needed the gray one. There was only one thing I could do . . .

The design was written down in Manhattan and hidden inside an old dictionary. No one knew my secret design, and I couldn't ask Harry to e–mail it to me because I'd never even mentioned it to him. However, the pattern was forged into my memory. Every detail. There had to be a good bespoke tailor in Dublin. Murphy would know. I'd talk to him tonight. Not that I'd tell Murphy about my bitch–proof suit either. All I needed was the name of a top tailor . . .

'So I'm leaving you in charge this afternoon,' Verde said to Emer. 'We're going back to Blue's hotel so she can change out of her suit. Oh and the clothes in my office wardrobe, throw them out or take what you want. I'm having a complete new look.' Verde glanced at me. 'Totally non eighties.'

Emer blinked. 'Even the black designer jacket you've never even worn and the —'

'Whatever,' Verde said.

Emer's deceivingly innocent hazel eyes brightened and I could almost hear her mind cherry picking what she'd take.

Verde and I left the office, then I ran back to grab a jacket to hide the wine stains en route to my hotel.

Emer was already raking through Verde's cast offs. Having a similar slim build, only softer, almost everything was the ideal fit for her.

I took a jacket neither of us liked. It was a yellow and green monstrosity that only a glow in the dark weevil would appreciate.

'Have fun with the makeover,' Emer said.

I gave an unenthusiastic mumble that she seemed to decipher better than me.

'Why are you complaining?' she said, shrugging on the black jacket. 'Everyone lives in their own kind of job hell. But at least in ours you get to wear better shoes.'

With these words of fashion wisdom ringing in my ears, I hurried to catch up with Verde who'd already secured us a taxi. We were at the hotel in minutes.

While I changed my clothes, Verde took an unusually keen interest in my suits which were hanging in the wardrobe. She was checking for labels, feeling the quality of the fabrics, and horror of horrors — holding up my black suit and admiring herself in the mirror.

No, no! If she even thought about trying on one of my bitch–proof suits I swear I wouldn't have been responsible for my actions. These suits were made to repel bitches not entice them.

I was just about to swipe it out of her clutches when she frowned, turned it around on the hanger, decided it was a no goer and then put it back in the wardrobe.

Phew!

That's the thing about the suits. They don't look impressive hanging up. It's when I put them on that the magic happens. Besides, they were tailored to fit my figure, not Verde's.

Her phone rang.

'Sears!' she said, giving me the thumbs up that he'd had the balls to call her. 'You got my message. Yes, dinner tonight. No hidden agenda.' She laughed lightly. 'Of course I'm lying, but you're man enough to handle it, Sears, aren't you? Good. See you tonight.' She clicked the phone off.

'The cunning bastard doesn't trust me,' she said.

Trust her? I thought. She should come with a safety warning!

Chapter Six

Dining with the Enemy

A relaxing afternoon makeover with Verde was completely draining. I needed a rest, I needed some space, I needed a —

'I ordered us a latte,' Verde said, reading my mind. Two coffees arrived, served up while she was having her hair done. She'd opted for daredevil red to spice up her usual auburn, and although I'd had reservations about the vibrancy factor, it turned out to be stunning. Some clever cutting softened the style and took the harsh edge off her cut glass cheekbones. But no amount of daredevil dazzle was ever going to detract from her bitchy persona, but hey, you can't have everything.

The hairdressing colorists had tried to persuade me to become a blonde bombshell (far more dangerous than my own blonde apparently), but I told them I'd save that ace card and would be back to take them up on it when I'd exhausted all other tricks and really needed to play dirty. Until then, a shampoo and style would suffice. They did a great job of giving me an up do embellished with small, sparkly stars. Murphy had asked for devastating, and I intended to give it all I had. Which reminded me — I needed to phone Murphy and tell him the latest about Verde and Sears. I'd a sneaking suspicion we wouldn't be having dinner at our favorite restaurant tonight. I knew where Verde and Sears were dining. The temptation to book a seat for that spectacle would be too great for Murphy to resist.

And I was right.

'I'll wangle us a table, Murphy assured me when I phoned in secret from the loos of the makeover salon.

'We're on the last gasp and then we're out of here,' I whispered.

'What's Verde had done?' Murphy asked.

'The works — clothes, make up, hair, claws . . .'

'An improvement or not?'

'Definitely an improvement. She's looking years younger, while I've aged half a century.'

'I'm sure you'll look devastating tonight,' Murphy said.

'What's with the devastating? Are you up to something?'

'No, no . . . well, yes and no . . .'

'Spit it out,' I said.

He hesitated. 'You know I'm in the spotlight right now with my new collection.'

'Yes.'

'Well, when I saw you last night, and especially this morning, I thought to myself — Blue would be perfect.'

'Perfect for what?'

'There's something about you, something special, an elusive quality — and that gray suit you were wearing, it's . . . I don't know what it is about it, but it was just right.'

My heart began thundering like crazy. Had he sussed out my suit? He was a fashion designer after all.

'So I wondered if you'd like to be part of my fashion campaign,' Murphy said tentatively. 'Help me promote the collection while you're in Dublin. Come to a few parties, which you'd probably be going to anyway. Be my muse. Advise on bits of marketing.'

'Bits of marketing?' I said. 'Marketing doesn't have bits. It has strategies and tactics and —'

'See! I do need you, Blue. This collection has really taken off. I'm ready to make the jump internationally.'

'Which is wonderful, but you need someone who'll be there full time — and besides, I've never ever thought of myself as *muse* quality.'

'Then you do yourself an injustice. I think you'd be a very amusing muse.'

We both laughed.

'Blue?' Verde called through the door. 'Are you ready to leave?'

'I thought the deliberate clash of cheap and classy fabrics was extraordinary,' I said pretentiously into the phone, while walking over to Verde.

'It's Murphy,' I mouthed to Verde.

She motioned for me to hand over the phone. 'Let me speak to him. He's just the man I need.'

I'm sure I heard Murphy curse like a demon, before Verde said, 'Murphy! Hi. It's Vee–Vee. I need a favor and I'll pay you back with bells on. I simply have to look spectacular this evening. I want to borrow that evening dress you showed last night at the party. The red one —'

I shook my head adamantly.

'Hold on a sec,' she said to Murphy.

'One word — overkill,' I told her.

'What do you suggest?' she asked me.

I thought for a moment. 'Give me the phone. I'll talk to Murphy.' She handed it over.

'Verde's had a makeover,' I said, as if I hadn't already told him every colorful detail. 'She's a vibrant redhead now, so the red dress would be a faux pas.' I paused. 'Okay, I'll ask her.' I turned to Verde. 'He wants to know the truth. Can I tell him?'

She nodded and tapped her wrist watch. Time was wearing on.

'Verde's plotting to claw her way into Sears Pearson's affections,' I said to Murphy. 'So she needs a dress with a hot ass guarantee.' I paused and listened to his suggestion. 'Okay, thanks.' I hung up.

'He's sending over the gold one,' I told her. 'And the red one for me.'

Dark thoughts aside about how the evening would go, I was actually looking forward to it. In a parallel universe I was out dining for all the traditional reasons, like enjoying myself, on a genuine date, and not game playing to the max.

Murphy and I were seated at a table overlooking the dance floor. While he was chatting to the manager, I sat back and admired the restaurant, which was situated in one of the most refined hotels in Dublin. Everything was white linen, silver cutlery and sparkling crystal glasses. Couples were dancing to elegant music. I recognized most of the dances. Not that I'm a dancer, in fact, *not* being a dancer is how I came to dabble in martial arts.

I've no sense of rhythm, thus the jiu–jitsu classes instead of jitterbugging. The dance teachers hadn't been deliberately evil hearted when they'd advised me never to darken their studio again. They'd just been honest. So, almost to save face and prevent myself feeling like a total loser, I'd ventured into the martial arts class. Instead of fox trotting on a Monday, I fought like a tiger on a Tuesday. It's not as if I couldn't do the dance steps or I was clumsy. I'd learned the rumba, and was quite light on my feet even though I say so myself. But I was always dancing to another tune. The story of my life.

I hadn't ever shimmied with Morgan come to think of it. Probably just as well. My ineptitude on the dance floor would've been one more point to score against me. I'd tangoed with Harry. Not in public, but in our apartment when we'd had one too many glasses of wine during Thanksgiving and at New Year. And that didn't count.

Who danced properly these days anyway except at weddings and glitzy functions where impromptu couples and distant relatives had a go at waltzing — badly.

'Have you any idea why Sears was hunting me down today?' I said to Murphy, who looked particularly flamboyant (in a good way) wearing a deep burgundy suit and a beige shirt with cravat style collar.

'Probably for the same reason Verde's hunting him — to glean information. That's what coolhunters do, isn't it? Then again, he could be trying to entice you to work for him instead of Randolph.'

I smiled. 'Isn't that what you're trying to do?'

'Yes but my offer is genuine. Sears' agenda will have numerous spurious and shifty clauses,' he said, winking mischievously.

Sears and Verde hadn't arrived yet. I wondered if they'd been arguing. It was one thing to plan an evening together over the phone and quite another to come face to face with a bitter enemy. They could be wrestling in the street for all we knew.

Before my imagination could run riot any further, the golden couple themselves walked in. It was quite an entrance. Even some of the dancers did a double take. Sears and Verde looked like a million dollars and there was no hint of them having been fighting. Not a single, glossy red hair was out of place on Verde, and she looked a decade younger and fresher without the heavy makeup and less severe hairdo. As for Sears, what can I say? His dark evening suit was a classic cut and he looked so tall, blonde and handsome.

They seemed quite at ease with each other, but the evening was young. I was almost jealous that Verde had become the bait. The gold, cocktail length dress was a scorcher. It was similar in style to the shimmering red one I was wearing. In that other universe I'd be wearing the gold.

'Don't look over at them,' Murphy whispered.

I'd been gawping which wasn't cool. As Verde had said earlier, it really had been a very confusing day. Verde had been strangely friendly, Sears had hunted me like prey, and now they'd morphed into the perfect gilded couple.

'Verde looks quite good in my design,' Murphy said. 'The bright red hair suits her.'

'Do you think it's all a sham?' I said. 'Or is there a spark between them?'

Murphy viewed them over the rim of the dinner menu. 'Right, let's read their body language. They're walking up to their table. If he puts his hand anywhere near her arse he's interested in her.'

'Sears is not going to feel her ass in public,' I protested too much.

Murphy gave me a knowing look. 'Ah . . . you fancy him!'

'I do not!' I whispered snippily.

'You do.'

'I don't!'

'You look peeved,' Murphy said.

'I wouldn't even know what peeved looked like,' I told him.

He proceeded to give me an example, pulling a face that made me laugh out loud. 'That's waspish, not peeved,' I said.

Murphy had another go at it when a waiter approached our table.

'Is the menu not to your liking, Sir?'

'No, it's grand, the menu's grand. I've eh . . . I've got a fly up my nose.'

Kudos to the waiter for not batting a whisker, and shame on me for laughing.

'Do you need a hand with the insect, Sir?' the waiter asked. 'He probably came in on your jacket. Quite a mild evening.'

Murphy snorted once, loud and deliberate. 'No, that's him gone.'

The waiter left us to study the menu.

'You definitely looked a bit jealous,' Murphy continued.

I sighed exasperatedly. 'All right, I admit it, I'm slightly miffed. I don't want to date Sears, but it rubs my feathers up the wrong way seeing Verde with him. I don't know why.'

'Listen,' he said, 'he never touched her arse as she sat down. I was watching. He never even laid a hand on her. That's not a good sign. Take a quick squint over at them. See how he's got one hand in his jacket pocket?'

'Yes.'

'That's a sure fire, furtive sign. He's being secretive, not showing all his cards. He's waiting on the chance to tell her what he really thinks of her. He doesn't like her.'

I peered over. 'What does Verde's body language mean?'

'She's displaying all the classic signs of a praying mantis.'

'Oh, he's looking over here, hide, hide, hide,' I said, trying to disappear behind the menu. We knew we'd be seen eventually but we wanted to enjoy some of the drama before they realized we were here.

Murphy whispered conspiratorially. 'If he sees you and comes over during the evening then he's interested in you. The sooner he comes over the keener he is.' Murphy paused. 'Uh–oh! Sears has seen you and he's heading this way.'

I went to get up but Murphy clasped my arm like a vice. 'Sit your arse down and brazen it out,' he advised.

In seconds Sears was right beside our table smiling down at me, sapphire eyes as unfathomable as ever. I never knew if he could see right through me. It had always made me anxious.

'Blue,' he said, holding my gaze for longer than I could handle it. 'It's good to see you again.' Up close he was devastatingly handsome, and his smooth Manhattan accent made me pine, for a flicker of a second, for home.

'Have you met Murphy?' I said brightly, trying to take the focus off myself. 'He's a fashion designer —'

'We haven't actually met,' Sears cut in, and then he looked down at Murphy. 'But I know you by reputation.'

'Likewise,' Murphy countered.

Murphy got up and they shook hands tensely.

'Would you care to join us for dinner?' Sears offered.

'We wouldn't want to intrude,' I said. Murphy nodded in agreement.

Sears was having none of it. 'I insist,' he said in a tone that wasn't taking no for an answer.

I stood up and Sears' manners kicked into action. He pulled my chair back and touched the small of my back (without touching my ass) to guide me over to his table.

The look on Verde's face was priceless as we approached. Bile and resentment oozed from every well cleansed pore.

'I assume everyone knows each other,' Sears said, knowing fine well this was true.

'I'm sure we could write each others biography,' Murphy quipped, seating himself opposite Verde, leaving me to face Sears across the table.

'Shall we have a drink before ordering dinner?' Sears asked us.

'That's the first good idea you've had tonight,' Verde snapped at him, accusation lancing him to the core. She got up. 'Excuse me for a moment,' she said, and marched off to the ladies room to throw a hissy fit in private. Nobody tried to stop her or asked if something was amiss. We all knew how the game was unfolding.

Sears nodded to a waiter.

'I'd like a bottle of champagne,' Sears said to the waiter, and then looked for our agreement. 'Is that all right with everyone? I think this occasion calls for a celebration.'

Indeed it did, I thought. The fiasco had begun . . .

'So,' Sears said to me, leaning back in his chair, 'I hear you're coolhunting in Dublin for the summer. Think you'll find the future here this time?'

He wasn't being a total bastard but he hadn't been able to resist rattling my cage. Clearly his question had a double meaning. Was I going to get involved with Morgan again, and did I think I was good enough to challenge him in the coolhunting stakes? 'Yes,' I lied. 'I'm confident the future's here somewhere.'

I saw the pupils in those sapphire eyes become instantly larger. I didn't need Murphy to interpret that signal. Sears' interest was stirred, he was excited. Was he excited by me or the challenge of rising to the bait I'd cast? I didn't know, at least, not yet.

'Well, well, isn't this cozy,' a voice said darkly, taking us all by surprise.

I looked round and it was Morgan.

'Don't get up,' he said to Sears and Murphy, while looking at me. I saw his eyes rake me from top to toe, taking in the shimmering red dress.

'You don't waste any time, do you, Blue?' Morgan said, snidely accusing me of being out with two men.

'It's not like that,' I said. 'Not that it's any of your business.'

Sears stood up. 'What is it you want, Morgan?'

The air burned between them. Clearly time hadn't healed their past differences. I thought for a moment that a fight would kick off, but the moment passed.

Morgan sidestepped the question. 'Are you still intending to compete in the yachting challenge in Dun Laoghaire?' he said to Sears.

'Wouldn't miss it,' Sears said, smiling, the top yachtsman in him projecting confidence.

Morgan glanced at me. 'Well, I'll leave you to enjoy your evening. Hopefully you won't be barred from here for brawling in the gutter.'

'I wasn't brawling in the gutter,' I shouted at him, but he was already walking away.

Sears was looking at me for an explanation. Grrr! Where could I start? Well you see, Verde and I were drinking in a bar this afternoon, but it wasn't me who took a wild punch at the man, it was her. No, I wasn't even going to try and explain.

Luckily our champagne arrived, literally lifting our conversation from the gutter.

While Morgan joined a party of friends on the other side of the restaurant, the waiter poured three glasses of bubbly for us, and Murphy proposed a toast.

'To friendship and fair rivalry,' Murphy said, holding up his glass.

We clanked our glasses, and suddenly I didn't feel so distraught. Two glasses of champagne later, I was feeling a lot perkier.

Verde eventually emerged from the ladies room, looking the closest to happy we were going to get.

Murphy leaned near to me and said under his breath, 'I guess she finally managed to get the burr out of her arse.'

We ordered dinner, which I was more than ready for. The day had been total chaos and I was now ticking over on the bare fumes of that peach croissant. My stomach was as flat as the pancake I'd ordered for dessert. I've never needed to diet. Harassment works for me.

The conversation got round to the wine disaster on my bitch–proof suit, so I took the chance to ask Murphy if he knew the names of any bespoke tailors who could make me another one. He recommended someone really good, a friend of his. He also offered to make the suit for me himself, but I said I wouldn't dream of it.

'Why do you need a bespoke tailor for your suit?' Verde said. 'I know someone who could run one up for you. What difference does it make?'

'The difference is in the cutting,' I said. 'I'd like a traditional bespoke tailor to make a personal, one off pattern for me and cut the pattern himself. He may even sew the garment himself or have a specialist stitch it, but it's the actual pattern making that counts. It's what sets it apart.'

'You certainly know a lot about tailoring,' Sears said, sounding suspicious of the level I'd gone to for what would appear to be a nice, gray suit.

I smiled sweetly. 'Fashion's our business, Sears. I simply like a well cut suit.'

Verde and Murphy were none the wiser but Sears knew I was hiding something.

Tomorrow I planned to visit the tailor and ask him to start work on the suit. I'd given the wine stained one to the hotel laundry services. They wouldn't be able to get the stain out but it would be clean enough to take along with me to show the tailor exactly what I wanted. There was only one way to make a bitch–proof suit and luckily I knew how to do it. Tomorrow . . .

'Oh I simply adore this song,' Verde said.

Quite a few couples were taking to the dance floor.

Verde skewered Sears with a look. 'Well, aren't you going to ask me to dance?'

If ever a man would have preferred to have a tooth pulled rather than dance with Verde . . .

However, Sears did the polite thing and escorted her on to the dance floor where they proceeded to quickstep wonderfully.

Murphy took my hand and pulled me to my feet. 'Come on, Blue.'

I tried to anchor myself to the chair, but there was no stopping him. 'I don't dance,' I hissed at him.

'I'm a brilliant dancer,' he beamed. 'I'll keep you right.'

'No, you don't understand,' I protested. 'I've no sense of rhythm whatsoever.'

He held me at arms length and I thought he was going to back down, but no. It turned out that Murphy was indeed a good dancer and adapted his steps to fit my rhythm, or lack of it. The strange looks we got were burned into my memory forever. On one level, we appeared to be quickstepping well together — but we were dancing to a whole different tune.

As we skip stepped past Morgan I swear I saw the fire breathing out of his nostrils. Either that or containing the laughter was choking him.

Despite our differences, grudges, hates and spites, we'd all managed not to rip each others throats out. The evening was really picking up.

But hey — the night was young . . .

Chapter Seven

Self Promoting Glory Hogs

By midnight it had all kicked off. Too many glasses of champagne, too many past grudges and not enough water under the bridge spilled over into an argument between Morgan and Murphy.

For most of the night Morgan had kept his distance. He didn't come back over to our table or ask me to dance (seeing me quickstep with Murphy put paid to any chance of that), but he'd sharked past our vicinity all evening with a sneer on his lips and pretended he was enjoying himself with his friends. Morgan's buddies were a mixed bag of stuffed shirts and equally stuffed skirts. Perhaps that's why he overreacted when he crossed swords with Murphy en route to the bar.

I can't be sure who started the mud slinging, but I do recall Murphy bellowing at the top of his voice, causing everyone to glare — not at him, at Morgan.

'And as for you, Morgan Daire, you're nothing but a self promoting glory hog!'

Now back home in New York that remark wouldn't have made a dent, but in Dublin it was fighting talk. It was the equivalent of calling Morgan a pushy, big headed chump whose business only thrived on spin.

The comment didn't go down well, though I have to admit I didn't think the fight would kick off quite so fast. One minute they were trading insults, (with Morgan shouting that if anyone was a self promoting glory hog it was Murphy), and the next they were grappling towards the foyer.

I didn't imagine for a minute that Murphy would tackle Morgan with such ferocity. When I say ferocity, it wasn't actually vicious. It was more of a scuffle with excessive posturing, mainly on Murphy's part, and belligerent name calling. Morgan certainly had a fight on his hands though. It was actually quite impressive. Not that there was any particular style to Murphy's technique. Wildly chaotic is how I'd describe it, and soon the two of them were out in the foyer and then tumbling into the street, tussling and growling (or maybe that was just Murphy). His colorful burgundy suit was aglow from the lights of the hotel restaurant, and a small crowd had gathered to enjoy the fracas. In

New York we settled things in court, but in Murphy's world a swift wrestle settled many an argument.

Verde fixed me with an incredulous stare, and then we both ran outside. Hotel security had been alerted, but once a fight was off the premises it wasn't their duty to intervene. Someone had called the police and within minutes I heard a Garda car, siren blaring, racing across the nearest bridge.

'Morgan! It's the police!' Verde yelled. I remember thinking the Garda would have no problem locating where the trouble was. Verde's dress alone shone in the night like a warning beacon, and under the lights her vibrant hair looked like it was on fire. Though I should talk! My sparkling red dress seemed to be alive with sequins. Between the two of us, we could've guided small planes in to land at Dublin airport.

Morgan immediately let go of Murphy's arm which he'd attempted to twist up his back. I'm sure Morgan was only trying to restrain his opponent, who was bending like a very wriggly wormy thing, rather than cause any real damage. Self promoting glory hog insults aside, Morgan didn't hold a grudge against Murphy like he did against Sears. Had it been Sears instead of Murphy, I think the fight would've been as vicious as a bag of snakes. This brawl was far too preposterous to be serious.

106

Murphy had grabbed the collar of Morgan's shirt as they'd wrestled on the ground, and the fabric had ripped, tearing the collar from its stitching. If anyone looked like they'd been brawling in the gutter it was Morgan. Ah yes, sometimes there was justice after all.

The police car roared towards us, and Murphy and Morgan jumped to their feet seconds before it screeched to a halt. That's when Verde sprang into action. She was good. Very good.

'Thank goodness you're all right,' she said, gushing over Morgan and Murphy.

The leading officer recognized Murphy. 'Oh it's yourself, Murphy. You look flustered. Are you okay?'

Before Murphy could explain, Verde intervened. 'These two guys stepped in to rescue me when rowdy thugs tried to steal my purse.' She held up her gold sequined handbag.

The whites of Morgan's eyes glistened in the night. Was he hearing right? But she continued.

'There were five of them, officer,' she said, being slightly over dramatic, 'and if it hadn't been for these two men I shudder to think what would've happened.'

The officer gave Murphy a nod, and then turned all his attention to Verde. 'Are you hurt, Miss?'

'No, I'm fine,' she said.

Now it's probably totally inappropriate at this point to mention how gorgeous the police officer was, but really, this guy was lush. He was tall and incredibly handsome with a physique that did as much for his uniform as it did for him. But that's the thing — Dublin Gardai (policemen) were invariably good looking. I'd never yet seen one who'd been on the wrong end of the ugly stick.

'What did these hooligans look like?' the gorgeous Garda said to Verde. 'Big, were they? Five of them you say?'

'Yes.' She ran a hand through her hair, feigning mild disarray and doing what Murphy would call in body language terms – subliminal flirting or fluffing her bouffant and her booty. 'They tried to grab my purse but these men chased them away.'

'Good on ya, Murf,' the officer said, and then looked at Morgan. 'And you.'

While a few mutterings went on, the officer radioed into the Garda station. 'No, it was only a bit of a kerfuffle. Murphy the fashion designer and another man stopped a young woman from having her handbag stolen . . .'

If anything made Verde's night, that was it — the 'young woman' comment from the policeman. Her face lit up, and not just because she was standing in the full glare of the hotel lights. She did look good in her gold dress that flickered in the warm summer night. I came a close second in the glistening stakes in my red sparkler.

Sears was watching us from the restaurant foyer, leaning nonchalantly against the glass door. I wondered what he was thinking. Unfathomable thoughts as always.

'If you want a piece of advice,' the officer said kindly to Verde, 'wear something less dazzling the next time you're out on your own at night. Lovely as your outfit is, it's going to attract all sorts of unwanted attention. Think about wearing a nice ladies cardigan to cover some of the sparkliness.'

'That's very good advice, officer,' Verde said, smiling, and then buttoned her lips before any snippy comments ruined the good impression she'd made.

Morgan remained silent but I could see the anger in his eyes. He ripped the remnants of his shirt collar off and glared at Murphy.

'Cheap stitching,' Murphy muttered, having another verbal dig at Morgan.

The fight would've kicked off again, but I stepped in, tugged Murphy's arm and pulled him away, while Verde worked her charms on the policeman.

Morgan shot me a look. 'You should never have come back to Dublin, Blue. You're a magnet for trouble.' His husky voice sounded rich in the warm air but there was no mistaking the coldness in those green eyes.

'No more than you, Morgan,' I said.

'We were always a fair match for each other,' he conceded.

'There was nothing fair about our relationship. Nothing! You were a liar and a cheat back then. Nothing's changed.'

'I never lied,' he argued, and I could see the fire spark deep within his eyes bringing heat into their coldness.

I felt my nails dig into the palms of my hands with rage. 'You did! You lied! You cheated me out of my marketing plans for the new fashion designs. I should never have confided in you. Never have trusted you.'

'Those designs were mine!' he shouted, silencing everyone around him.

It was the tone of his voice that made me hesitate. It rang horribly true. Even the small crowd of bystanders paused to listen, not knowing what our differences were, but sensing that the void between us cut long and deep.

I felt empty for one heart stopping moment, and then the panic of realization hit me hard.

He took a step closer. 'Yes, that's right, mine, not yours. You thought you'd found something new. Well you hadn't. I didn't steal the ideas from you. The designs already belonged to me. I'd been working on them for almost a year under another name.'

I looked desperately at Murphy. This couldn't be true, could it? For six years I'd believed he'd ripped me off. Now he was telling me the designs were his all along. There was no shred of bluff or bravado in his revelation and I feared he was telling the truth. I felt everything in my world tilt.

Morgan sneered. 'What? Didn't Murphy tell you? I thought he'd have been bursting to tell you that gem.'

My mind flashed back to what Murphy had said earlier about Morgan's secrets — one of them was a corker. Was this it? That Morgan was secretly a women's fashion designer? Murphy and I hadn't had a chance to exchange any gossip while Verde and Sears were nearby. I'd assumed we'd huddle in a darkened corner later and I'd hear every scandalous detail of Morgan's secrets, but the brawl had put a different spin on the end of the night.

Morgan's eyes were boring into me, daring me to defy him. I looked again at Murphy.

'Morgan's telling the truth for once,' Murphy said, the words almost choking him. 'The designs were his. I've only just found out.'

I felt the fight knocked out of me as I realized my mistake.

Then like some fictional criminal from a television drama who feels the urge to confess all and give a full explanation of what had happened, Morgan told me everything. I could only stand there and weep silently, inwardly, to myself. I'd never give him the satisfaction of seeing how hurt I was. It wasn't just that I'd made a mistake. It was the six years. Six years!

'I didn't think anyone would take my collection seriously if they'd known it was mine,' Morgan began, his voice a dark whisper. 'I'd only been testing the water, releasing a few garments to see how the market reacted. But of course you came along and decided it was going to be the next big thing in fashion. You're just not as sharp as you think you are.'

Clearly.

Murphy stepped in immediately to sweep me up from the depths of my own silent despair. 'Here's the name and address of that bespoke tailor you were looking for,' he said, taking some folded notes from his pocket and pressing them firmly into my hands with a look that said to me, and only me — this was not what the notes contained. 'I phoned and arranged an appointment for you to meet him tomorrow morning.'

I played along. 'Thanks, Murphy,' I said, smiling tightly. I unfolded the notes and almost froze when I saw what they were. Hiding my reaction I rolled the notes tight and clenched them like a baton, ready to run like blazes if Morgan tried to see what was written on them. Trouble didn't begin to describe what would occur if he'd known that I was clutching the financial details of his business — the ones that Harry was primed to analyze for Murphy and me. I was one breath away from Morgan and holding the statistics of his business in my grasp. If only he'd known. Murphy had also included the details of the bespoke tailor and the early morning meeting, so it wasn't a complete lie.

I blinked out of the moment and realized Verde was talking to Sears, and that the crowd of bystanders had melted away into the colorful shadows of the nightlife. The police officer beckoned Murphy over for a final well done slap on the back, leaving me standing alone with Morgan who was too close for comfort. I couldn't think straight. The man oozed lust, unintentional I'm sure, as he looked particularly annoyed.

I tried to put some distance between us, but as I stepped back, one of the heels of my ridiculously high shoes got caught in the cobblestones. It was stuck firmly and I had to step out of the shoe to try and wrench it free. The blood rushed to my head from frustration as I bent down, hoping I wasn't baring my frillies in this short dress while the police were still around.

Apart from trying to balance on one wobbly high heel, I was also holding tight to the virtual window into Morgan's financial situation. It was a fine balancing act and I'd have pulled off if it hadn't been for the mild wind blowing up my nethers, alerting me that my panties were probably on show to the police. I jerked up and tumbled back, and I would have fallen if Morgan hadn't stepped in and swept me up in his very capable arms.

Potent emotions raced through me. His sheer strength took my breath away, making me feel like a modern day damsel in distress. Up close, Morgan's masculinity was a thrill to behold. His liquid emerald eyes gazed into mine as he held me tight, and I'd the strangest notion that the past six years had been forgotten in that moment. This was how we used to be all those years ago when we were together. He'd lift me up as if I belonged to him and I never once felt the urge to deny it. I've always loved my career and wouldn't ever want to give it up, but there's no denying the raw instincts that kicked in whenever he swept me off my feet. Back then, nothing had ever compared to Morgan's love for me. Nothing had since.

The dark pupils in his eyes sparked dangerously, a giveaway that I had an effect on him too. The long black lashes lowered slowly as he tore his gaze away, and then he looked again at me, long and hard and close. Instinctively I'd put my arm around his shoulder and I could feel the powerful muscles underneath the fabric of his shirt. I'd defy any woman in my circumstances not to be affected by the devilishly handsome Morgan Daire.

'You should never have come back to Dublin, Blue,' he repeated in a whisper. The words brushed against my cheek and then died in the night air. Something was missing. And then I saw what it was. Reflected in his eyes was me. The woman that I'd become. As things were, I didn't belong in Morgan's arms, especially as I had the dubious information in my grasp.

He moved closer and I thought he was going to kiss me, his resolve weakened by a few heady whiskeys. His lips were a breath away, but he suddenly changed his mind, put me down safely, retrieved my shoe and helped me to step back into it.

Would I have let him kiss me? Succumbed to a long, lingering and passionate kiss? You really want me to lie? Blame the champagne. That's what I would've done. Or would I? Maybe I'd have spurned him, and refused to bend so easily to his hot, masculine will.

'Come on, Blue,' Murphy said, pulling me away, saving me from the mental torment of wondering whether I'd have kissed Morgan. 'We've been offered a lift home in the police car. I may even encourage them to let rip with the sirens.'

Morgan had already started to walk away, so I took Murphy up on his offer and went over to the police car.

It was the perfect ending to a bizarre evening. Sears and Morgan went back to their own worlds in their own way, and we took Verde with us in the police car.

The three of us sat in the back seat, one on either side of Murphy.

'I hope you won't let this unfortunate incident put you off Dublin,' the gorgeous Garda said to Verde.

'Not at all,' she assured him, still with that flirtatious lilt in her voice.

I looked out of the window as we drove over the bridge. For a moment I caught a glimpse of Morgan's car heading away along the quays like a dark shadow in the night. A painful sense of loneliness washed over me. Had I really traveled all this way to upset myself again over this man? Was I really that smitten with him? Or did I just need to settle things in my own mind before I could truly let him go?

'Are you okay?' Murphy whispered in my ear.

'I'll be fine,' I said and gave his arm a squeeze.

Verde had linked arms with Murphy who made no attempt to unravel himself from her. It was a casual gesture that created the strangest sense of contentment between the three of us.

With one of us on each arm, Murphy chatted to the gorgeous Garda who even gave us a quick blast on the mew–maws to make our evening complete.

The police kindly dropped Verde off at her townhouse near the quays, then Murphy got out at his place, and finally they took me to my hotel. The looks I got from the hotel reception staff were filled with questions, but thankfully none of them asked if I was a wanted criminal or mentioned my police escort arrival. Instead they said that my gray suit had been cleaned, though the stain was permanent, and it would be brought up to my room shortly.

Upstairs in my room I flicked on the local radio to drown out my thoughts. I didn't want to think. I just wanted a cup of coffee and to drive out the images of Morgan's beautiful dammed eyes and the effect he had on me. Those thoughts had to go. They were far too torturous.

The radio filled the silence. I used to love listening to it when I'd lived in Dublin before, and hoped it would obliterate the sound of my own annoyance.

The radio stories and local gossip on some of the shows were fascinating. You'd never hear anything like it in Manhattan. Things like telling listeners to bring in their washing because the weather forecast was rain, or passing on a message from one listener to another about a shopping bargain. It was like hearing people chit chatting over the garden fence in an era when there was actually time to do that.

I made myself a strong coffee, slipped my shoes off but kept my dress on. I really liked it. When was I ever going to be this sparkly red again? Nope, it was staying on. Whatever the fashions of the future turned out to be, I'd firmly recommend that every collection included a red, sequined dress. The ubiquitous red sparkler I'd call it. Yes, that sounded good. Every woman deserved to be a firecracker on heels at least once. It would be the new little black dress of the future — only sparklier.

I was sitting on the bed with my feet up, sipping my coffee and listening to the radio, and almost choked when I heard the radio announcer mention Verde. Not by name, but he could only be talking about one person.

'*And a news story just in . . . popular clothes designer, Murphy, a man of many talents, was involved in a skirmish this evening with a bunch of raucous hooligans who tried to steal a lovely young American lady's handbag in the city center. Another man, loosely identified as businessman, Morgan Daire, laid into them too. The hooligans were apparently chased away and the lady in question was unharmed. The identity of the young lady is unknown, though she was allegedly wearing an eye dazzling gold party dress with more sparkles than your average firework. That she could be seen from here to Dun Laoghaire on a clear night is neither here nor there . . .*'

I was still laughing at this when my phone rang. It was Sears.

'Can I come in?'

My stomach did a somersault. 'What?'

There was a knock on the door.

'Can I come in?' he repeated casually.

I turned the radio off and opened the door.

He was standing there looking like a heartthrob off the silver screen, carrying my newly cleaned gray suit on a coat hanger. Without any invitation he walked in and laid the suit down on the bed.

'Ah, you're having coffee.'

'Would you like one?' I said, hoping I didn't look as flustered as I felt.

'Black, one sugar.'

While I poured the coffee, his vivid blue eyes studied me. I was glad I'd kept the dress on. It flickered like fire in the glow of the soft lighting and made me feel that I was a match for him. He was still dressed for dinner, though he'd loosened his tie and wore his jacket unbuttoned. Yes, Sears was a splendid sight, but a complicated man.

I handed him the coffee. He took a sip and wandered over to the window, but instead of looking out at the wonderful view of the city, he ignored it and focused only on me. There was invitation in his eyes.

'You looked stunning tonight, Blue.'

I felt the color flush across my cheeks. His words hung there in the silence and I didn't know how to fill it. To have Sears standing there in my room was fascinatingly unnerving.

'The trip to Dublin seems to agree with you,' he said. 'I've never seen you look so . . . vibrant.'

'Two–thousand red sequins and too much champagne will do that to a woman,' I said lightly.

He smiled at me.

Many women would've taken advantage of the situation and flirted with him like crazy. Maybe I was crazy not to. Then again, I knew that Sears disliked blatant flirts. To ensnare a man like him you had to take a different approach. Verde was proof of that. She'd spent the entire evening using every feminine trick in the book on him to no effect. Sears was flirt proof. But I was Sears proof. At least I thought I was.

'I'm going sailing tomorrow,' he said. 'I've hired a boat for my stay in Ireland. It's moored in Dun Laoghaire marina. I'm driving down there in the morning to try it out in preparation for the race.'

'Think you'll beat Morgan?'

No change in those fabulous blue eyes that almost made me ache just looking at them. 'That's the plan.'

'Morgan can sail like the devil,' I warned him.

'And I can sail like the wind. It should make for an interesting challenge.'

'Indeed.'

'Would you like to come with me tomorrow? I've already twisted Verde's arm up her back to release you from her clutches for the day. I thought it would give us a chance to talk.'

'About what?'

'The past . . . the future.'

'Business or pleasure?'

'Aren't they the same thing in our world?'

I nodded.

'If you're interested, I'll pick you up after breakfast, say around nine, and we'll drive down to Dun Laoghaire.'

Then I remembered. 'I can't. I'm going to see Murphy's friend, the bespoke tailor, at the crack of dawn tomorrow, so I'll have to pass.'

'Ah yes, the bespoke tailor.' He put his coffee down and stepped closer. 'Whatever are you up to, Bluebell Byrne? Or is it a secret?'

'It's a deep, dark secret,' I said, smiling as I exaggerated the meaning.

'I thought only Morgan Daire had secrets like that,' he said, looking at me as if he knew a lot more than he was saying.

'Want to tell me some of his secrets?'

'I only divulge things like that when I'm sailing. So if you change your mind call me. My number's on the card that Randolph gave you.'

'Is there anything you don't know?'

'Yes.' He stepped closer. 'What does a woman like you see in Morgan Daire? He'll only break your heart again. You're no match for what he'll do to you.'

'I can take care of myself these days.'

An enigmatic smile was his silent reply.

'Thanks for the coffee, Blue,' he said calmly and then headed towards the door. 'Remember, if you change your mind . . . I could do with someone on deck who's fit and agile. Judging by your performance on the dance floor tonight with Murphy and your entertaining sprint down Grafton Street when you gave me the slip, I'd say you were the perfect sailing companion.'

I couldn't help but smile. 'You saw my mad dash down Grafton Street?'

'Didn't everyone?'

We both laughed and then he opened the door to leave. 'But I could've caught you,' he said quietly. 'And maybe one day I will.'

Then he was gone.

I closed the door and leaned against it, wondering how I was ever going to get some sleep with my mind whirring from the night's events. Was Sears right? Was I really no match for Morgan?

Suffice to say I couldn't sleep, so I e–mailed the financial notes to Harry and chatted to him via the webcam he'd suggested I set up so he could see that I was okay. He looked great, and I found myself almost envying his contentment and felt a pang of longing for Manhattan. I bolstered myself with the assurance that Manhattan would still be there when I'd finished what I'd set out to do in Dublin.

'Which is what exactly?' Harry said, knowing fine, but getting me to remind myself.

'To futurehunt the fashions that will blaze a trail forward instead of rehashing the past,' I said.

Harry moved the webcam around pretending it wasn't picking up my message. 'Sorry, the cam went a bit wonky there. It didn't pick up anything about you settling an old score with Morgan Daire. Must be all those red sequins causing a chaff effect.'

I sighed so hard that the webcam's microphone crackled with static from the force of it. Harry was right, of course. Not about the sequins, but about me losing sight of my goals.

'Okay,' I said. 'Tomorrow I'm going to push ahead with the fashion work. I'm going to search this city for what's hot and find something new and exciting. I'm going to deal with the ghosts of Morgan Daire one way or another. And I may even go sailing with Sears for the sheer hell of it!'

'Good. I'll have a look at those figures you gave me and get back to you.'

'Any idea whether Morgan's business looks prosperous or not?'

'Blue,' he said calmly, 'if there's one thing that's in no doubt it's that Morgan is rich, very rich — and it also looks like his company is considering some sort of merger with a company right here in New York. No idea who, but I'll fish around and find out.'

Well that did it. No sleep for me. Instead I sat on top of my bed drinking copious amounts of coffee and hot chocolate while preparing sketches of my bitch–proof suit to take to the tailor.

The night sky never really reached full darkness, only a subdued twilight. It's something I loved about Dublin during the summer. It was as if the nightlife merely paused to catch its breath before giving way again to the dawn.

The morning arrived with a clear blue sky. Perfect for sailing down the coast. But I had other things to be pushing ahead with. Murphy called to confirm that the tailor, Octavien O'Flannigan, would see me bright and early, extremely early, fitting me into his busy schedule.

'That's obviously not his real name,' Murphy explained. 'He changed it for business purposes. He's actually Octavien *O'Leary.*'

At 7:30am I was outside his premises in a cobbled nook in Dublin. I felt quite excited about meeting Octavien O'Flannigan, bespoke tailor extraordinaire.

Armed with the stained remnants of my gray bitch–proof suit and design drawings, I rang the doorbell. I heard it tinkle far inside the building and minutes later the door opened and a distinguished, white–haired Irish gentleman beckoned me into the labyrinth that housed the most magnificent selection of tailoring materials I'd ever seen.

He was immaculately dressed in a suit with waistcoat and pocket watch, and I was glad I'd chosen to wear my black bitch–proof suit so I didn't feel too far out of my depths. Somehow I had to persuade this lovely gentleman to make me a replica of my gray suit without spilling the beans on what made it so special. I got the impression he was as sharp as a tack and pulling even a few strands of wool over his eyes would not be easy.

'Mind your step,' he said, as we went down a narrow wooden staircase to the heart of his business. Everything about it was plush — from the deep claret colored carpets to the polished wooden paneled walls and shelves, it was a classic perfection. It smelled of the merest whiff of traditional beeswax, and was probably the most silent place in the entire city.

'Murphy tells me you need a ladies suit made while you're here in Dublin,' he said.

'Yes, the one I had got stained with wine. I've had it cleaned but obviously it's ruined and I need a replacement.'

Fascinated blue eyes viewed me, and then the suit, as I unwrapped it and put it on his work table.

'Hmm,' he murmured. 'I don't usually tackle ladies tailoring, only gents, but this looks . . .'

My heart stopped. What? What did this expert in tailoring see in my suit?

'Interesting,' he said finally, and then looked right at me, studying me for several moments.

'You're up to something, aren't you?' he said.

'Who me?' I said, sounding guilty as hell.

He tapped the side of his nose with his finger. 'I can sum up a customer in jig time. And you young lady have the look of a woman with mischief on her mind.'

I went to protest, and probably make a run for it rather than reveal the secrets of my suit to someone I'd just met. I decided I'd rather forgo having the suit made than risk it being found out.

'Oh, relax,' he said, smiling. 'A broken heart will do that to you.'

'A broken heart?' I said, but he was transmitting and not receiving.

He looked into my eyes. 'I can see the hurt. Yes, I can see it deep, deep, down inside. You were wronged by a man long ago. Never really got over it, did you?'

I went to speak but he rattled on.

'But now you're all hunky–dory and set on revenge. Yes, and you'll beat him too.'

'You can see all that just by looking at me?' I stammered.

'Nah, I was only pulling your leg to make you smile.'

'How did you know all those things?'

He smiled at me. 'Murphy's an awful gossip–monger.'

He must have caught the killer glint in my eye as I pictured what I'd do to Murphy for telling tales about my love life.

'Relax, Murphy never told me anything really private. He just said that you'd been away after a love went wrong years ago and were back to kick some arse.'

I couldn't help but smile.

'Okay, let's get started on this suit,' he said, rubbing his hands together. 'We've got a couple of hours to get the bones of it put together, and then I'll have my stitchers finish it off. But I'll cut the pattern and sew the buttons on personally, and you'll have it in oh . . . four days. How's that? Same price you paid for the original which I believe was a fair bargain.'

'Thank you,' I said, still reeling from the onslaught of Mr O'Flannigan's welcome.

'Seriously though, this is a well cut suit. Fine stitching, beautifully balanced design, and lovely material. It'll hold its shape and yet give with the body. I've got several fabrics that are similar. You can pick from them. I take it you want the same color of gray?'

'Yes.'

He took out his measuring tape. 'Right arm first,' he said, measuring from my shoulder to wrist bone. 'Who made this for you by the way? They certainly knew what they were doing.'

'A bespoke tailor in New York.'

He measured the length of the jacket from the back of the collar at the nape of my neck to the hem. Pockets, lapels, everything was measured precisely and compared to his idea of what was an ideal garment.

'I'm impressed,' he said. 'Murphy says you work in the fashion industry, coolhunter, futurehunter or something?'

I explained what I did.

'And you think you'll find the fashions of the future in Dublin?'

'Hopefully.'

He nodded thoughtfully as he studied my drawings, and began to sketch his own version of the pattern with such precision and lightning speed that I was lost in sheer admiration. Then we chose the fabric from the wonderful selection of materials. We opted for a fine, mid gray fabric that was an ideal match for the original suit, and a gray silk lining.

We chatted as he worked under the bright lighting above his pattern cutting table. Although polished and pristine, the table bore the hallmarks of a lifetime of wear. And I probably told him more about Morgan and me than I'd intended.

'I'm nearly as old as my name suggests. I'll be seventy–nine this summer. I'll retire in five or six years. I've seen all types of romance in my time, so take a bit of advice from an old boy like me. Don't wrap your hopes and dreams and resentments around this man who did you wrong in the past. Get on with what you want to do, what you need to do. And if he's worth it, fate will bring him back like a pin to a magnet. And if not . . . it was never meant to be, and there will be someone else out there for you. Believe me I know what I'm talking about.'

Now I should mention that Mr O'Flannigan had a well trimmed white mustache that set him apart from the crowd, mainly because there was only half of it.

'Whatever you do,' Murphy had warned me, 'don't stare at his missing mustache Apparently his girlfriend shaved half of his mustache off when he was sleeping. She's the jealous sort and wrongly thought he'd been putting himself about with the women.'

'Okay,' I'd said hesitantly. 'But why doesn't he just shave the other half off?'

'Because then she'd have won. No, no, he'll let it grow back and keep the other half while it does. It'll embarrass her more than him. A man can't be seen to be giving in. Stubbornness can sometimes be a virtue from a man's perspective.'

And maybe that was the problem with Morgan — stubbornness, male pride and sheer bloody mindedness. If so, what could I do about it?

'Are you off now to do your fashion hunting?' Mr O'Flannigan said, sounding enthusiastic as we finally headed back upstairs, satisfied that he had everything he needed to create the suit.

The warm sunlight poured into the premises as he opened the door. It was barely 9:00am. The air felt like one of those summer days when no one should be working.

I looked up at the sky. It was a clear, cloudless blue. 'No,' I said, changing my mind about my plans for the day. 'I'm going sailing.'

Chapter Eight

The Ultimate in Temptation

We drove down the coast with the sunroof open and the wind in our hair.

Sears had picked me up at my hotel after I'd called him. I'd barely had time to change out of my black suit into something more casual for the day's sailing trip. Rummaging through my clothes, I'd grabbed a summery cream and light floral print tea dress. Sears had lingered in the doorway of my hotel room while I got ready and had assured me that despite what he'd said about needing a fit and capable deck hand, I'd not be required to climb the rigging, hoist the main sail or even haul up the anchor. So I chose the classic dress for its wafting about on the deck of a private yacht quality rather than shorts and a t-shirt.

Sears wore a white linen shirt, sleeves rolled up to expose those lithe, pale gold forearms, and sand colored trousers, classic cut of course. To the casual observer we looked like we belonged in another era, the 1930s perhaps. Only the modern sports car, a silver bullet on wheels, gave any hint of our true slot in history.

I looked at Sears in profile, golden blonde hair ruffled sexily by the wind. Even with my sunglasses on, he had a glow about him that I envied — and admired. No doubt about it. The day was a scorcher and so was Sears. But could you really live with a man like this? Honestly, could you? He'd be an awful lot to live up to. Verde's attitude to men used to grate against mine, but now I understood. She'd said about Sears, 'I'd like to borrow him for a few weeks for happy memories, then give him back to the wide blue yonder.'

Now this may have seemed cold hearted, conniving and geared only towards sheer lust, but her argument was — 'what's wrong with that? Sometimes forever isn't very long, Bluebell, and it doesn't need to be. A quick forever every now and then is good for girls like us.'

That's the bit that bothered me. *Girls like us.* Was I anywhere near being like Verde Valmont? Jeez, I hoped not. Though to be fair, Vee–Vee had been less of a bitch recently. I'd even go as far as to say she was quite good company.

The coast road leading down to Dun Laoghaire gave a magnificent view of the harbor with its sparkling emerald water and colorful boats anchored in the Irish Sea. I caught a glimpse of Morgan's mansion in an exclusive part of the town as we drove past. It hardly seemed real that I'd ever stayed there. His house stood out from the others. Like him, it had a dark, brooding quality, with castellated battlements, as if it was always ready for a fight.

Sears parked the car and we walked the short distance to where his hired yacht was moored. It was all white hull and turquoise sails and polished wooden deck. After collecting some paperwork, we boarded the yacht. I barely had a moment to enjoy the splendor of the occasion, the warm sea breeze and bright sunlight when my phone rang.

'It's Emer,' she whispered anxiously. 'Is Sears there? Did you succumb to his invitation to go on that boat of his?'

'Eh, yes and yes.'

'Can he hear me?'

'I hope not,' I said, taking the precaution of placing the phone to the ear furthest away from him, while casting him a smile that all was fine.

'Right,' Emer said, taking a deep breath. 'Verde's shitting shoehorns.'

'Is she?'

'Yes. There's been a ruckus here in the office.'

Sears busied himself, preparing the boat for sailing. I walked nonchalantly to the bow, feeling the wind waft gently against the fabric of my tea dress —

and sensing the possibility of a great day out sinking without a trace.

'What happened?' I said quietly.

'Well, Morgan Daire was here looking for you. Verde told him you'd gone sailing with Sears and he nearly hit the roof. He accused her, and me, of lying. He even refused to get involved in my lie detector test. We could've proved to him we weren't telling fibs.'

'You've got a lie detector machine?' I found this incredible. Why would a seasoned liar like Verde want a lie detector anywhere near her?

'No,' Emer said, sounding mildly annoyed. 'It's not a machine, it's my grandmother's jewelry. Remember I told you about it. The gemstones change color when you hold them in your hands. She taught me years ago how to use the colors to test whether people are blatantly lying.'

'I thought you said that the colors showed what state of mind you were in — you know, happy, jealous, desperate —'

'They do, but you can glean a lot more out of them with a bit of jiggery–pokery. I'll show you when you get back to the office. Meanwhile, watch your back with Sears.'

He walked towards me, smiling and curious to know what the phone call was about.

'I think we should include the handbags and the shoes,' I said.

Emer caught on instantly. 'Oh right, Sears is loitering nearby. Okay, I'll talk and you listen.'

I listened.

'Morgan's livid. Jealous as hell that you're helping Sears to win the yachting event at the fashion extravaganza.'

'I'm not,' I protested.

Sears frowned.

I smiled and indicated that all really was fine.

'So then it all comes out, all the dirt and daggers and underhand dealings,' Emer said breathlessly. 'And here's the biggie — apparently Sears has already found a load of future fashion styles in Dublin. He wants you to join forces with him to bring down Randolph's company. He's going to try and steal you, get you to work with him. Tempt you over to the dark side. Sears wants to be the new Randolph. To monopolize the fashion marketing business back in New York.'

'Is that why he's invited me sailing?' I whispered.

'Yes. I'm not saying Sears doesn't like you in his own mercenary way,' said Emer. 'But Sears is the type of man who'd sell his granny in a raffle if he thought he'd make a profit from it.'

I gazed up at the seagulls flying high above me and realized that in more ways than one, I was in serious jeopardy of being shit on from a great height. But there was an alternative. One that made me feel a whole lot better about myself. What if Sears did like me and was only being a bastard to Randolph and co. This was possible.

'Where's Verde?' I whispered.

'Gargling. She's shouted herself hoarse arguing with Morgan. My ears are still ringing.'

'Morgan seemed okay last night.'

'Did he? According to Verde it ended with a street brawl. And he's found out about Sears staying the night in your hotel room.'

'He did not!'

'It's okay. We all succumb to temptations like him. Raffling grannies aside, I would, if you know what I mean. I *would*.'

'I *didn't*. You can test me with your jewelry when I get back.'

'No, no. If you're adamant I'll take your word for it, Blue. Apologies for the lurid accusations but that's the gossip that's been flying around here this morning. What a fiasco!'

I heard a gurgling noise in the background.

'Hold on, Verde's saying something.' More gurgling. 'Oh right, yes, okay.'

'What did she say?'

'Randolph's business is on the line. We need to be the first to find these new fashions, not Sears. Don't trust him.'

'I won't.'

More garbled noises from Verde.

'Verde says to try and find out what Sears knows about the new designs. She couldn't wangle anything out of the bastard, even with that gold dress on, or the promise of it coming off.'

I was so engrossed in the conversation that I never noticed Sears untie the ropes that moored us to the jetty. It was only when we began to sail away from the harbor's edge that I realized it was too late to make an excuse to jump ship.

'Remember, if Sears tries to sweet talk you,' Emer warned sagely, 'he's probably talking a shower of shite. So keep your guard up and your knickers fastened.'

'Will do.'

'Thanks, Blue. We're in a bit of a bind here. Us girls are relying on you.'

'I won't let you down,' I assured her.

'You're a star,' she said and hung up.

Sears emerged from below the deck carrying a picnic hamper. 'I thought we could have a late champagne breakfast,' he said, smiling, and with his shirt unbuttoned to display a sculptured golden torso that would make most women weep with desire. He smelled delicious too — clean and fresh with just a hint of cool citrus cologne.

Warning bells played a deafening descant. Champagne, luxury yacht, drop dead gorgeous man. The ultimate in temptation. I was in at the deep end. And if Sears was the lying monster Emer warned me about, I'd deal with him when we got safely back to shore.

In the meantime, I decided to play him at his own game.

'The sea air's brought a glow to your cheeks already,' he observed, popping open the champagne and pouring two glasses overflowing with the bubbling liquid.

Rage will do that to you I thought to myself, clinking my glass against his in a quietly furious toast, as we sailed out into the open sea.

By the second glass of champagne he was asking me my thoughts on fashion design in Dublin and wondering how I'd got on with the bespoke tailor.

'That gray suit of yours must be something special,' he said.

'I like a well tailored suit, that's all.'

He smiled and then dropped his gaze. 'We both know you're lying,' he said, still with that languid smile. 'I think the suit is part of the new future designs.'

I gave a silent cheer. He hadn't figured out the purpose of my suit after all. 'You're wrong. The suit's got nothing to do with the new designs.'

The doubt flickered in those sapphire blue eyes of his. He sensed I was telling the truth. And it was true. The suit had nothing to do with the futurehunting. I just didn't tell him what it really was.

'Okay,' he conceded, downing his champagne and getting up to adjust the sails as the wind changed course and became more blustery. His white linen shirt blew back to expose his taut torso, the fabric flowing behind him. 'What about the future, Blue? Do you seriously think you'll find new designs here?'

'According to the gossip–mongers, you've already found plenty of them,' I said. There was no use in beating about the bush. We were both searching for the same thing in the same city.

'Gossip–mongers? One of them wouldn't be Morgan Daire, would they?'

I took a no guts, no glory approach in my reply. 'He said you were planning to bring Randolph's company down, and replace him with your own company, having secured my services to help you succeed,' I said boldly.

The muscles in Sears' jaw tightened. 'Did he indeed?'

'Do you deny it?' I challenged him.

A second's hesitation. 'No, I don't deny it.'

I should've felt that I was winning but I sensed that Sears had yet to play his ace card. What would it be? I would never have guessed.

'Did Morgan mention anything about his joint merger with Randolph's company?' he said, nailing me straight with that lethal blue gaze.

Any color the fresh sea air had given my complexion drained in an instant.

'That's right, Blue. Morgan's planning a merger with Randolph. When the deal goes through, Morgan will own half of Randolph's business. And you know what that means . . .'

I certainly did. I just couldn't bring myself to say it. Sears said it for me.

'It means that Morgan Daire will truly own you. You'll be working for him, and Randolph, but once the silver fox retires to Honolulu, Morgan will call all the shots.' He paused then added. 'I can't see you ever being the boss' wife. It's just not your style, and I doubt that it's Morgan's style either.'

Inside I was reeling, cut to the bone.

'Does Verde know?' I said quietly, feeling I'd had the stuffing knocked out of me.

'Yes.'

The wind caught the sails, filling them with air. The opposite had happened to me. I mulled over the situation while Sears adjusted the rigging, his strength and skill handling the yacht with ease.

So here's what I thought. Morgan was going to own half of Randolph's company. Effectively he'd own Verde, Emer and me (or be our boss, which in some ways is the same thing). On the other hand, Sears was going to create his own business to rival Randolph. Sears wanted me to join him. With Morgan, all the power would be his. With Sears, my skills and ability would be acknowledged.

'I'd want you to be an associate in my company,' Sears said, reading me clearly. 'There would be a position for Verde if she wanted it, though she's no match for you as a futurehunter, she's got her own skills that are valuable to our sort of work. I'd take Emer too. I like Emer. With me, the three of you would be assured your careers. With Morgan, well . . . he's a man who wants all the power.'

I was still holding my champagne glass. He went to top it up but I didn't want any more champagne. Neither did Sears. He put the bottle aside.

'Listen, I'm sorry things have worked out this way but —'

'Are you?' I could hear myself take my anger out on him. 'Why couldn't you do a merger with Randolph rather than set up a rival company? You seem hell bent on destroying him, and in the process, us.'

'I was loyal to Randolph for a long time. He'd promised me a place on the board of directors. Then he gave it to Verde because of her bedroom tactics. She's not even any good at futurehunting for new trends. Randolph said I should stay, but I sensed he'd do the same thing to me again, maybe with Marina DeMar or Azuree, maybe even you, Blue. So I left.' He paused, looked right at me and said, 'If you'd been cheated out of a hard earned directorship because Randolph couldn't keep his dick in his pants, would you want to do a merger with him?'

'No, I wouldn't,' I said, understanding his reasons. If Randolph had screwed me over for someone he was screwing behind his wife's back, I'd want to kick his business' ass.

'I haven't found any outstanding new designs, not yet,' Sears confessed gently. 'I thought maybe we could team up. We used to be a great team when we worked together in New York.'

'We were. I always wondered why you left.' Then I said, 'Why does Morgan want to own part of Randolph's company anyway?'

'Surely you can figure that out. It's for you. If he can't have you in his private life, I hear he wants to have you in his business life.'

I blinked.

'Don't look so surprised. You know he was crazy about you. But you've always had a bad sense of timing, Blue.'

'What does that mean?'

'Ask Verde. She knows all about Morgan's secrets.'

This put me on edge. I needed that glass of champagne after all.

'I've never wished you any harm, and I never will,' he promised. 'You have to believe that.'

I did. Deep down I sensed he was telling the truth.

Sears dropped the sails and locked the rudder in place. The boat drifted gently through the waves which were lapping against the hull. He sat on the forward deck with me. In that moment of sheer tranquility on the sea, with no one else around, so much could have happened.

Instead, he put his arm around my shoulder and I leaned against him, and we sat quietly gazing out to sea, with the sunlight glinting off the water. We were both enjoying a rare thing in our lives — a moment of calm. Any anger I'd felt towards him had gone. I truly did understand his business motives. Honestly, in his shoes, I'd have gone after Randolph's blood too.

The calm didn't last very long. Sears noticed the change in the sea first, and then I saw it too. The waves were becoming stronger, as if something was churning it up from underneath. Storm clouds appeared from nowhere, shading out the sun.

Sears jumped to his feet and secured the sails.

'There's a storm approaching fast. Go below decks, Blue.'

'I want to help. Surely there's something I can do.'

'Put a life jacket on immediately,' he shouted, his voice buffeted by the wind.

I did as he suggested and stashed my phone safely below decks before going back up to be with Sears.

He tied the sails down, started the engine and turned the boat around to head back to shore. I held on tight as the yacht banked sharply, the hull cutting through the water.

Underneath his shirt I saw the muscles in his back tighten as he used all his strength to turn us around full circle. I knew he was a proficient yachtsman, but a sense of dread chilled me to the bone. I shivered from the coolness of the breeze without the warmth of the sun. Above us, the sky had darkened to a threatening gray with swirling clouds that moved at a ferocious pace.

Then we heard the roar of a speed boat heading towards us from the coast.

Morgan was approaching at high speed. His black hulled boat crashed through a huge wave, powering forward against the will of the sea.

Chapter Nine

Absinthe Makes the Heart Grow Fonder

Morgan's boat raced towards us as the storm gathered pace. His dark hair was soaked by the sea spray and from the rain that was now falling like Irish mist. He was wearing a black wet suit — or at least the skin tight bottom half of it. Stripped to the waist, the muscles in his arms were taught as he steered the speed boat head on into the waves until he was within shouting distance of us.

'Turn her around,' Morgan yelled at Sears. He was of course meaning the boat and not me. 'Head further along the coast then bring her in to shore.'

Sears had firm control of the yacht and was reluctant to take Morgan's advice. After all, he was a seasoned yachtsman who'd sailed in all weathers and in more locations than Morgan ever had.

'I know these waters,' Morgan shouted adamantly. 'The currents here have a mind of their own.'

And so unfortunately had Sears. Unwilling to let Morgan call the shots, he continued on his intended route which logically seemed like the fastest way back to the harbor.

I should explain that deep water and wild seas hold no fear for me — within reason of course. Born in New York, I'd spent plenty of time swimming and diving off the coast since I was a kid. It was one of the few things Verde and I had in common. In fact, the only time I think her and I truly clicked was two years ago during an all expenses paid trip to an exclusive resort north of New York that Randolph had organized for his key staff. As I remember it, Verde and I were the only two who hardly saw dry land that whole weekend, preferring to spend more time in the beautiful blue, Atlantic water than at the free bar. To the cynical eye, which would include me, Verde never gave the impression of being an action girl. But let me tell you, chic fashions and killer heels aside, that woman can swim. The holiday weekend was like a pocket in time when we'd got on great. Unfortunately when we went back to work her bitchy demeanor returned as if it had never been away.

But my point is that I'm fine in the water, which was just as well because a humongous wave washed over the front of the yacht and took me with it. Luckily I was wearing the life jacket and bobbed to the surface pretty quickly gasping for air.

Sears was totally distraught. I could hear him shouting to me and immediately attempted to throw me a life line — a ring buoy tied to the end of a rope which was secured to the yacht. I tried to make a grab for it but missed, so he reeled it in to throw it again.

The engine of Morgan's speed boat had gone silent. The next thing I saw was Morgan swimming towards me, powering through the water like a man possessed. He grabbed me as if I was a rag doll, and in the flowery tea dress I half looked the part, especially as I'd lost my shoes. Using a life saving technique, he grabbed me from behind, tits up, and swam with me to the speed boat. Here I was unceremoniously deposited into the boat, followed by his angry frame climbing in with practiced ease.

Strangely, he didn't say a word. Not one. Though he did give me a look that would've withered lesser mortals. Thankfully I was made of sterner stuff, or I was possibly more stubborn than he gave me credit for.

Either way, I sat there like a bedraggled ragamuffin in a dress that had become vaguely transparent and clung to every embarrassing part of my female shape. I'd intended wearing a bra with this dress. Yes, yes I had. But having to get ready at lightning speed, and with Sears nearby, the bra had been forgotten because I couldn't find one that suited the tea dress. I'm not particularly well endowed and the style of the dress hadn't necessarily warranted a bra. I certainly hadn't factored in the chance that I'd be swimming in the Irish Sea. Wafting on the deck was all I'd envisaged. I did have panties on though. White ones. But of course white panties become see–through when they're soaked, so all modesty was cast to the wind.

The growl of the speed boat seemed to match Morgan's mood as he started up the engine. His half naked body was glistening wet, all honed and toned, a darker and slightly more untamed physique in comparison to Sears' build.

The bottom half of the wet suit looked like it had been poured on to Morgan's hips and thighs, emphasizing every long, powerful muscle. The top part of the suit lay discarded in the boat. Clearly he'd chosen to hurry to our rescue rather than waste time zipping himself into the remainder of the suit.

I wondered what was going through his mind, apart from the rage, jealousy and resentment.

His bare torso tensed as if he were reining in what he really wanted to say but had made his mind up to remain silent.

'I heard you had an argument with Verde in her office,' I called to him, making myself heard above the noise of the storm and the roar of the engine.

'I'm sure you were given a fair account of what happened.' His tone was heavy with sarcasm. 'I'm certain I was painted as a right jealous bastard!'

This was true. I couldn't deny it.

'Apparently you accused them of lying,' I reminded him.

The muscles in his broad back tensed like steel cords. 'Yes,' he said.

'Is it so hard to believe that I'd go sailing with Sears?'

He turned and speared me with accusation. 'The woman I knew would never have set foot on his damned boat. Storm or no storm, it was asking for trouble.'

'I'm not the woman you used to know,' I shouted at him.

The boat lurched and pounded through the waves.

He didn't say another word. Instead he led the way safely back to shore. Sears followed in his yacht and moored at the jetty.

Morgan's strong hand pulled me out of the speed boat and on to the boardwalk.

Sears secured the yacht and joined us. His white shirt was soaked and his trousers too, though I was obviously the one who was completely drenched.

'Didn't you think to check the weather forecast?' Morgan ranted at Sears.

'Of course! No storm was forecast,' Sears retaliated.

'This is the Irish Sea,' Morgan said. 'The weather here can be unpredictable. You're not familiar with the coastline. You're clearly not up to the sailing challenge.'

Sweeping his wet blonde hair back from his face, Sears spoke in a low, resentful whisper. 'I will be,' he promised.

Morgan sneered and walked ahead of us down the wooden boardwalk to where Sears' car was parked.

Sears put his hand on my waist. 'Are you all right, Blue?'

'Yes, I'm okay,' I said quietly.

'I'll take you back to Dublin,' said Sears.

Morgan turned on him. 'No you won't. She's soaked to the skin, probably in mild shock and barefooted. I'm taking her to my house to get dried off. Then I'll drive her back to Dublin.'

I was shivering but trying not to. I'd have gone back with Sears, but Morgan's offer was more sensible.

Sears reached into the glove compartment of the sports car and gave me my handbag. He'd also retrieved my phone safely from his yacht. 'I'll call you later,' he said, got in the car and drove off under a downcast sky.

I was still standing there in my bare feet. Rain fell like mist all around me.

151

Before I could object, Morgan lifted me up and carried me to his car, and then drove the short distance to his house that overlooked the harbor with a panoramic view of the bay.

Pebble stones lined the driveway in front of the house, and although the lawn was neat and tidy, there were no flowers in the garden. There used to be roses, lilies, love–in–a–mist and other summer flowers. Now it looked like someone had pruned the life and color right of it.

I got out of the car and went to walk to the door, but again I got whisked up into Morgan's arms and carried inside. He'd effectively carried me over the threshold, though not quite how I'd ever imagined.

He put me down on the polished wooden floor of the hallway. It was the strangest feeling to be standing in Morgan's house after all this time. I stood there looking around me, feeling like I was a familiar stranger back where she once believed she belonged.

A wide staircase led upstairs, and to the left was the spacious lounge with its real, open fire where I'd had many a romantic evening in my other life with him.

The fire looked like it hadn't been lit in a long time, perhaps due to the warm weather, but it was set anyway should someone care to light it.

I noticed the decor was different, more muted. The pale gold and antique aqua–green color scheme had been eclipsed by a darker shadow of its original self. Heavy brocade curtains had been added to the front bay windows and cut out some of the daylight, as if it was an intrusion.

The house smelled different too — a sort of nothingness with a hint of sea air. It used to be filled with vases of fresh flowers and the scent was lovely.

'No flowers?' I said, not meaning to speak my thoughts aloud. My voice sounded clear in the silence of the house.

'I'm too busy these days,' he said, striding past me in the hallway and handing me one of his shirts — a dark emerald green shirt that although folded and laundered still had the distinctive scent of Morgan on it. I'd never known a man with a scent like his. He was always clean but not groomed to perfection. He had a few rough edges. His cologne lingered on the memory yet was barely noticeable. It was as if it affected me on a subliminal level. Just a whisper of masculine fragrance.

'I suggest you go upstairs and get dried off. You know the way. There are clean towels in the en suite bathroom.'

I nodded and padded up the stairs, aware of his eyes watching me, aware too that my dress left little to the imagination. Like I cared! He was acting like an arrogant asshole. Okay, so he was giving me free rein to use his house to get my act together, but he had an ulterior motive. Oh yes, I could sense it brewing under the surface of his forced civility. I think I may have even seen it under the surface of his wet suit too.

I tried not to look at his big, sumptuous double bed with its luxurious satin cover as I walked through to the bathroom. In fact, I tried not to think of where I was and focused on cleaning myself up and getting the hell out of there.

I won't even begin to describe the state of my hair when I saw it in the bathroom mirror, though my waterproof mascara had proved to be a worthwhile investment and had only blurred slightly at the edges giving me a more smoldering look than when I'd first applied it early that morning. The visit to Mr O'Flannigan's shop seemed like ages ago. It was astounding what you could fit into an abnormal day in my life. And the day was still young. No doubt there would be more mayhem and bedlam before the sun set on this one.

As if on cue my phone rang.

'Blue, it's Emer. Sears phoned to say you'd been washed overboard and were now barefoot and at the mercy of Morgan.' She took a deep breath. 'Okay, so he didn't put it quite like that, but are you all right?'

'I look like shit,' I said, stepping out of what was left of my dress which resembled a wet rag. 'And Morgan's acting like a sullen bastard.'

'Oh thank jeezus you're all right,' Emer said. 'Obviously we'd no worries about you falling into the sea. You and Verde used to swim like a couple of barracudas. No, it was being alone with Morgan that flustered us. We feared you'd had the fight knocked out of you.'

I put the green shirt on and helped myself to one of Morgan's silk ties to belt it into quite a sexy little number. 'Nope, in fact, I'm spoiling for one. I've had just about enough of Morgan's attitude. Who does he think he is? If he imagines that because he dived into the sea to rescue me I'm going to be putty in his hands he can go and take a flying fu —'

'I've lit the fire and made us some tea,' Morgan said darkly. He was standing at the door of the bedroom wearing dry clothing and had heard every word.

'Did he hear you?' Emer whispered.

'Oh yes.'

'Brazen it out, Blue. Brazen it out and get yourself back to Dublin. Jump in a taxi or something,' Emer advised. 'I know you've no shoes on, but that's happened to me during many a wild night out. Taxi drivers don't bat an eyelid.'

It was good advice I thought. 'You know, I think I'll do that,' I said to her.

'Have your tea first though,' Emer said. 'Get some heat in your bones. But don't let him pounce on you.

155

His body will be all pumped and pulsating with adrenalin. Men love to think they've rescued you. It makes them feel useful.'

'Yes,' I said, my tone telling her Morgan was still there.

'If you can't get a taxi,' Emer said, 'remember, there's always a man willing to give a half naked woman a lift to wherever she wants to go.'

'What did Emer have to say?' Morgan asked. He'd obviously heard her high pitched lilt advising me how to outmaneuver him. 'Did she tell you to keep your distance in case I made a pass at you?'

He stepped closer, too close for comfort. Without my shoes on I felt smaller than ever and he towered above me, one red hot male. But I was determined to be strong willed and resist him. I wasn't going to give in so easily.

I stepped back to put some space between us, but I slipped on the polished wood floor and almost fell on to the bed. *Almost.* I managed not to, but the momentum of Morgan's body nudged me just enough to tip me back on to the midnight blue satin bedspread.

Strong arms leaned over me, supporting his body weight just short of actually touching me. His face was so close I could see the gold flecks in those gorgeous green eyes of his. Eyes so deeply green and forbidden they reminded me of an absinthe cocktail.

'Tell me I don't have an effect on you,' he murmured, 'and I'll leave you alone forever.'

If there was a prize for lying I'd have walked away with the trophy — with a rosette. 'I have no feelings left for you,' I fibbed defiantly.

He pushed back off the bed as if I'd mentally slapped him across the face. Or dented his ego. Probably both.

'I won't ever compromise you again,' he said.

Bearing in mind Verde's estimate of how long forever was, I thought I could always renege at a later date if I changed my mind and wanted to take him up on his offer of unbridled passion.

'I'll put my car keys downstairs,' he said, walking out of the bedroom. 'Leave the car with Verde. I'll pick it up later.' Then he added the bitter twist. 'I'm sure Sears will be waiting for you in Dublin.'

You have to remember I'd endured six years in the romantic wilderness because of this stubborn man. That's a lot of pent up anger. Unfortunately it erupted to the surface with more force than I'd intended.

'There's nothing going on between Sears and me,' I shouted at him as he hurried down the stairs.

'You looked pretty cozy with him on his yacht,' he said over his shoulder. 'And I hear he stayed the night in your hotel room.'

I hurried after him. 'Sears did not sleep in my bedroom.'

'Who said anything about sleeping?' he countered smugly.

'You big headed, arrogant bastard!'

'Hit a raw nerve have I?'

I don't remember leaping at him. Perhaps I was just a bit giddy from having had nothing to eat all day except a liquid breakfast of champagne on the yacht. Then there was the small matter of having been through the clutches of the Irish Sea, topped off by false accusations hurled at me by someone who had no right to judge me. No right whatsoever! And there was the fact I was standing three steps up on the stairs above him while he'd already reached the bottom. It was possibly the only time I'd ever have a height advantage over him.

Anyway . . . Morgan got a surprise. He'd once told me that nothing surprised him. Well, I beg to differ. I saw the whites of that man's eyes boggle as I flew at him.

Obviously I was no match for the brute and he sustained no noticeable injuries, except to his pride. Oh and the accidental punch on the nose. His nose. It was worth the leap just for that. Taking the punch like a trooper, he grabbed hold of my wrists to prevent me pummeling my fists on his chest. Shamefully, I was cursing like a demon.

As he pinned me to the hall floor I calmed down again because I realized that I'd managed to get myself into the same position I'd been in upstairs in the bedroom, only flatter, and with his body pressed firmly against me. I could feel every muscle in his body. And I do mean *every* muscle.

His hot breath was a whisper away from my lips, and in the heat of the moment I felt something stir in his trouser pocket. And yes, my first thought was probably the same as yours, but then it played a tune, and I realized even Morgan Daire wasn't that versatile, and it was in fact his phone.

We both got up and I held my hand out indicating I wanted the car keys as promised. He handed them over and then took the business call.

I picked up my handbag and headed out of the house. The car was parked out front. Luckily I can drive most things on four wheels. Don't ask me why. A quirk of nature. Just don't ask me to park the damn things.

There were no strong arms to carry me across the pebble stones to his car this time. I was on my own. But I was okay with that. My temper was still simmering so it was better that he kept his distance.

I put the keys in the ignition and started up the car first time, revving it hard and scattering a few of those pebbles as I drove off.

Driving in bare feet wasn't exactly a novelty. Like many women, I'd slipped my high heel shoes off and driven in my stocking soles when my feet were sore or the heels were so precious I didn't want to scuff them. Bare feet were just one step further. But I wasn't going to drive all the way to Dublin without shoes. There were plenty of shops in Dun Laoghaire that sold them.

I drove into the center of the town, parked right outside a shoe shop, ran in, bought a pair of low heeled pumps and ran back out again.

It was an easy drive up the coast road to Dublin, where I abandoned the car in as legal a parking space as I could maneuver near the Temple Bar office.

When I went in Emer was looking out the window and complaining in an irate voice. 'What eejit parked their car over there? It's blocking the entry to the old cobbled lane.'

I dangled the car keys and looked guilty.

'Quick give them to me. I'll go and move it.'

'Thanks,' I said.

Verde waved me into her office. She was having a webcam meeting with Randolph in New York.

'Randolph, Blue's just arrived.'

The silver fox watched me as I sat down near Verde.

'Ah, Blue,' Randolph said. 'Very nice. Different. I like it.'

It took a second for the realization to sink in. He was complimenting me on the shirt and tie that I was wearing as a dress.

'Not sure about the hairdo though,' he said, frowning. 'Maybe I'm just not used to seeing you so . . . *bohemian*. Keep up the good work though.'

'Will do, Randolph,' I said, smiling.

'And I hear you were deep sea diving in Dun Laoghaire. Getting ready for the sailing extravaganza, eh?' he said.

Verde sighed and motioned to me that his hearing was on the blink again. 'Blue and I have lots to do. I'll keep you posted, Randolph.'

He nodded, gave a cheerful wave and clicked off the webcam.

Verde looked at me, studying my fingertips.

'What is it?' I said, glancing at my nails to see if they looked weird.

'I'm just checking your fingers for scorch marks,' she said dryly. 'Seems like you're always getting burned by the men in your life. When will you ever learn?'

I smiled. Point taken. 'How's your throat?'

'It feels as rough as the inside of a parrot's cage. Nothing that a stiff drink wouldn't fix. Shall we?' she said, indicating that we head out.

'Yes, if it includes food,' I said.

'I know just the place . . . '

Outside the offices we fell into step as if we'd done it a hundred times. Verde took hold of my arm to help her navigate the cobbles in her skyscraper heels. There was an open air cafe bar in the nearby square where we sat down in the afternoon sunshine and watched the world go by until a waiter approached with our menus.

Verde ordered two Irish martinis, for herself of course.

I was ravenous and would've eaten almost anything on the menu. I opted for a large green salad served with minted new potatoes, fresh, crusty bread and a large pot of tea.

'What are you having to eat?' I asked Verde.

'I'll have the same as you,' she said. 'Without the tea.'

The waiter kindly informed us of the day's special offer — two courses for the price of one. 'There's pudding to go with the main course. Today's special is chocolate trifle.'

Verde smiled wryly at me. 'What the hell, huh?'

The waiter jotted down our order, including two chocolate trifles, and off he went. The food was served up surprisingly quickly considering how busy they were. Verde took a sip of martini, and while we enjoyed our meal, I told her the details of what happened in Dun Laoghaire.

'Did you wrinkle Morgan's duvet for him?' she asked wickedly.

I burst out laughing.

'Come on, you know I'm dying to ask.'

'No, I didn't,' I said, explaining what went on in his house, including punching him on the nose.

'It couldn't have been hard enough,' she said. 'He was on the phone to Randolph while I had the webcam meeting. He sounded fine.'

'Sears said that Morgan has secrets.'

'Morgan's got lots of secrets,' she said. 'I warned you, didn't I?'

'You did. So what are they?'

Verde sighed wearily. 'Well, you know that Morgan plans to buy into Randolph's company. It's been on the cards for a while.'

'Yes, and Sears plans to set up a rival company.'

'I suspected something was going on with Sears. Back stabbing is a way of life in our world. Better the devil you know than the one you don't know. I'd rather work under Morgan, metaphorically speaking of course.' She sighed again. 'I used to think that Sears was straightforward but he's not at all. I take back what I said about him. Sears is more of a mystery to me now.'

'Sears said I should ask you about Morgan's secret. He said it's got something to do with my bad sense of timing.'

Her blue eyes widened. 'Oh yes, that secret. The most intriguing is the ring.'

'What ring?'

'Your ring — the one Morgan was going to give you when he proposed.'

Chapter Ten

Irish Martinis and Bad Behavior

'Proposed?' I said to Verde.

'Morgan had a ring for you. I saw it six years ago.'

I stared at Verde, realization crushing me into silence.

'You're good at your job, Blue, but your sense of timing is shit. Morgan was planning to take you away the weekend you accused him of stealing your fashion marketing ideas. He was going to propose. But you fucked up big style and ran back home.' She shook her head at me. 'Things could've been so different.'

'How do you know? Morgan's hardly going to confide in you,' I said, feeling the anger building up inside me.

'Credit me with some savvy, please. Morgan may be the secretive sort, but you know what I'm like at inveigling information out of men.'

'Why the hell didn't Morgan say something? Okay, so we'd had a fight and I'd accused him of stealing my ideas, but if he felt strongly enough to marry me wouldn't he have tried to sort things out between us?'

'He thought you'd fallen for Sears,' said Verde.

I frowned. 'Why? Because Sears stuck up for me and gave Morgan's business a financial beating? Sears was the only one who tried to help me when I got back to New York. The only one. But we were just friends.'

'Morgan didn't see it that way. He assumed you were more than friends, and maybe you'd been cheating on him with Sears all along.'

'And so the bridge was burned. He let me go?'

'Morgan's the jealous type. Stubborn as hell. Nothing has worked out for him since you left. Now you're back. The merger is his way of securing you.'

Verde continued talking but I flicked on the mute button. My thoughts rewound to that night six years ago. Morgan had acted differently. I remembered that, and he seemed secretive. I'd thought it was because he'd stolen my ideas, but looking back it could've been his nervousness at asking me to marry him. A bad sense of timing? Oh yes! An explosive mix of emotions that night had sealed both our fates.

'The ring was a sparkler by the way,' Verde said. 'A real diamond dazzler. Morgan hasn't been serious about any woman since. And believe me, I've tried.'

She sipped her martini. 'Though I wouldn't want to be married to Morgan. It wouldn't ever work. I'm far too impulsive and shallow for him. Too badly behaved. He would never let me away with any indiscretions. Now Murphy . . .'

'Murphy! You fancy Murphy?'

She wafted her hand airily, brushing aside any seriousness. 'I'm just using him as an example. Though I was quite impressed with his attack on Morgan last night. Preposterous but daring.'

I nodded, but I was completely torn about Morgan's proposal, or my bad timing of it. I couldn't finish my meal.

'I'm sorry, Blue,' Verde said.

Strangely, I believed her.

'I heard he gave the ring back to the jewelers,' she said. 'He didn't throw it in the Liffey or anything like that.'

I sighed deeply. 'Maybe you're right. Being married to Morgan would be difficult. He wouldn't ever allow bad behavior or scandal. Or drinking martinis in the afternoon or scoffing chocolate trifle.'

'That wouldn't suit girls like us,' Verde said with a foxy smile, and pushed her second glass of martini over to me. 'Cheers.'

I raised my glass. 'Cheers.'

Suddenly Emer came running over to us. 'Dire news, fuckin' dire!'

I looked concerned but Verde sipped the remainder of her martini. 'What's wrong?' she said calmly.

'Randolph's done us a favor,' Emer said loudly, causing several people to stare. 'He's gone and organized a New York news team to turn up at the fashion extravaganza, ensuring international publicity for the event. Photos of it will be featured in some of the glossy magazines.'

'I'm liking Randolph's favor,' said Verde.

'Not when you hear who the media journalist is who is heading up the team,' Emer said adamantly. 'She's the one who'll be covering the whole story. It'll be relayed to New York and everywhere else besides.'

'Who is she? The devil herself?' I said flippantly to Emer.

'Worse! She's a total bitch, and she hates the bejeezus out of us.'

Verde's face became pale, well paler than usual, as she suspected who it was.

And then it dawned on me too. 'No, it couldn't be. Randolph wouldn't be that stupid.'

'Yes,' Emer said, and then spat the words out bitterly, 'it's *Magenta*.'

In that instance, there was no risk of Verde's metabolism being fucked to Kansas. She pushed the chocolate trifle aside. 'Fuck Randolph!' she roared. 'Magenta can fuck off!'

'No, it's too late,' Emer insisted. 'The deal's done. Money has exchanged hands. Favors have been pulled in. Morgan's agreed to it as well, though I doubt he understands the type of noxious viper who's going to be heading to Dun Laoghaire.'

And so we were stuck with the horrible specter of Magenta on the guest list. Her news team were going to be in Dublin covering some big, important celebrity event and while they were within spitting distance of us, they were going to cover the fashion extravaganza. This was bad because the extravaganza was our main publicity event of the summer. Even I needed it to help me secure some of the future fashions. All the top new designers from Ireland had been invited. None had turned it down yet. But Magenta had the power to ruin it by writing scathing reviews. All our hard work could be wasted.

We paid our cafe bill and walked back to the office. Verde linked arms with me again, and I felt the weight of the disappointment dragging her down. I began racking my mind for something to thwart Magenta. Come on, I urged myself, she's got to have an

Achilles heel within range of her designer stilettos. And then I remembered.

'Magenta hates fancy dress parties,' I said, my words bursting out with enthusiasm as if I'd struck gold. Such was the effect this prize bitch had. Verde could be bad, but she was nothing compared to this dark hearted viper.

Verde squeezed my arm tight. 'That's right, Blue! She loathes them, bordering on paranoia.'

'You were planning to have a lavish dinner dance as the extravaganza's finale,' I said to Verde.

'Yes, but the plans aren't finalized yet,' Verde said, eager to hear what I had in mind.

'Well,' I said, 'I think a ball would be more spectacular — a *masquerade* ball.'

Verde's face lit up. 'You're brilliant!' she said, her eyes twinkling with excitement.

My idea was that when Magenta found out we were having a fancy dress finale she wouldn't turn up, or at least she'd cut her time short. I'd take photographs of the ball and we'd use these for our own publicity. Good publicity.

'A masquerade ball would be wonderful,' said Emer. 'I've always wanted to wear a fancy dress mask with exotic feathers and stuff. Outside of the bedroom anyway.'

Both Verde and I looked at Emer.

'Don't look so shocked,' Emer said, trying not to laugh.

The three of us disappeared into the offices with renewed hope and began working on our plan. I did, however, dash back to my hotel to shower and change my clothes — and tame my hairdo into something less bohemian.

By the time I got back to the office, the thought of Morgan's proposal didn't have as devastating effect on me as I'd feared. In fact, just finding out that Morgan had intended marrying me somehow helped me feel better. At least he'd taken our relationship as seriously as I had. There had to be a shred of hope in there somewhere.

'I've changed the wording on the invitations,' Verde said as I walked into her office. 'Guests now have to wear a masquerade mask along with their glamorous evening wear.'

I noticed she'd created a theme (come on, Verde had to have a theme) for the masquerade ball. It was *fashion*, *fantasy* and the *sea*. The mystique of the masquerade suited the niche in her nature that thrived on mystery.

'It's brilliant,' Emer said. 'Magenta will hate it. A masquerade ball filled with mystery and surprise events.'

'We'll need to get Morgan's approval for the change of plan,' Verde said.

This was true. After all, it was Morgan who was holding the extravaganza. He'd originally agreed to deal with the construction of the huge marquees where the various fashion shows would be held. Runways, changing areas and huge screens to relay every aspect of the shows were his domain, as was organizing the catering and the sailing challenge. For the past five years Morgan had held a sailing spectacular in Dun Laoghaire. This year he'd teamed up with Verde who'd added the fashion shows. Designers from all over Ireland were set to show their latest collections — a perfect showcase for them and equally advantageous for fashion futurehunters like us.

We took a coffee break while Verde phoned Morgan. She put the call on speakerphone so that Emer and I could hear what was said.

Emer broke out the contraband — crumbly cream biscuits. We took one each and listened to their conversation.

His tone was dark and cold. I got the distinct impression that if Verde had suggested a three ring circus he would've agreed to it. Something seemed to have taken the wind out of his sails. It couldn't have been the altercation with me could it?

'Basically, all the guests who were going to attend the dinner dance now have to wear a masquerade mask,' Verde explained to him. 'They would've been wearing evening dress anyway. Adding a mask to their ensemble is easy. I think most of them will relish the fantasy. A hint of mystery appeals to the quality of the night in all of us.'

'Yes, fine, go ahead,' he said.

'We'll keep everything else as planned, including the mermaids,' said Verde.

I frowned and mouthed to her, *Mermaids?*

'Hold on, Morgan. Blue's here and she doesn't know about the mermaids.'

The silence from him was dramatic. Emer bit her lip and pulled an *uh–oh* face.

Verde didn't falter. 'Two top models are going to be dressed as mermaids and dive into the sea to open the extravaganza. Morgan's organizing two diving platforms for them. It's going to be the opening highlight.'

'Sounds like a winner,' I said to her.

Morgan's dry tone resonated down the line. 'Had I known about your aquatic daring, Blue, I'd have built a third platform just for you.'

'My loss,' I said. 'Another time perhaps.'

Silence again.

'Well,' Verde said brightly, cracking a hole in the wedge that was firmly stuck between us, 'do you want us to get a masquerade mask for you, Morgan? Or will I let you sort that out for yourself?'

'I've already got one that I'll wear,' he said, taking us all by surprise.

Emer nearly choked on her crumbly biscuit. She raised her eyebrows and whispered. 'Probably got a selection of them for his boudoir conquests. No offense, Blue. I don't count you as a conquest. You're more of a challenge.'

'Great,' Verde said to him. 'I'll push on with the plans. We'll send out the invitations as soon as they're ready.'

'Do you think his mask's got exotic feathers sticking out of it?' Emer whispered. 'He'll look like a cockatoo.'

Even Verde was trying not to laugh.

'I'm glad you find it amusing,' he said haughtily.

'Oh we're not laughing at you,' Verde lied.

'And tell Emer there are no feathers involved,' he said curtly, and then ended the call.

'He's just full of surprises,' Verde said, sounding genuinely intrigued. She looked questioningly at me.

'Morgan didn't have any dressing up tendencies when I was involved with him,' I assured her. 'Then again . . . he was good at being secretive.'

'All men have secret sides to them,' Emer said in a mildly warning tone. 'It's like a horrible lucky dip when you get to know the real them. I've had a few nasty surprises I can tell you.'

We were going to prattle on about this, probably for some considerable time, when I remembered about the jewelry.

'You promised to show me how the jewelry works as a lie detector,' I said to Emer.

'I did, didn't I? Well, the first thing you have to learn are the color combinations that indicate a change in attitude.'

Emer brought through a selection of rings and pendants, and went on to explain her theory about the yellows, blues, purples, greens, grays and black, and how they could be interpreted for the purposes of telling whether someone was lying or not.

'The jewelry was never designed for this purpose,' I said.

'No, no, definitely not,' Emer said. 'But the colors change according to the body's temperature. I had this wild theory that when someone's lying they become stressed and the temperature of their skin increases. So then I thought — okay, maybe it could help me tell if someone was pulling the proverbial wool over my eyes.'

'Is it accurate?' I asked her.

'It's not especially accurate,' she said. 'It's more for fun, but it sometimes helps me to glean the vibe that's coming from a person.'

I had picked up one of the rings. The stone was purple when I first held it, but by the time Emer had finished explaining her theory, it had changed to a lovely turquoise blue.

'How appropriate for you Blue,' Emer said, sounding delighted. 'You're probably feeling quite calm and less harangued than earlier in the day. If you'd been wearing this during your fiasco with Morgan when he had you pinned to the floorboards of his big house, that ring is very likely to have told a different story.'

'What we need is someone who's a good liar so you can try out the technique,' said Verde.

'Preferably not one of us because we know each others secrets,' I said.

Emer nodded. 'We need a familiar stranger who's not averse to slanting the truth.'

With no tall, handsome strangers in the vicinity, we continued to theorize about the various scenarios that would turn the jewelry into wild and wonderful color combinations. It was all quite silly and frivolous, accompanied by more coffee and crumbly biscuit contraband. We had our moments, the three of us. Okay, so they were as rare as a surprise pay increase from Randolph, but sometimes amid the vile reality of our cut throat careers, a niche of niceness fought its way through.

'Imagine the color the ring would've been when you were on the yacht with Sears — prior to the storm,

the bit where the two of you were relaxing on the deck,'
Verde said.

Yes, I'd given them far too many details, but that's
how the conversation had gone.

Emer elaborated. 'And you'd been tempted by
Sears' smooth, golden, muscular physique. The ring
may have glowed like a sunbeam,' she said, laughing.

Our laughter ended when someone knocked on
the office door which was wide open. We turned to find
Sears standing there in the doorway, silhouetted by the
honeyed glow of the late afternoon sunshine pouring in
through the windows. He was wearing cream colored
trousers and a light turquoise shirt that made his eyes
look bluer than usual.

'Sears,' Verde said, the first of us to spring into
action. 'What a surprise. We were just talking about
you.'

'I heard,' he said.

I felt myself cringing. How long had he been
standing there? How much had he heard? Despite our
closeness earlier on the yacht, I was embarrassed to be
caught talking about him.

'I just wanted to see you were okay,' Sears said to
me.

'Yes, I'm fine, thanks,' I said.

There was an awkward silence. Then Verde and I
realized that Sears had never actually set foot inside our

offices, mainly because he'd been our arch rival in the futurehunting stakes. However, things were different. Our rivalry had been tempered. He'd even danced with Verde.

'Come on in and sit down,' Verde said.

'Would you like a coffee?' I said to him.

'Eh, yes, great,' he said, relieved that he was getting a fair welcome.

'We're just deciding on some pieces of jewelry,' Emer said. 'What do you think of these?' She handed him two of the rings.

I noticed that the stones were yellow and blue, and then I hurried off, made the coffee in minutes, and took it back through and sat it on the desk near Sears.

He was turning the stones over in the palms of his hands. 'The three of you are up to something. What is it?'

'Nothing,' Verde said.

He smiled. It was such a sensational smile. I thought Emer was going to pass out. 'I know you're lying, so what are you girls up to?' he said lightly.

Emer finally sighed and confessed everything.

Sears laughed. 'It'll never work.'

'It may have worked, a bit,' Emer said, sounding slightly flustered, though I suspected the peachy glow on her cheeks was more to do with Sears being drop dead handsome than anything else.

'Since you're here,' Verde said, veering the conversation away from Emer's lie detection theories, 'you should know that we're planning a masquerade ball for the fashion extravaganza.'

'A masquerade ball? Sounds exciting,' he said, glancing at me to see my reaction.

'You'll need to wear a fancy dress mask,' Verde said. 'Are you up for it?'

'Wouldn't miss it. There are few things more alluring than seeing a woman's eyes look at you from behind a beautiful mask.'

'Speaking from experience?' I said.

He looked right at me. 'Hoping to.'

The air sizzled, at least, that's how it felt to me.

'Blue punched Morgan on the nose today,' Emer told him, breaking the moment, though not intentionally. 'And she drove herself back from Dun Laoghaire in his car.'

Sapphire eyes looked at me. 'You've had a full day then.'

'I have, and a full evening ahead. We're going to Verde's house to rake through her numerous evening gowns to choose something to wear for the ball.'

'We'd invite you along but it's a girls' only night,' Verde said to him.

Sears smiled. 'I just came by to see if Blue was all right.' He made a move towards the door. 'I'll look forward to the masquerade ball.'

He was still holding the jewelry in his hands and I noticed that the stones had turned a deep, clouded black. 'I'm glad you're okay,' he said to me again and gave the jewelry back to Emer who was so busy looking at his face she never saw how dark the stones had become.

Verde picked up her purse. 'Let's call it a day.'

I collected my laptop, and then the four of us left the offices together, stepping out into the warm, early evening light. Temple Bar was buzzing with life — colorful and lively. Morgan's car was parked just ahead near the cobbled lane.

'I'm parked in Dame Street,' Sears said, walking on.

'We'll speak soon,' Verde told him. 'Drop by the offices anytime. Don't be a stranger.'

Verde, Emer and I got into Morgan's car. I started up the engine and we drove off waving to Sears as we passed him by. To say that he looked surprised was a blatant understatement.

I felt slightly guilty about driving Morgan's car, especially as I'd punched him on the nose earlier, but it was the quickest way to get to Verde's townhouse which was a short drive away along the quays of the River

Liffey. We could've taken Verde's car, but somehow it was more fun to zoom along in Morgan's prized car.

'Did you notice how black the jewelry had become with Sears holding it?' I said to them.

Verde was surprised. 'Really? Is that good or bad?'

'Sears is so hot I'm surprised it didn't melt, never mind turn black,' said Emer.

'What do you suppose it means?' I said.

'Were the stones shiny black or murky black?' Emer asked me.

'Murky. Definitely murky.'

'Hmm,' she said ominously. 'It means don't let the blonde hair and golden good looks fool you. Sears Pearson is a passionate force to be reckoned with. He's probably a scorcher between the sheets.'

We cut through the busy traffic, and headed along the edge of the Liffey to the stylish townhouse Verde had rented during her stay in Dublin. The hot, burnished sun was going down in a blaze of glory, making the reflections on the river glisten like liquid gold. Again I was reminded how beautiful this city could be.

Verde turned on the car radio, and I opened the sunroof, and the three of us drove along as if we were the greatest girlfriends in the world. And maybe we would be. Stranger things had happened. One or two of them had certainly happened today. Emer sat in the back seat of the car singing along to the radio, and although Verde didn't join in, she ran her fingers through her vibrant red hair, letting the warm breeze blow away the effects of a long feisty day. She turned to me smiling and laughing. 'If only Morgan could see us now.'

I smiled and nodded.

Oh if only . . .

Chapter Eleven

The Beautiful and the Spellbound

A gorgeous scented perfume reminded me of myself when I walked into Verde's spacious bedroom. It was the perfume I'd worn in Dublin years ago when I bought the haunting fragrance in one of the city's perfumeries. It was a mix of floral essences.

'I recognize that fragrance,' I remarked, feeling slightly sad. Sights, sounds and even photographs can churn up memories, but there's something so emotional about a perfume from the past that really affects me.

'You should do,' Verde said, flicking on the spotlights that illuminated the wardrobes and walk in cupboards. 'It was you who got me hooked on that perfume.'

I remembered giving a bottle of it to Verde as an unintentional gift because it had too many memories for me. I'd been going to throw it away when she'd grabbed my hand and wrestled it out of my determined fingers. The power yoga had a lot to answer for I now realized.

'I finished the bottle you gave me in New York and only just found the perfume again in one of the Dublin department stores. I simply couldn't resist buying it. But it's really more your signature scent, so take it with you if you want.'

I did want to and yet I was wary of the memories it evoked. Long, dark evenings together with Morgan. Languid summer mornings with him in Dun Laoghaire. I decided to see how I felt about it as the night unfolded.

Verde held up another bottle of fragrance. 'I've been wearing this recently — a violets of the night concoction edged with a hint of modern sensuality,' she said with a wicked twinkle in her eyes. 'Far more me.'

I looked around the room which had more wardrobes and walk in cupboards than I'd ever seen. The only giveaway that it was a bedroom and not a fashion designer's collection store was that it had a bed in it somewhere beneath the silk scarves, handbags, accessories and eclectic array of blouses and other luxury separates. Only Verde could be so glamorously untidy.

Although the bed was in disarray, it had no unclean clothes on it of any kind. It simply looked like Verde had been hurrying to get dressed, and had tried on several outfits before deciding what to wear. The choice of colors was overwhelming, and I'd probably never have made it into work if I'd been her.

Even more overwhelming was the eye boggling number of evening dresses in the wardrobes and on rails in the cupboards. There had to be a masquerade ball gown for each of us here.

'Okay, Blue,' Verde said, 'you're the special effects expert. What do we wear that will be the equivalent of poking Magenta in the eye with a sharp stick when she sees us at the ball? That's on the wildest chance she has the nerve to turn up and her fancy dress paranoia doesn't get the better of her.'

I took a deep breath. 'I know we'd all love to wear our personal favorites, but Magenta puts a different slant on things. With international publicity looming, we'll definitely have to look like we're capable of being on the cutting edge of fashion futurehunting or we'll be attacked without mercy. So here's how I see our plan of defense. First of all we have to stand out from the crowd, in a good way. Most of the women will be wearing black evening dresses, or white or neutrals.'

'Won't many of them wear outrageous colors?' Verde said.

'No, this is a masquerade ball,' I said. 'It's not an excuse to turn up looking like a pantomime dame.'

'Okay,' Verde said. 'What's next in the color schemes women are most likely to wear to the ball?'

'Red to be daring or green to be different, so we can't wear those. Then there's the pastels — pinks, peaches, eau de nil, the lighter shades.'

Verde was starting to look concerned. 'So what does that leave us with?'

I smiled. 'The colors of the night, the sea, the elements and metallics. All of which will look fantastic with a masquerade mask.'

Verde almost cheered. 'Blue Byrne, I love it!'

'*And*,' I emphasized, 'we're also going for *beauty*, not sexy, not dynamic. Whatever we choose has to make each of us look beautiful or be damned.'

'Do you think we can pull it off?' Verde said.

'Oh definitely,' I assured her. 'Especially as we're wearing masks.'

We laughed, and that's when I realized I must've blinked or something because Verde and I were on our own.

Emer had completely disappeared into the depths of a walk in cupboard which was full of glamorous clothes. Would we ever see her again, I wondered, or was she lost forever in a twilight world of silk, organza and sparkling gold sequins (yes, Murphy had let Verde keep the dazzling gold cocktail dress), clouds of deep blue chiffon and jewel colored satin? The withdrawal symptoms when we finally extricated her from this den of fabulous fashion iniquity would be horrendous. Even

I was in dire jeopardy of being lured into its mesmerizing clutches.

'It's an impressive collection of evening dresses,' I said without a word of a lie. Though I bit my tongue rather than ask if she'd accumulated them in Dublin or had she brought half of her home collection with her from Manhattan.

As if reading my thoughts she said, 'All the designers who've signed up for the fashion show in Dun Laoghaire have been plying me with dresses for the past several months.' She held up one particular dress that was a vision of shimmering sensuality. 'This one has me spellbound, though when I tried it on it's just not me. But it's certainly a keeper. I get goose bumps just looking at it.'

She handed it over and I felt it work its magic on me. Spellbound? This dress could've put a hex on most red blooded males. Even I was going to have a problem leaving Verde's house without it.

Emer emerged from the cupboard laden with dresses. 'The last time I was this mesmerized was when I was seven and got lost in Santa's grotto. I warn you, Verde, I may even have to move in here.' Then she held up a very unusual gown. 'Was this dress designed by someone with a grudge against women's arses?'

Verde smiled. 'It did make my ass look weird. Love the detailing on the bodice though.'

I ventured into the walk in cupboard which was lit with spotlights.

I could hear Emer enthusing to Verde. 'This one has definitely beguiled me. And I'm in raptures over this one.'

The voices became slightly muffled as I was lured into its tantalizing depths. Would I ever be the same again, I fretted? Then all resistance faded as my world dazzled with every color and fabric imaginable. The talent of the designers was breathtaking. The masquerade ball aside, there were surely some designers of the future to be found here.

Between the three of us, we tried on dresses for longer than seemed humanly possible without sitting down for a tea break. We were the nearest thing to perpetual motion in the world of fashion.

We finally narrowed them down to a small selection of dresses that were the right color and design. Wondering if we'd have to fight each other in close quarter couture, we each chose our favorite, hoping not to clash. Luckily we all liked different dresses. Although the spellbound gown suited none of us, it was still one of our favorites. We reluctantly put it aside.

Verde's dress was the color of the night. It had layers of purple, violet and deep azure chiffon. A light sprinkling of gold sparkled on the fabric as if someone had cast a handful of stardust across it. The color made her blue eyes more vibrant and the soft flow of the chiffon made the most of her figure.

She gave us a twirl.

'It's really grand,' Emer said.

Verde looked at her reflection in the full length mirror, turning to view the low cut back. 'I've never worn an evening dress this color, but it's quite breathtaking.'

The dress had a vintage vibe going on, like something out of the 1920s era, an art deco look — and although we were futurehunters, Verde's red hair brought the whole thing up to date.

'It's fantastic,' I agreed. 'But we've still got to find a mask to go with it.'

'You could design and sketch something suitable, couldn't you, Blue?' Verde said. 'Maybe Murphy could put it together for us.' She reached over to her vast collection of makeup and found a box of luxury cosmetic face paints. 'We could experiment with these.'

While Verde painted a gleaming gold design around one eye, Emer and I tried on our dresses. Mine was a futuristic fantasy in aqua blues and deep sea greens that I thought reflected the theme of the extravaganza. The fabric shimmered and sparkled in all the right places giving my figure a boost in the beauty stakes.

'With your blonde hair that dress is perfect,' Verde enthused.

'Wait 'till Morgan sees you. His eyeballs will be out on stocks,' said Emer.

'And look at you,' I said to Emer, who was wearing a metallic bronze dress. The fabric moved like liquid metal and draped over her figure, clinging to every slender curve. Emer had silky, light brown hair that touched the top of her shoulders, and a pale creamy complexion. She really suited this wonderful bronze creation. She appeared almost statuesque even though she was the same height as Verde and only marginally taller than me.

'Verde paused from painting her face to study Emer. 'I've got some bronze, copper and gold face colors that will work a treat with that dress.'

We ended up painting each others faces to spectacular perfection with stars, moons and fairytale designs winging out from our eyes, creating the look of a mask.

I took photographs of us for inspiration to sketch the designs for the masks later on.

'I'm getting quite excited at the thought of going to the ball,' Emer said, picking up the bottles of various perfumes on Verde's dresser. 'I love it when a hint of perfume has an alluring effect that men find hard to resist.'

'It's like subliminal catnip for men,' Verde said.

'I like to layer my perfume. That's my secret,' I said.

Verde relaxed back in her chair, gold starry eye makeup sparkling. 'Explain.'

'Well, I'll dab on one of my favorite scents, and when it's dry, I'll layer another scent on top. I rarely wear one scent. I've always layered my perfumes to make them different and to create certain effects.'

Verde studied the array of perfumes on her dresser. 'Is there anything here that would have the desired effect?'

I had a look. 'Hmm, that perfume there has quite a good ambery tone.' I lifted up one of the other bottles. 'And this one is especially potent.'

Verde took them both and went to spritz her usual lavish amount of fragrance over herself.

'No, just wear a small amount of it on the insides of your wrists. Don't wear it on your neck or behind your ears. Keep it to the pulse points on the wrists, not the kissing zones. Once it's dry, add a layer of the other fragrance on top.'

Verde applied the first perfume to the inside of her wrists, let it dry, and then added a top layer of the other perfume. Emer copied her. I varied mine slightly by using the gorgeous floral scent, risking the memories flooding back.

191

'Write down any other combinations I should try out,' Verde said.

'Not that Verde has to use wiles to attract men,' Emer joked.

I scribbled them down on a piece of paper and gave a copy to Emer too. I'd listed my favorites that worked well for me.

'Gold dust,' Emer said, clutching the paper in her hand triumphantly. Then she put it away in her purse.

'What time is it?' Verde said suddenly.

None of us knew.

Before we could check, my phone rang. It was Murphy.

'Where are you? I was looking for you at the hotel. I've a party emergency and need you to grace my arm tonight at an impossibly ostentatious, arty farty party to promote my fashions.'

'I'm at Verde's house.'

'I need my muse, Blue. Can you come tonight? It starts within the hour. Short notice I know, but I thought I'd find you at the hotel,' Murphy said.

'Um, okay . . .' I said, and then looked at Verde and Emer. 'Would there be space for three muses on your arm at the party tonight?'

'Absolutely. Are you thinking of bringing Verde?'

'Yes, and Emer.'

'Great,' he said. I could hear the relief in his voice. 'Now if I can sort out something for you to wear. Full length evening gowns. This event's a killer.'

'You said it was ostentatious?' I ventured.

'It's so over the top it's in danger of being up its own arse. But it's one of the key hoops I have to jump through. If my designs go down well at this event, it'll be a boost to my reputation in the home market and abroad.'

'We can do ostentatious,' I promised him.

Taking me at my word, Murphy said he'd send a car to pick us up in forty–five minutes.

I wish I'd had a video of the mad flurry that followed in Verde's bedroom. It would've surely cheered me up watching reruns of it on a miserable day. I'd never seen Verde move so fast, and the gleam in Emer's eyes peering out from the fantasy of bronze and copper face paint was just short of maniacal.

Obviously we weren't going to be wearing our masquerade ball dresses, so these were unceremoniously stashed and other dresses selected at the speed of a January sales bargain hunting spree. But we decided to keep the face paint makeup on. We'd slot right into the party scene.

I chose a shimmering silver sheath dress that out dazzled the red number I'd worn last night (which Murphy had insisted I keep too). The metallic aqua, gold and silver makeup around my eyes went well with my silver dress, and I pinned my hair up to show the long, diamante straps at the back.

Meanwhile, Emer poured herself into an emerald satin and velvet fantasy of a dress, and helped herself to Verde's array of styling products to give her shiny brown hair volume and texture.

'I think Murphy will be satisfied with this level of ostentation,' Emer said, including the two of us in her critique.

Verde stepped out from behind a rail of clothes looking utterly magical. 'I know, I know,' she said before we could comment on the dress she was wearing. 'But when am I ever going to get the chance to wear it? Murphy's party is ideal. I'd never get away with it anywhere else.'

Verde was wearing the dress that had spellbound all of us, and to be honest, it looked fantastic — and so did she.

'You look like you've fallen out of a starry sky,' Emer said. It was the perfect description. 'Not of this world, but not an alien either if you know what I mean. I love the fabric. It's finer than silk.'

Verde ran her hands down the flimsy material of the dress. 'I've never seen fabric like this before. Have you, Blue?'

'I've no idea what the fabric is,' I said, genuinely flummoxed.

A loud knock at the front door of Verde's house interrupted us. Like three spies, we crept through to the hall to see who it was.

Verde sneaked a look through the security peephole and reeled back when she saw who it was.

'It's Morgan,' she whispered urgently. She shushed us into another room. 'Hide! I'll get rid of him. He's not spoiling things for us tonight.'

Emer and I ran for cover. The room was in darkness, but we kept the door open so we could hear what was said.

Verde opened the front door.

'Morgan. Hi, what a surprise.'

'Rather overdressed for a night in don't you think?' he remarked.

'Totally, but I'm not staying in. I'm going out to a wild party. One of Murphy's events.'

There was the briefest silence before Morgan responded. 'I came to pick up my car. I see it's parked, *randomly*, outside. If you give me the car keys I'll give you a lift to your party before heading back down to Dun Laoghaire.'

Emer and I stared at each other. We didn't especially want Morgan to see us like this. We were feeling confident, in the mood to be daringly outrageous. A disapproving stare from Morgan would kill the mood dead. That I'd abandoned his car randomly in the street outside guaranteed at least one icy glare from him. And I didn't even want to think what he'd say about our masquerade makeup. No, it was better all round if he just went away and let us enjoy ourselves.

We could tell from the unwelcoming tone of Verde's voice that she felt the same as us. 'Car keys? Yes, they're in my bag in the bedroom. No subtle hint to lure you there intended. Wait here, I'll get them, though transport's already been arranged thanks.'

Instead of waiting at the door he stepped inside the hallway. 'That perfume is familiar.'

'Gorgeous, isn't it,' she called to him, rummaging through the whirlwind of clothes and chaos we'd created in the bedroom, trying to find the keys where I'd left them on top of her dresser.

Emer and I stepped back into the shadows, keeping the door of the spare bedroom open slightly so we could watch him without being seen. His tall, broad shouldered figure shaded out the light from the hall lamp as he walked past following the sound of Verde's voice.

'Blue used to wear it,' he said, almost wistfully.

I could've cheered when Verde quipped, 'Yes, Blue gave it to me as a gift once. Such a haunting scent don't you think. It must rip the memories right out of the past for you. Perfume can be lethal that way.'

A sigh of withheld anger sounded clear before he responded. 'Is Blue going to Murphy's party tonight?'

'I really couldn't say.' She handed him the car keys.

He turned and walked back along the hallway to the front door, then stopped and confronted her. 'Let's get one thing straight, shall we. Blue and I are over. We were over a long time ago. Just because she's back in Dublin, it doesn't change anything.'

When it came to a verbal dagger fight, he was no match for Verde tonight, especially as she was on her own turf.

'My thoughts entirely. I told Blue to forget all about her silly relationship with you. She was young and foolish. We all have mad flings we'd rather forget about. I advised her to find someone new and exciting. She deserves a fresh start, don't you think?'

I clenched my fists in a moment of triumph, and Emer drew a winner's score in the air for Verde.

'Strange how you'd been set on twisting the knife into her the night she flew back to Dublin,' he reminded her. 'Or did I misinterpret your motives? I was sure you'd set her up for a fall.'

'I had. I don't deny it,' she said plainly, without any hint of being cornered by him. 'But things are different now. We've reached a better understanding of each other. Blue knows I'm a prize bitch, always have been, but unlike you, she doesn't judge me on it. We've all got dark sides to our natures. Mine just happens to be a little more vicious than sweet, but without that quirk I wouldn't be able to stand here and face up to the likes of you.'

He laughed, sort of, as if she'd outmaneuvered him.

'Well now that we've cleared the air between us, yet again today,' he emphasized, 'perhaps you could do me a favor. When you change any other aspects of my plans for the extravaganza, you should discuss it properly at a meeting.'

We heard the business bitch bite back. 'Certainly. Oh and by the way, the next time you and Randolph want to strike a deal for publicity, you might want to involve me and Blue in your short sighted decisions.'

'What's that supposed to mean?' he demanded.

'Magenta. The media journalist —'

'What about her?' he snapped.

Verde lowered her voice. 'She's a viper. She hates us and will do everything she can to make the event look bad. Your precious extravaganza is going to get mauled to shreds in the media. You're going to need Blue, Emer and me to try and fix it. Now, if you'll excuse me, I've a party to go to.' She hustled him out the doorway.

I pictured the look on his face. There was no quick comeback from him. He understood exactly what she meant.

'Can the damage be undone?' he said finally. 'Can Magenta be canceled?'

Verde laughed. 'Cancel Magenta? No. You and Randolph invited her. She'll be at the event. But we're working on a way to deal with her.'

'I'm sure you can handle the situation,' he said, and stepped outside.

Verde closed the door behind him.

Peering out the window I could see the doubt on his face as he got into his car and drove off. His self assured ego was probably thinking about the mistake he'd made if Verde was telling the truth about Magenta.

'Phew!' I sighed. 'I thought he was going to walk in and find us hiding here.'

'What is that man's problem?' Emer ranted.

'He's still got feelings for Blue, and I think it's driving him to distraction,' Verde said.

Just then, the peep of a car horn outside jolted us into action. It was time to party. With the promise of a delicious buffet and a wild night of socializing ahead, we hurried out into the night. Murphy's three muses were on their way — and so was the potential for trouble.

Chapter Twelve

Scents and Sensibility

'Remember,' Emer said as we drove up to the party, 'no brawling tonight. Don't let Murphy get into any fisticuffs either.'

Verde and I nodded. We also agreed that if we stood out like beacons in the night, in an embarrassingly awkward way, we'd make a run for it and hope that no one at the party recognized us. This was our back up plan. Our face painted masks were not for the faint hearted.

But we needn't have worried. It turned out that we blended into the party scene just fine. I'd never been to this venue before, but it was very stylish and numerous paintings were exhibited on the walls. It wasn't busy, but apparently most people had chosen to be fashionably late and throngs were expected to turn up within the next half hour.

Murphy's eyes widened when he saw us, and he let out a cheer of sheer glee.

'You look beautiful,' he said, standing back to admire us. He was especially taken with Verde — and no wonder in that dress.

'Breathtaking,' he said, eyeing her from top to toe. 'That dress is a knockout!'

'Spellbinding, isn't it,' Verde said, angling her body to show how the sparkles caught the light.

'It certainly is,' he said, and then directed us towards the heart of the venue where there was a lavish buffet, bar and alcove seated areas. Verde, Emer and I sat down on a deep, red, velvety couch that curved inside one of the alcoves. It was so comfortable and I felt myself relax.

'I have to organize the models before everyone else arrives,' Murphy said. 'They're going to mill around. No runway show tonight.' He checked the time on his watch. 'If you're hungry, I suggest you help yourself to the buffet before the gannets arrive and leave nothing but the crumbs.'

He went to hurry away and then turned back. 'Without wanting to put the proverbial dampener on things, can I ask the three of you to behave yourselves, at least until everyone's had a fair drink in them?'

'We promise,' I said, and off he went quite happily entrusting his reputation to us.

'Right, I'm making a beeline for the buffet before I wilt with hunger,' said Emer. 'Lunch was a blur and dinner was forgone in favor of mesmerizing wonder. I'd rather try on evening dresses than stuff myself with pizza, but I get ratty when I'm hungry, and I don't want to nip someone's nose off if they say the wrong thing to me — especially in this posh frock.'

So we helped ourselves to the buffet. Lunch had indeed been a blur, and two crumbly cream biscuits were the last thing I'd eaten all day.

We took the food back to our table in the comfy alcove. I'd opted for sparkling mineral water instead of a glass of wine. I'm really not much of a drinker, despite the overindulgence in champagne recently.

Again, I felt the harassment of the day ease away. It was a hot, languid evening and through the windows I could see a burnished sunset stretching over the city. The doors to the venue were open, inviting guests in, along with the heady warmth of the night. Thankfully no one seemed particularly perturbed by our appearance. Murphy's models were already wafting around, and a few of them could've given us a run for our money in the extravagant fashion stakes.

But we'd obviously caught some people's attention because two men approached us. They invited us to join them for the evening, which was very sweet, but apart from being Murphy's muses, and just wanting to eat our dinner, we weren't there to find ourselves a man.

Remembering we'd agreed there would be no brawling tonight, we turned them down politely, explaining we were part of the fashion promotion so as not to offend them.

After they'd gone, another man approached us with a similar offer. By now we were narrowing our popularity down to two things. One — our dresses and makeup sent the men's pulses racing and they couldn't resist us. Or two — the perfume was working like catnip.

'I'm going for the catnip effect,' Emer said. 'I think the perfume technique is hitting its target. Men are being lured by our sultry scent.'

Verde wasn't sure. Neither was I. Even though I was responsible for concocting the enticing aroma, I was hoping there was another reason we were so popular, like being dazzling and fascinating, something laudable like that. Catnip effect just didn't have the same ring to it.

'I'm telling you,' Emer insisted, 'I have a sense for things like this. There's a gleam in those men's eyes. It's the catnip effect for sure.'

We sat there half joking and half wondering and enjoying our meal when a stunning looking man came over and approached me specifically. He had light brown hair that the sun had lightened naturally, and blue–green eyes with long, dark lashes I'd have killed for. After a few minutes chatting, I turned down his offer to join him at his table for a drink, but promised him a dance later on.

'He was lovely,' Emer said to me.

I nodded vaguely.

'Wake up, Blue!' Emer said loudly. 'That bar code on your arse is nearing its sell–by–date. Six years in the fuckin' wilderness because of Morgan Daire! It wouldn't be me, I tell you. Hell would freeze over with a cherry on top first!'

Personally, I thought wilderness was a bit harsh. They knew I'd had a handful of disastrous hot dates back in New York after splitting up with Morgan. I looked at Verde.

'Emer's right. You've put yourself on ice waiting for him. Morgan ruined romance for you.'

Emer gasped at the audacity of Verde. 'You should talk! Where's the wonderful man in your life, Verde? Where is he? I've worked with you for over two years and I've never seen him. I've seen a few lustful dates come and go but nothing special.'

'I'm not looking for anything special,' Verde said casually. 'I've enough on my mind career wise.'

'Honestly, sometimes I despair for the two of you. I really do,' Emer said, sounding exasperated.

Verde spread her arms and shrugged her shoulders. 'I'm ambitious. But that's my choice.'

Emer put her fork down. There was a strawberry spiked on it, untouched, and as strawberries are her favorite thing in the world, or so she'd said when she speared it at the buffet, I had to conclude that she was serious about what she had to say. 'I'm intensely ambitious.'

Verde raised a skeptical eyebrow.

Emer clenched her fist. 'I am! My ambition is to marry an architect.'

Verde and I exchanged a questioning look.

Emer was insistent. 'You don't see many architects lying in the street roaring drunk, down on their luck or scandalized in the newspapers. Architects do very well for themselves. I'm after one of those. They've got lovely names too. Names like Adam, Phillip, Jefferson. Men like that have got time for you. Certainly, they're often in business for themselves, but they're not forever doing mergers and takeovers like Morgan and Randolph. I couldn't be arsed with that. Your life as a wife would revolve around their power struggles until the day they retired. No thank you, that's not for me. Give me an architect any day.'

'If that's all you want, you're really not ambitious,' Verde concluded.

Emer shook her head. 'You don't get it, do you? I'm not like you two. Truly no offense, but my ambitions are stronger than yours. My ambition is to be happy. And for me that will come from being happily married. You and Blue are likely to end up with a Morgan or a Sears. But imagine you had a spot on your nose. A great big pimple from eating too many sweets. If you woke up in the morning beside the likes of Sears, could you let him see you looking like that? Could you really do that with Sears?'

Our faces answered her question.

'No, I didn't think so. You'd be doing a stealth move across the bedroom to dab concealer on your nose before he woke up. For me, that type of relationship would be too exhausting. No, I'll have my architect. Life would be sweeter.'

'Why don't you get one now? Why wait?' I said.

'Because I want some wonderful life experiences under my belt first. I want to have stories to tell my kids — and things to talk about to my husband and our friends, so I won't feel like I never did anything extraordinary. I mean, here I am in Dublin dressed outrageously with my face painted to look like a masquerade mask. What a story that'll be.'

Verde seemed suddenly subdued. Was she thinking what she'd do once Emer had gone? No one had lasted this long working with Verde ever before.

'How long do you think you'll continue working for Randolph's company?' I asked Emer.

'Two years and then I'll be off to be happy forever.' She paused then added, 'Verde will be fine when I get married. I'll be able to watch both your careers progress, and all the trouble making you'll cause in the press, maybe even on the television. And I'll say — I know them. They're my friends, Verde Valmont and Blue Byrne.'

'I'm glad you won't just slip out of our lives,' I said.

'You and Verde are never getting rid of me. Even when I'm up to my arse in nappies, I'll be on the phone saying — don't you be showing yourselves up on national news and stuff like that.'

'But there's no guarantee that your marriage will be a happy forever one,' Verde said. 'Your husband could turn out to be a real nightmare.'

Emer shook her head in disagreement. 'Nope, it won't happen. You both know I'll pick the right man because my radar is accurate to within a gnat's bollocks. So he'll be lovely and I'll look after him and the kids — and be happy. And I'm ferociously ambitious about that.'

Verde seemed pensive.

'You thought about it,' Emer said to her. 'You thought — is there an architect out there for me? You wondered if you could settle for a bit of happiness with a man like that.'

Verde smiled, but wouldn't admit it.

'You did, Verde. You did,' said Emer.

'I'm sure Blue thought about it too,' Verde said, foisting some of focus on to me.

'No, Blue's different. She's got a glitch in her nature that stops her choosing the right man. We're all wired differently. Blue's unique, and because of that she'll often make the wrong choices.'

My heart sank. Emer meant no harm but something struck a chord with me. Deep down I knew she was right.

'No offense, Blue,' Emer apologized, 'but your romantic vision is so narrow it only focuses on Morgan, or maybe Sears. You seem blinkered to every other eligible man you meet.'

Morgan wasn't mine anyway, I thought darkly. And Sears never had been.

'For example, there was a lovely man asking you to dance and have a drink — and what did you do?'

'I brushed him off because of Morgan Daire,' I said honestly.

Verde straightened the straps of her spellbinding dress and tried to sound decisive when I really thought she was upset for me. 'Okay, tonight, for one night, Blue and I will say yes to any decent men who want to dance with us.' She turned and looked at me.

'All right,' I agreed. 'We'll see what happens. This will be the night we say, yes. But I want a built in Cinderella clause. We won't take any of them home at the end of the night.'

A high fives between the three of us sealed our agreement.

Emer ate her strawberry and decided to go back to the buffet for more. I went with her.

'Bastards,' she muttered when she saw the caterers had added the most sumptuous cake. It was sitting as a centerpiece with a big, juicy strawberry perched on the top layer of whipped cream. The cake itself was displayed quite high, and even with a long spoon, and standing on her tiptoes, Emer was having a problem retrieving that damned strawberry.

It didn't help that I couldn't stop laughing as I held on to her waist to anchor her while she tried to reach it.

'Can I give you a hand?' a man said from behind us.

I turned to find a handsome looking man poised to help Emer. I stepped back, letting go of her waist.

She wobbled slightly and he put his hands where mine had been and steadied her in an instant.

'Oh!' she gasped, realizing she'd been grabbed by a tall, dark, handsome stranger who didn't think it odd that a grown woman was climbing half way up the posh buffet to steal a strawberry. 'I was just —'

But he'd taken the spoon from her hand, and retrieved the strawberry. Then he lifted her down, and with his face so close to hers he said, 'luscious, isn't it?'

'Oh yes,' Emer said, not even looking at the fruit.

'You smell delicious,' he whispered.

That was the last we saw of Emer while she ate her cake at his table. She kept secretly waving over to us, and mouthed that he was a lawyer.

By now the fashionably late guests who'd wanted to make an entrance, had arrived en masse.

'I'm going to get some cake before it disappears,' I said to Verde. Do you want any?'

After a fifteen second thoughtful pause she nodded. I went over, got two slices, and uninterrupted by any stray lawyers on strawberry alert, came straight back with them.

While we ate our cake, we were approached by three different men. Had this been an era where we'd had dance cards, they'd have been filled within the first part of the evening. Anyway, we agreed to dance with each of them later on.

'I can't take my eyes off you,' Murphy said to Verde, finally breaking free from his obligation of meeting most of the guests. He sat down beside us.

'It's the dress,' Verde said to him.

'No, it's the woman who's wearing it,' he insisted.

That's the moment I saw the spark between them. It was a light flirtation, and then it was gone again.

'What's that perfume you're wearing?' he said to me. 'I don't recognize it. What's the name of it?'

'It's a special concoction of various scents,' I said, smiling.

'We're keeping it a secret,' Verde said teasingly.

He shook his head and laughed. 'The pair of you are up to no good. I love it! All muses should have secrets.'

So of course with it being Murphy, we told him all about our perfume ploy and that we weren't taking it seriously. It was just a bit of fun.

'Fun it may be, but if your frivolity turns out to work — and it certainly has an effect on me, then I'll consider bottling it and making it the signature scent for my designs. Though we definitely won't use the phrase *catnip for men* in the advertising copy,' he joked. But hidden within his joke was a note of future possibility.

He stood up and offered his hand to Verde. 'Are we dancing? No one's taken to the floor yet. Will we get this party off to a fine start?'

Verde took his hand and off they sauntered, after he'd made me promise the next dance to him.

I sat back and watched them take to the floor. He was wearing a dark blue dinner suit with a regency shirt, giving him the flamboyant designer look that was part of his style. Verde was the perfect match for him in her spellbinding dress. Everyone in the room stopped to watch and admire them.

'Would you like to dance?' a man said politely, taking me aback. I'd been so busy watching them dance I hadn't noticed him approach. I instinctively went to say no, then I remembered the agreement. Here was a charming man who had summoned up the courage to ask me to dance with him.

'Yes,' I said. 'Though I have to warn you — I'm not a very good dancer.'

He smiled. 'That's perfectly fine.'

On the dance floor he didn't seem to care that I was dancing out of step with everyone else, and we waltzed to the best of his ability. He said he was an art collector and traveled all over the world in search of artifacts. He certainly wouldn't have made the grade on Emer's list unless he'd found some way of being home in the evening for his dinner from wherever he was.

When we'd finished dancing I looked over at Murphy. He was still waltzing with Verde. It was only later that I got a chance to talk to him.

'You seem rather taken with Verde,' I said.

He acted uneasy. 'I do, don't I,' he said, almost against his better judgment.

'What's wrong? You're not pretending to like her, are you?'

'No, it's just . . .'

The look on his face said it all. Now I understood. 'It's the cross between a heartless android and a cobra thing.'

'Exactly,' Murphy said.

'Verde's got another side to her. I used to loathe her, but now we're getting on okay.'

'Yes, but I distinctly remember you saying there were times when you wanted to like her and thought she liked you,' Murphy reminded me.

'That's true. But things happen. Deep, deep, down she's quite witty, intelligent and generous.'

'I've always seen her as a cold hearted, inhuman bitch. She's a headache in high heels.'

'She is,' I said. 'That's what makes her Vee–Vee.'

He shook his head and looked down. 'I just don't want to have my heart fried and skewered. It's such a risk. Of all the women — Verde Valmont.' He put his hands up to his face. 'That woman could go through a man's heart like acid. And yet . . . I do like her.'

'I tell you what. Give yourself some time. Don't rush it.'

He nodded and took a deep breath. 'The party's going well, isn't it?'

'Up until now.'

He frowned at me.

'I promised to dance with you,' I said, smiling. 'Seeing me quickstep with you is sure to clear the dance floor.'

He immediately linked my arm through his and led me through the crowd. 'Don't say anything to Vee–Vee.'

'Say anything about what?' I teased him.

He laughed, and then off we went, skip stepping across the dance floor out of sync with everything and everyone in perfect unison.

Chapter Thirteen

Magnets for Trouble

Murphy and I were just about to attempt a mambo when a man cut in and asked me to dance.

Giddy and almost breathless from dancing with Murphy, I was still smiling as I turned around to see Morgan standing there. He hadn't been on the guest list for the party, but for someone like him the lack of an invitation wasn't going to stand in his way.

I squeezed Murphy's hand, assuring him it was okay to let me go. Dance with Morgan Daire? Oh yes, he deserved the shortfall of my ability to keep in time to the music. With Murphy it was different, and in fact we were getting better at being out of step. We were becoming quite good at it.

'Would you like to dance with me?' Morgan repeated. The lingering gap as my thoughts strayed had forced him to ask again.

'Yes why not?' I replied, knowing there various reasons why I shouldn't dance with him. Being pinned down by him on his bed earlier that day was one of them.

Murphy reluctantly let go of me, and I felt Morgan take me in his very capable hands. The music was softly blending in the background gearing up for the next dance.

'Is there a valid reason for the unusual face paint?' Morgan said, eyeing my makeup. 'This doesn't appear to be a fancy dress event.'

He had to ask! He just had to. Every other man had accepted me as I was, but Morgan needed to challenge the validity of my appearance. He'll never know how close I came to walking away from him right there and then. The only thing that stopped me was the thought of dancing with him. I was a bit like Emer. I wanted some wonderful life experiences under my belt. I'd traveled all the way from Manhattan to Dublin mainly, but not only, to deal with old wounds and challenge Morgan on his home turf. And here I was, all dressed up like a shimmering silver fantasy in his arms, waiting for the music to start. There was no benefit in backing down. A memorable experience was about to be created.

I looked up at Morgan, into those green eyes that demanded an answer about my makeup. So I told him the truth.

'I'm wearing this because you agreed with Randolph about inviting Magenta to the extravaganza. We're practicing our look for the masquerade ball. I believe Verde has already explained about the trouble Magenta will cause.'

He looked at me like he wished he'd never asked.

The music began. It was a two dance medley. A slow, romantic waltz would soon give way to a lively foxtrot.

'Can you do the foxtrot, or will we call it quits after the waltz?' he said.

'I can foxtrot,' I said defiantly. Whether he could do a Murphy and adapt to my version of the foxtrot was another matter. That smooth black suit of his and dark gray shirt were in jeopardy of getting a ruffling they'd never forget.

He led me into the center of the floor where there was no hiding place if I messed up the steps. We began to waltz, and I hoped my silvery dress would provide a dazzling display to distract from my dancing.

For the first few minutes I felt tense within his waltzing hold. He was a good dancer, though Murphy was better. It unnerved me being so close to Morgan, somehow forgetting how tall he was as his broad shoulders towered above me.

'You smell . . . lovely,' he said.

I thought he smelled good — freshly showered, probably having done a mad dash back home to get changed into his evening wear and then drive back up to the party. His shirt smelled brand new.

'I wanted to apologize to you for any brutish behavior today,' he said, sounding as if he meant it. 'When I heard you were going sailing with Sears . . .'

'Why would you even care?'

His eyes focused directly into mine. 'You know why.'

'No, I don't. I thought we were finished long ago,' I said.

'Were we? If that's true then why are you here?'

'Randolph sent me to work with Verde.'

He gave a wry smile. 'Randolph said you fought like a tiger to win this assignment.'

Damn! Randolph had told him about the meeting in Manhattan.

'I did,' I said, trying to sound calm. 'I wanted to find the latest fashions. My marketing experience indicated that Dublin was a likely source of great new designs.'

'So it had nothing to do with seeing me again?' He sounded disappointed.

'I didn't know you'd still be here,' I said lightly.

The silence showed I'd wounded his pride. I hammered another point home while he was on the ropes. 'When I saw you again you were barely civil to me. Murphy was delighted to see me. But you showed no hint of being pleased to see me whatsoever.'

'You were game playing — wearing the same clothes and the same hairstyle from the night you'd left here years ago. What did you expect?'

I stopped dancing and we stood there facing each other. He was still holding me in his arms, as if we'd paused mid dance, frozen in time, while we challenged each other's motives.

'Maybe I expected you to see me the way you used to. To remember how we used to be. I hoped you'd apologize for the things you'd said to me the last time we'd been together.'

'It was you who ran back to Manhattan, not me,' he snapped.

'You said there was no place for me in Dublin, no future for us,' I told him bluntly. 'In my position, would you have stayed?'

'No, but neither would I have turned up again looking like the bloody ghost of Christmas past!' he shouted.

People around us glared, and he began dancing with me again as the waltz ended and the music quickened pace for the foxtrot.

I thought for a moment he was going to call it quits and forgo the fiasco of the foxtrot, but no, he got a firm grip of me and got ready to trip the light fantastic. Out of the corner of my eye I saw Murphy watching us.

Then we began, with him in time to the music and me somewhere else. I felt his grip tighten as he tried to force me to keep in tandem with him. It was our life in miniature set to music — always just out of step with each other.

Hand on heart, I can say that I danced my socks off. I genuinely tried to nail that rhythm. Perhaps that's why it was quite so awful. With Murphy I'd kept the wrong timing in sync throughout the dance. I'd been consistently wrong. With Morgan I managed several variations of bad timing. He had to repeatedly adapt like a man possessed. Luckily I couldn't see the full picture because he had me so tightly held in his grip of bloody mindedness to make me dance the foxtrot with him to the bitter end.

I was aware that someone with a video camera was capturing every moment, and other dancing couples were tactfully giving us a wide berth. They weren't clearing the floor out of admiration. It was out of necessity. They didn't want to risk being anywhere near us.

We circled like a whirling dervish around the floor to a song that seemed to be the extended version of the original. But what the heck! Everyone was getting double the value to see a moment in social dancing history that few would ever forget. Yes, it was one of those wonderful life experiences Emer had mentioned.

Murphy was howling with laughter. He was literally holding on to an ornate pillar gasping for air, splitting his sides laughing.

When the music stopped, Morgan glared daggers at me, his eyes accusing me of intentionally making a complete farce out of the foxtrot, and then he stomped off.

The music started up again quickly, and everyone went back on to the floor as if drawn by an invisible magnet. A few were smirking or sneering in disapproval.

No one was laughing out loud like Murphy. He was even making me laugh.

Emer hurried over to him. 'Ssh!' she said. 'You're taking the good off your promotion.'

Verde grabbed Murphy in the nearest thing to an arm lock and together we hustled him away to a quiet corner.

'Tell me someone has videoed that pleeease,' he said, still laughing like a demon. 'That's going to be on my all time favorite list of home entertainment. Did you see Morgan's legs? They were all over the place.'

Even Verde was starting to laugh. 'Stop it! People are looking at you. Stop laughing,' she said.

'Is Murphy all right?' a manager asked anxiously.

Emer barred his way. 'Yes, he's right as rain, thank you. A helium balloon burst and the vapors went right up his nose. The effects will wear off in a minute.'

After some officious finger snapping and muttering we saw two members of staff surreptitiously snipping the ribbons that secured the helium balloons on display and collect every one of them. The last we saw of the balloons they were being taken through the crowd into the back of the venue where they were never seen again.

Judging by the way Morgan stomped off we were unlikely to see him back here again any time soon either.

The four of us sat down in the alcove and Murphy got us a bottle of champagne before dashing off to attend to his models. Overall, his fashions were well received and a few lucrative business transactions were sealed.

Verde's wrist cracked as she downed her second glass of champagne. 'Tomorrow I thought you and I could hit the streets and see what trends are leading the pack,' she said to me. 'Dublin does have something different to offer. There are several innovative designers who're showing at the extravaganza so we can cherry pick from their ranges too — and that includes two or three trends from Murphy's collection.'

'Murphy's really going to be big on the international scene,' I predicted. 'The flamboyance and fresh perspective is a great combination. I'd certainly wear most of his collection. We won't be going back to Randolph empty handed that's for sure.'

'I love the beautiful top that model is wearing,' Emer said, pointing towards the model nearby. 'It's unique without looking like it's from outer space. I could see myself wearing it somewhere special.' Her expression became wistful. 'I'd love to go out on one of the yachts at the extravaganza.'

'Go sailing with Morgan or Sears?' I said.

'Yes. Just to say I'd sailed at the event. Though I'm certain hell would freeze over before either of them offer to take me out on their big, fancy yachts.'

I made a mental note of Emer's wish before we were interrupted.

'You promised to dance with me,' one of the men from earlier prompted me. 'I'd like to hold you to your promise,' he added, smiling.

I think if I'd have hesitated for one second longer, Emer would've jumped at the chance. This was the first man who'd approached me — sun lightened brown hair, blue–green eyes.

Emer whispered to me. 'If he's an architect, I'm stealing him and leaving Verde and you in the lurch two years early.'

We'd been dancing for about ten minutes when I noticed Emer making frantic hand signals to me from the alcove. Shit timing as always. I made my excuses and hurried over to her. Before I had a chance to ask her what was wrong she blurted out, 'Verde's dress has disappeared!'

I blinked. 'What? Like in a puff of smoke? Whoosh and it was gone.'

Emer pulled me aside. 'I'm serious,' she hissed. 'Verde's distraught.'

Obviously I didn't think her dress had gone up in a puff of magic smoke. 'Okay, what happened? Did someone steal her dress?'

Emer pointed an angry finger at my ear. 'You're not listening. The fuckin' fabric has disintegrated. Not all of it, but the straps are gone and the seams have given way. It's like trying to hold a paper tissue dress together. It was a sample evening gown. Not a proper dress. It was designed to show off a new type of futuristic fabric.' She stuffed a small instruction tag into my hands. 'This was inside the dress. It lists all the things you should never ever do with this dress.'

'Such as?' I said, skimming over the details.

'Such as everything Verde did from the moment she put it on. And of course both of us tried it on too which weakened the seams and the fabric. It was an accident waiting to happen.

'So it just disappeared?' I said.

'Yes. We were sitting there having our champagne when she spilled some of it down her dress. Well! Within seconds the straps looked like wet tissue paper, and the weight of the bottom of the dress made the top half fall down. Her chesticles were on display before she'd even put her champagne glass down. Then when she made a run for the ladies loo the other half was like gauze. She could hardly hold it together.'

I gasped. I did. I gasped. There were so many things nowadays that were hard to fathom. New formulas and fabrics were being created all the time.

'What's Verde wearing right now?' I said anxiously.

'Murphy. Oh and he's loving it. His hands were everywhere. I mean *everywhere*. All in the name of covering her modesty of course.'

'Didn't he give her his jacket?'

'*Eventually*,' Emer said, giving a knowing wink. 'Bloody men. Anyway, she needs a dress. Yours or mine. Murphy's models came straight here in the agency bus fully dressed in their fashion, so they've nothing here to spare that she can put on. The management don't have any ladies clothes and Verde refuses point blank to wear a table cover, so it up to you and me.'

The look on Emer's face wasn't giving both options. She meant I had to give my dress to Verde.

225

'Awe, come on, Blue. You'd be wearing Murphy's jacket. You know how paranoid I am about my thighs. You've got a great pair of pins. His jacket would be like a short dress on you. With those high heeled shoes you're wearing it'd show your legs off brilliantly.'

And so of course . . .

Verde, Emer and I had to walk the full length of the venue with me wearing Murphy's jacket and very little else. Verde wore my silver dress. Everyone paused to stare at us as we walked past. Word had got around about Verde's dress falling apart.

'Luckily we've got these masks painted on,' Verde muttered to us. 'At least people won't recognize us again.'

I wasn't so sure. Two Manhattan magnets for trouble and a fiery, Dublin PA tended to flag attention.

The car we'd arrived in was waiting outside to whisk us off. Murphy stayed to finish the end of his promotional night, but his muses had certainly made their mark on the evening.

We went back to Verde's house where I changed into my own clothes and then took a taxi to my hotel. And all before midnight. The Cinderella clause had worked after all.

After making myself a cup of coffee, I checked my e–mails. There was one from Harry. It said that he'd done the number crunching and had discovered that

226

Morgan was so wealthy he could buy and sell Randolph. I'd always known Morgan was affluent, but this put him in another league. Harry also revealed that Morgan's finances had increased dramatically during the past four years from sales of his fashion designs — and now he was getting ready to make his designer name public. Morgan Daire Designs, Dublin, was due to be launched very soon.

I quickly accessed the list of designers who were exhibiting at the extravaganza. I remembered Verde mentioning that someone had booked a slot on the runway schedule, but the fashion company's name had yet to be confirmed. It was penciled in under the initials MDD, which I now interpreted as Morgan Daire Designs. Morgan was exhibiting his fashions at the extravaganza. That was one event I wasn't going to miss.

I e-mailed Harry thanking him for the information, and then I phoned Verde to tell her everything.

'I've had my suspicions,' she confided. 'As I've said before, Morgan's full of surprises. We won't have long to wait to find out what he's been secretly designing. It's just over two weeks until the extravaganza. All will be revealed then.'

'He's been trading in accessories,' I said while typing his details into my computer, trying to access anything about his business on the Internet. 'According to a few snippets on the web, his company is into accessory design — handbags, shoes, scarves and jewelery.'

'There's a fortune to be made in those markets,' Verde said. 'Morgan's such a shrewd businessman.'

We agreed to keep this information quiet and see what type of runway fashions Morgan displayed at the event.

Before going to bed, I stepped outside on to the balcony and breathed in the cool night air. It was colder than earlier, and the sky had a threatening undertone. There was a strange warning in the night, a change in the atmosphere — and I sensed that things were never going to be quite the same again.

Chapter Fourteen

Fortune Telling in the Rain

It was pouring rain outside my office in Temple Bar. The weather had changed overnight. Yesterday's sea squall in Dun Laoghaire had been a hint of forthcoming rain. The weather in Dublin could be completely unpredictable, but that's what I loved about it. There was always an element of excitement in the air. I could sense it today, despite the rain, though it was typical that the first day Verde and I planned to hit the streets in search of the latest fashion trends, it would be umbrella weather.

From my window overlooking the square and cobbled streets, the rain had brought more color to the environment in the form of bright red and yellow umbrellas, and vibrant raincoats, jackets and lightweight waterproof boots. Through the rain running down the window everything appeared like a primary bright watercolor painting whose colors had blurred into artistic perfection.

A market stallholder was selling lots of umbrellas and rain jackets, and I knew that Verde and I would be adding to their revenue when we ventured outside.

I'd been sketching designs for the masquerade masks. Murphy insisted he'd make them if I gave him the sketches, and with the ball looming ever closer I'd started drawing the designs as soon as I got into work.

'Can I have more curly cues at the corners of the eyes?' Emer said, leaning over my shoulder and putting a cup of tea down on my desk.

I scribbled an embellishment on to the design. 'How about that? I'll mark that these should be decorated with bronze and copper colored sparkles and glitz.'

'Fantastic, Blue. You're a star,' she said.

Verde was on the phone to Sears doing her utmost to find out from him where the hotspots of future fashions were located in the city. I got the impression he'd told me the truth on the yacht yesterday. He hadn't found anything of great value, not yet, and any information he'd gathered he wasn't prepared to share with us.

She walked into my office, and I motioned to her to cut the call short. She did, telling him they should keep in touch.

'We'll mine our own diamonds,' I said to her. 'I've made some contacts in the city. We'll research those first.'

'Great,' she said, and then turned one of my sketches around on the desk to look at it. 'These are wonderful, Blue.'

'Do you want more curly cues?' I offered. 'Maybe some elongated, gold metallic wings at the edges?'

She'd been going to say no to the curly cues, but when the offer of winged edges came up she jumped at it. 'Oh yes,' she said, watching as I sketched them into the design.

'These masks are going to be spectacular. No one will have anything like them,' said Verde. 'In fact,' she added thoughtfully, 'we need some artwork for the new posters to advertise the masquerade ball. We'll use your sketches, if that's okay with you, Blue?'

'Fine by me,' I said. I planned to have the sketches finished later today and whiz them over to Murphy so he could start making them.

Verde went over to the window and gazed out at the rain. 'Shall we?' she said to me.

I nodded. I'd walked into work in a pair of stylish black boots as it was already threatening rain when I left the hotel. I wore them with my plaid bitch-proof suit that both Verde and Emer had admired. The neutral colored plaid had an uncanny habit of blending with its environment. In the city, the stone and gray tones reflected the colors of the buildings. Near the coast it appeared cooler, with a hint of sea green, even though the fine green thread in the fabric was barely noticeable, as if it affected the subconscious without the conscious seeing it. It was like painting a portrait of someone with blonde hair. To make them appear more blonde all you had to do was add a few flecks of green to the hair. Standing back, the green disappeared from the conscious view, but had the effect of making the hair look blonder. The suit had that hidden quality. There were fine Prussian blue and amethyst threads in the mix along with the green. In a way, the plaid bitch–proof suit had a chameleon effect, and created a sense that you belonged wherever you were.

Leaving Emer to man the office, Verde and I ventured out, scurrying like mad across the wet cobblestones. Verde was wearing a pair of fashionable boots in a neutral shade that she kept in the office for rainy days. The heels were mildly sensible. She didn't need to hold on to my arm to steady herself on the cobbles.

We shivered slightly under the canopy of the market stall and chose two umbrellas and knee length rain jackets. Verde's were yellow and mine were red. Inexpensive and designed not to last, they still kept us warm and dry.

We laughed at each other as we zipped ourselves into the silky plastic jackets and put our umbrellas up in a fumbling haste. Umbrellas and I have never seen eye to eye. If this umbrella lasted a day it would be a personal record. Usually they'd blown inside out within minutes.

Then there's the drenched cat syndrome that inflicts some women and completely bypasses others. I've never been able to fathom what it is that I do wrong. I envy women who are able to wear a smart business suit and if it dares to rain, they simply put up an umbrella that keeps their clothes dry and their hair immaculate — as if they'd just stepped out of their office. How do they do that?

Verde falls into that fortunate category. This morning her hair was in a chic chignon. I didn't doubt that when we got back from our futurehunting street adventure she'd put her umbrella down and her hair would still be perfect. But I'd lay bets that my updo would be wet and straggly and somehow the rain would've got through to my suit.

Verde's bright yellow umbrella gave her face a golden glow and I could see the red of my umbrella radiating around me. It was possibly the only time we'd ever be beacon bright and merge with the crowd into the sea of gleaming umbrellas. Colorfully incognito is how I'd describe it.

But there's always someone who recognizes you, isn't there?

'Hello, ladies. I thought it was you. You're invariably dazzling in gold and red somewhere on the streets of Dublin.'

We tilted our umbrellas back to look up at the man who was standing in our way. It was Murphy's friend, the gorgeous Garda. Decked out in his resplendent police uniform, he was smiling down at us.

We didn't know his name. We didn't need to. He spoke as if we were long time acquaintances.

'What mischief are you ladies up today may I ask?' he said cheerfully.

Verde became a bit flirty. I didn't blame her. Deep down I was glad he'd caught us at the start of our street trekking rather than at the tail end when my hair would've looked bedraggled. Such was the effect of the gorgeous Garda.

'Oh we're just heading out to look for the latest fashion trends,' Verde said, thinking he'd be none the wiser about our business.

But we were wrong.

'Well,' he said, sounding very sure of himself, 'if you wander up that way, over the Ha'penny Bridge and on to Henry Street, I think you'll find some amazing shops and boutiques that'll inspire you.'

Verde looked at me, and he obviously misinterpreted her expression, mistaking her — *can you believe this guy* for *what the hell is this man talking about?* So he took her politely by the shoulders and turned her around until she was compass point in line with the direction she should go. 'Right up there,' he said, pointing.

'Then,' he said, taking a deep breath, 'come back the way you came and head up that way, to Grafton Street and Dawson Street. There are high fashion shops with jewelery, handbags, and everything you need to work out what the new trends are likely to be. Be adventurous too — take a look up the little side streets that run off the main thoroughfares.' He checked the time on his watch. 'At around eleven this morning there's a new shop opening in the Grafton Street area so that could be worth a look.'

'Thank you,' Verde said.

He smiled. 'You're very welcome.'

'You seem to know your fashion,' I said.

'It's good to take an interest in what's new,' he said.

Then Verde and I had the same thought. She spoke first.

'We're having a fashion extravaganza and yachting event in Dun Laoghaire in a couple of weeks time.'

'There's a masquerade ball,' I told him.

Verde nodded. 'Would you like an invitation?'

He hesitated but his face lit up at the thought of it.

'We'd be delighted if you'd be a guest,' I said.

'That would be grand,' he said, clearly taken aback. 'A masquerade ball? I'll look forward to that. I've policed the sailing event before, but it'll make a nice change to be part of it this year.'

We took his contact details and promised to send him an invitation.

'I'll see you at the ball,' he said, and waving, went on about his duty.

'That man is luscious,' Verde said as we headed over the Ha'penny Bridge, as he'd suggested, jostling with numerous others and their umbrellas crossing the Liffey.

'Good job he's not an architect,' I said.

'Emer would steal him and —'

'Abandon us two years early,' we said in unison, laughing, and hurried through the rain, our umbrellas angled against the stormy day.

We found quite a lot of inspiration in the Henry Street area of the city, and also on the other side of the river when we headed back to Temple Bar and up to Grafton Street. The gorgeous Garda had been right. A new shop was opening and we were among the first to set foot in it. It was stocked with fresh and exciting fashions, created by several designers who'd joined together to bring their work to the commercial hub of the city.

Overall, our morning's work had been worthwhile, and even though it was still raining, we were filled with enthusiasm as we hurried back to our offices.

En route we picked up something for our lunch. Numerous eateries catered for every taste and we opted for sumptuous fresh baked, thick cut bread sandwiches with delicious fillings. We got some for Emer too. Mine were bursting with salad ingredients, and we bought fresh fruit salad for dessert.

Holding our umbrellas over the food to keep it dry, we didn't expect to be approached by a complete stranger near the bottom of Grafton Street. It was one of the city's fortune tellers. I don't know why we stopped. Perhaps it was something in the man's manner, or something he sensed from us that made him call out to us in the crowd.

Verde and I stopped, huddled underneath our umbrellas, and decided what to do.

'I've always wanted to have my fortune told,' Verde whispered to me. 'Do you think it'll take long?'

He peered out from under his black umbrella. 'No, not long,' he said, overhearing her. 'You can ask a few questions and I'll answer them for you.'

'Okay,' Verde said, stepping nearer to him.

I went to step back so she could talk to him in private, but she said there was nothing secret that I didn't know already.

She began by asking about the extravaganza. Would it be a success?

The man gazed at her for a good thirty seconds, which isn't long, but seems long when a stranger is gazing right at you. Then he said, 'Yes for some, and no for others.'

Verde was taken aback. 'Will it be a success for me?'

'Yes, but water and danger will play a large part in it,' he said.

'It's a sailing event as well as a fashion event so water will be involved,' she explained.

He cut in. 'I understand that, but I'll say again. For you personally, water and danger is waiting for you.'

'And you,' he said, looking directly at me.

My stomach flipped, especially as he hadn't turned a single card, studied our palms or anything like that. He'd only looked at us, presumably using his psychic powers to glean this information.

Now of course Verde and I were unsettled. We wanted to know what sort of danger, how to avoid it and what would happen.

'The danger is in the water — and in your pride and competitiveness.'

'We're not actually competing in the sailing event,' I said, just to clarify.

'This doesn't involve boats, only the water,' he said darkly.

'Okay,' Verde said. 'Can we avoid this danger?'

'Yes, you could, but you'll choose not to.'

'Are men, arrogant men, involved in this scenario?' I said, thinking perhaps that Morgan or Sears had something to do with it.

He shook his head.

We were flummoxed.

'Right,' I said, recapping. 'We're going to do something dangerous involving water, and although we could avoid it, we won't. So can you see what will happen?'

The rain was battering off our umbrellas, and his. He thought long and hard before saying, 'Your daring will pay off. You'll both be all right in that sense.'

I know we were getting carried away by this, but I'd defy most women to be okay about having a fortune teller set their nerves on edge, whether you believe in it or not. You had to be there. It was the look his eyes, as if he could see right into our lives.

So anyway, Verde comes right out and challenges him. 'How about cutting to the point? What is eventually going to happen?'

He smiled and tipped his umbrella back to have a closer look at us. The water ran off it like a waterfall down the back of his long dark coat. In the grand scheme of things, he was a fine looking man, very roguish and rugged.

'If I were to give you any advice it would be this,' he began, 'both of your futures could've been here in Dublin, on these shores, but it's not to be. Your futures lie far from here.'

I don't know about Verde but my mind shot immediately to thoughts of Morgan and me. If my future wasn't here, did that include him? Then I realized that Morgan would be moving to New York or at least splitting his time between the two cities when he merged with Randolph's company. I also took into account that the fortune teller could hear that we were American and therefore it was likely our future was far from Dublin.

He was still talking. 'Both of you will make your mark on the world.' He pointed firmly at me. 'You especially. Don't ask me why. I can't see any more than that.'

'If we believed in any of this, we could change our future if we wanted to, couldn't we?' said Verde.

'Yes that's the whole point in me telling someone their fortune. It's their future *as things stand* but it's not cast in stone. The purpose is to tell you probable outcomes and for you to make the right choices. You decide your future. It's what you make of it.'

A gust of wind suddenly blew my rain jacket wide open, and it flapped behind me like a cape. I'd unfastened it to reach my purse to pay for my sandwiches and hadn't bothered fastening it again because the rain had somehow managed to get through and dampen part of it anyway.

His eyes focused like a hawk on my plaid bitch–proof suit. Then he looked into my eyes, and then back to the suit.

'Your suit means a lot to you, doesn't it?' he said finally.

'It does.'

He was momentarily unsettled and then smiled quietly. 'Very clever,' he said, 'very clever. I don't understand why, but that's what I sense.'

Verde frowned, and then brought the topic back to the advice he was giving us. 'Can you give any advice on eh . . . men for instance?'

'You mean romance?' he corrected her.

'Yes,' Verde said.

241

'Or did you?' he questioned her.

'Yes, I meant romance.'

He shook his head. 'There lies your answer. Plenty of men in your life. Few with the potential for romance. So choose wisely.'

Our lunch was starting to get soaked, and so were we, standing there in the rain. 'How much do we owe you?' Verde said, opening her handbag.

'If I'm right about the water and the danger, come back and tell me, and pay me then,' he said. 'If not, there's nothing owed to me.'

Verde wouldn't hear of it and forced what she thought was a fair amount into his hands. 'You were right about the romance,' she said boldly. 'There are those who would call me cold hearted and flighty —'

'I didn't,' he said politely.

'No, but it was inferred — and you're right, but I'm working on it, and I do have another side to my nature.' She was babbling, almost arguing with herself. 'I suppose you'd advise me to show my better side more often.'

What he said took us both by surprise. 'Not until after your event down the coast. Don't drop that ferocious guard of yours until that day is done.'

'Okay,' Verde said, taken aback.

'Thanks again,' I said, and began to walk away with my rain jacket flapping in the wind.

'Nice suit,' he called after me.

I turned and looked over my shoulder. He smiled, and I smiled back at him, and then Verde and I disappeared into the crowd of umbrellas again.

Chapter Fifteen

Dinner or a Date

Emer sucked the air in through her pursed lips, and peered at us over the edge of her sandwich. 'Water and danger are waiting for you at the extravaganza? Ooh, that sounds ominous.'

We were having lunch in my office and watching the world go by through the window. Emer had made us a lovely big pot of tea.

Verde's hair was still in a chic chignon. In contrast, my hair had created its own bedraggled style from the rain. The front of it had more curly cues than Emer's masquerade mask. However, I planned to enjoy lunch and then smooth it into submission with Verde's array of hair products that she kept in her desk.

'What do you think it all means?' Emer asked in a mysterious tone.

'It could mean anything,' I said, searching for a hidden message, though gut instinct warned me that we needed to be wary. I wasn't really into this sort of thing, but I thought it would be wise to keep an open mind, especially as he'd nailed the fact that my plaid suit really did mean a lot to me.

'I'll be interested to see if he's right,' Verde said, seemingly unfazed by it all.

'I've had my fortune told lots of times,' Emer said. 'I've been told I'll marry a tall, dark stranger and live near the sea, by someone who reads the tealeaves. But it's more for a bit of fun than anything else. I've been told all sorts of things.'

'Like what?' I said, pouring myself more tea and wondering if it was possible to read our fortunes from the dregs of the teabags.

'Well, I've been told that my future husband will be a policeman — but that's never going to happen.'

'A *policeman*?' I said, casting a glance at Verde.

'Yes,' said Emer. 'But I'm settling for nothing less than my architect.'

'What if that was the wrong choice?' I said.

'It won't be,' Emer insisted. 'You see, despite what anyone says, my gut instinct keeps me right.' She shrugged. 'Maybe I'll have a wild fling with a policeman, but I won't marry him.'

My computer alerted us that Randolph was trying to make contact. We took the webcam call on my laptop computer.

'Don't let me interrupt your lunch, ladies,' Randolph chirped. 'It's good to see you tucking in.'

'Hello, Randolph,' Verde said. 'How's things your end?'

'Good. I've just had a call from Morgan. He wants to push the merger through sooner than planned. It could be a done deal by tomorrow.'

'Why the rush?' I asked him.

'Morgan says he wants everything sorted out before the extravaganza. I agree with him. The merger's going ahead anyway, so why drag our heels?'

A man's voice resonated from the doorway of the office, sounding like someone objecting at a wedding. 'Why hurry? The merger date was set for after the sailing challenge.'

'Sears!' Randolph's voice boomed over the webcam. 'It's been a while.'

I held my breath. I could tell from the tone of the silver fox's voice he'd been caught off guard but was trying to hide it behind blustering bravado. This was the first time they'd come face to face since they'd fallen out. Even though it was via the webcam, I wondered if the confrontation would turn bitter and nasty.

'Yes, it has,' Sears said, stepping into the office. He was wearing an expensive rain jacket, and his hair was wet. He pushed it back from his face and took out swatches of fabric samples from his pocket. They were completely dry. He handed them to me.

'The ladies made me feel guilty for withholding information about new trends in the fashion market,' Sears explained to Randolph.

I studied the samples. There were four batches, and each one had around twenty different fabrics in it. At first glance they were great. This would save me having to gather bits and pieces to put together my future design presentation. Sears had always been great at sussing out fabrics, and this information was of real value to me.

'Thanks Sears,' I said, smiling at him.

Randolph commanded Sears' attention. 'Old differences aside, we used to make one hell of a team. Ever thought of coming back into the company?'

'I've thought about it, yes, but I've always been one for leaving burning bridges alight and not looking back,' Sears said.

'I used to have that fire in me,' Randolph said proudly. 'Still do when I'm cornered.'

'Perhaps we'll meet up when I get back to Manhattan,' Sears said to Randolph.

The silver fox nodded. 'Let's do that.'

Sears went to leave, but before he did, he leaned close to me and spoke in a private whisper. 'Will you have dinner with me tonight?'

Sapphire eyes urged me to agree, so I did. 'Yes, I will,' I whispered.

'I'll pick you up at eight.'

'What have you done with your hair this time, Blue?' Randolph boomed. 'Quite the chameleon aren't you? Very pretty, and what's that you're wearing, some sort of suit is it?'

I gave him a long length view. 'It's a plaid suit, Randolph.'

'Nothing plain about it. Love it! Add it to the future collection. It could be very popular.'

'What, my suit?' But he wasn't listening.

'Get some photographs of it. I've got clients nipping at my heels for something fresh and exciting. There's something about that suit that's right on the money, Blue.'

I mouthed to Verde that this was *my* suit, not a designer's. I couldn't have the secrets of my bitch–proof suit coming out.

Verde tried to explain to Randolph. 'Blue's suit is —'

But Randolph wasn't listening properly.

'I'll deal with it,' Verde said to me. 'I'll tell him the suit was stolen in the night.'

After Sears and Randolph had gone, Emer made us a fresh pot of tea.

I was just about to enjoy my fruit salad and a cup of tea when my phone rang.

'Blue Byrne? It's Octavien O'Flannigan. Could you pop round for a quick fitting? Your suit's going to be ready sooner than I thought.'

I smoothed my hair into a chignon using some of Verde's hair products, and slicked on my amber–gold lipstick (an unusual color, but it gave a natural looking, sun–kissed glow). Then I put my rain jacket on, grabbed my red umbrella, and hurried out into the rainy day, heading to the cobbled nook to try on my new gray suit.

Mr O'Flannigan smiled at me when I arrived. He still had half of his white mustache. The other half hadn't sprouted at all, or perhaps he'd shaved it to keep the pot boiling under his little drama with the lady in his life.

'Come in out of the rain. What a day,' he said, his twinkling blue eyes taking in my plaid suit when I took my rain jacket off.

The labyrinth still smelled of traditional suiting fabric and a hint of beeswax, and was as silent as ever. We went downstairs and over to his brightly lit work area. My original sketches of the suit were lying on top of a buff colored portfolio alongside sketches he'd drawn himself. Pieces of the new pattern he'd created were displayed under the spotlights, and I was fascinated by the detail he'd included in the paper pattern.

He held the suit up. It looked perfect. The fine quality of the mid gray fabric was exquisite. 'I've taken the liberty of making a slight improvement to the inside seams of the skirt. I understand you didn't want anything changed, but outwardly it will look the same, though I think you'll find that the skirt will hang better and move easier when you're walking.'

'Wow! You've done a wonderful job, Mr O'Flannigan.'

He smiled with delight and pointed out that he'd sewn the buttons on personally. He'd worked round the clock on it, eager to get it finished.

'If you'd like to try it on, there's a changing room through there,' he said.

I couldn't wait to put it on, and when I did, it fitted like a dream. The slightly softer seams made a big difference to how the suit felt when I was wearing it. I stepped out of the changing room so he could see.

He hurried over and began checking the sleeves, the hemline, and generally fussing over every detail.

'It's fantastic!' I told him. 'The best suit I've ever had.'

He primped his half mustache and appeared suitably modest. 'I aim to please,' he chirped. 'And though I say so myself, I don't think it needs any alterations.'

He was right. It was perfect in every detail.

'Nothing leaves my premises until it's done right,' he said. 'But I think your suit is ready for you to take away.'

Yes! I had my favorite bitch–proof suit back! And better than ever!

'I can't thank you enough, Mr O'Flannigan.' I paid the very fair price we'd agreed, and frankly I thought this was a real steal considering what I was walking out of there with. I had no intention of wearing it in the rain, and got changed back into my plaid suit while Mr O'Flannigan carefully wrapped the new suit up for me.

'I'm delighted that you're delighted,' he said, probably using a little catch phrase. But we both genuinely were, and it lifted the mood of my entire day.

He also wrapped up my old gray bitch–proof suit, and put all my sketches into the buff portfolio. 'I'll give you a copy of the new pattern I made,' he said, folding it carefully and adding it to the portfolio.

I thanked him. This would be so handy when I needed a new suit made.

'That plaid suit you're wearing — I've never seen one quite like it. Stunning,' he said admiringly, and then corrected himself. '*Quietly* stunning.'

I caught a glimpse of the suit in a mirror. The deep claret carpet had brought out the fine amethyst threads. Lit by the blue daylight bulbs he used above his work table to create a natural light, these gave a violet–blue tint to the plaid.

He stood back and studied me thoughtfully. 'I think I've figured out what it is about your suits that makes them special. It's not what's *right* about them — it's what's *not wrong* with them.'

I smiled. His conclusion was the nearest to being accurate that I'd come across.

Before leaving I handed him a personal invitation to the extravaganza. I didn't know whether he'd want to go, but I thought I'd make the offer.

'A masquerade ball! Oh I'd love to go. Thank you, Blue. I shall look forward to it.'

He showed me to the door, helped me on with my rain jacket, and said he'd see me at the ball. Then he looked again at the invitation. 'I see there's a speedboat race. Can anyone enter?'

'Eh, yes. It's an open race, though competitors have to register their intention of entering at least three days before the event.'

He rubbed his hands with glee. 'Wonderful, wonderful. Put my name down on the competitors' list. I've always wanted to enter this type of race.'

I tried to be tactful as I said, 'So, you're into speedboat racing?'

'For my sixty–seventh birthday years ago, I decided to have a few lessons and took to it like a duck to water. Wish I'd done it ages ago. For my birthday last year I splashed out and bought myself a small speedboat. Oh I know what you're thinking. What's a man my age buying a small speedboat for? I should've gone for a bigger one. But you see, the smaller boats are nippier through the water and can turn a lot quicker.'

He'd got it half right when he said he knew what I was thinking. Visions of Octavien O'Flannigan let loose in the Irish Sea in a speedboat didn't bear thinking about. 'I'll put your name on the competitors' list,' I promised. Who knows, I thought, maybe he had a natural talent for sailing.

'I've been to the sailing event the past few years. Never entered before. Morgan Daire's the organizer and he usually walks away with the trophies, but perhaps he'll be one short this year,' he joked.

As I'd already confided in him previously about Morgan being my ex, I thought I'd bring up about his design work. 'He's venturing into fashion design.'

'Prrrph! He's playing at it. Needs a better finish on his garments — the ones I've seen anyway. He's kept it all under his hat. Hasn't wanted to risk criticism. But word gets around. You can't keep a secret like that indefinitely. I hear he's launching publicly soon. He'll still need a crisper finish on his hemlines. That'll come with experience.' He paused and then confided, 'I hear he was out on his speedboat yesterday, diving into the sea to rescue some silly, young woman who'd gone yachting during a squall.'

'Really?' I said searching his eyes for any hint that he knew it was me. Nothing. I'd got away with it.

I thanked him again for making the suit, put my umbrella up and hurried out into the rain that was bouncing off the cobblestones.

On the way back I popped into a new jewelry exhibition in an art gallery I'd seen a few days ago. When futurehunting for fashion, you have to include accessories and peripherals — jewelry, handbags, shoes, scarves, makeup and hairstyles. You need to have a good eye for color and design, fabric textures, and know what was fashionable throughout each of the last ten decades (at least) on an international basis. Then, when you see something that looks good, you ask the crunch question — what era would that item belong in? If you have a problem slotting it into a niche decade, there's a chance you've found something new and original or that has a timeless quality to it.

The jewelry exhibition was quite busy. I noticed a few items of jewelry on display that had a timeless quality and one or two pieces that could possibly be part of a future trend.

Gold was the key trend. Not just any gold. It was lustrous *green gold*. 'It's specially created,' one of the exhibitors told me. 'The gold is mixed with silver and other metals to make a yellowy–green colored gold alloy. It has to be mixed just right for maximum effect.'

I was so excited about this and thought that the color was beautiful.

The art gallery let me try on a couple of the rings, fantastic engagement rings, and I have to say, the hint of green in the gold made the diamonds and other gems sparkle like green fire. Very flattering and so unusual. I loved it. I also thought that it was typical of fate skewering me with a big pointy finger as if to say — aha! You missed out on an engagement sparkler from Morgan Daire. Your sense of timing really is shit!

I took some notes about the jewelry designers, and then headed back to the office, sheltering the bag containing my new suit and the portfolio.

Walking in the rain, and having just tried on engagement rings, my mind began to dwell on what might have been with Morgan. Frankly, I'd pushed the thought of him having a ring for me to the back of my mind since Verde had told me. I felt that if I thought about it too deeply I'd be overwhelmed with bitterness and loss, thinking how close I came to being his wife.

For the truth is, if we hadn't had the fight that night and he'd asked me to marry him, I'd have said yes. I'd have planned my wedding, the dress, the whole thing. I would've become Mrs Morgan Daire.

Keeping a firm grip on the umbrella, I took a deep breath and walked on, even though I could've wept more buckets of tears than there was rain. But sobbing in the middle of Temple Bar, even on a stormy day, wouldn't have been acceptable. Instead I pushed the hurt, caused by the chance I'd missed, back into the shadows where I didn't need to think about it, and hurried into the offices to finish sketching the designs for the masquerade masks.

Emer was shouting down the phone to someone. 'No, those are spurious lies! Verde Valmont didn't deliberately flash her tits at the party. If there's one person who's got nothing to trumpet about in that department, it's her. Her dress disintegrated. She wouldn't dream of flaunting her chesticles, so you can fuck off!'

Verde was sitting at her desk rolling her eyes at me. 'The local press got wind of what happened to my dress at Murphy's party.'

'The only thing doing a disappearing act,' Emer yelled down the phone, 'is your career if you dare print an untruthful word of it.' A long pause. 'Well, apology accepted.' Pause. 'Yes, it's an easy mistake to make especially as technically her wares were on display.' Pause. 'Listen, if you're that hard up for good stories for your newspaper, you should get yourself down to Dun Laoghaire for the extravaganza I told you about. *Everyone's* going to be there. We've ensnared quite a few celebrities. Two top models, whose names are household fodder for the glossy mags, are going to open the proceedings by diving into the sea, skimpily dressed as mermaids.'

Verde motioned to Emer to hand over the phone so she could speak to the journalist.

'This is Verde Valmont. Have you ever heard of Magenta Malone? She's going to be covering the event with her news team.' Pause. 'You have? Well, that harridan is planning to steal your thunder by scooping the latest gossip and behind the scenes goings on. If I were you, I'd pick up the gauntlet and make sure you get the stories and photographs before she syndicates and sells them.'

The journalist took the bait. They were particularly interested in the mermaid daring do.

Having dealt with the journalist, Verde and Emer asked if I got my suit, and I told them yes, but didn't make a big deal about it so as not to raise suspicion. As I've said before — to highlight it is to risk reducing its effectiveness. I shook the rain from the bag that it was in and nonchalantly hung the suit up in my office.

The afternoon passed in a blaze of colorful designs and sparkles as I added the finishing touches to the masks.

'They're all bewitching,' Emer said.

Verde leaned over my shoulder to have a look at the sketches. 'I love the gold and silver on mine, but the bronze, copper and emerald colors of Emer's mask are stunning. And yours, Blue — aquamarine, sea greens and silver — exquisite.'

'I'm sure Murphy will make a great job of them,' I said. 'I promised I'd e–mail the sketches off to him this afternoon.'

Verde nodded and then smiled knowingly. 'Where's Sears taking you for dinner tonight?'

There was no point in denying it. Verde and Emer knew fine he'd asked me out.

'Are there no secrets in this world?' I said jokingly.

Verde's eyes sparkled wickedly. 'Not in our world, Blue.'

'What do you think he's after?' Emer said in a hushed tone. 'Apart from all your secrets and a flip in the duvet?'

'It's just dinner. Nothing more.'

Verde looked at Emer. 'Do we believe her?'

Emer sighed. 'Unfortunately she could be telling the truth. She could be having a romantic dinner with one of the most gorgeous men I've seen, who really likes her. And at the end of the night she'll turn down his passionate advances.'

'Sears won't be making any advances,' I protested. 'I think he just wants to talk.'

'Oh!' Emer gasped suddenly and looked behind her. 'What was that?'

For a second she fooled me.

'Ah, it was just Blue's big chance for a hot night of passion flying right out the window.'

We laughed, and somehow even the torturous thoughts of missing out on being Mrs Morgan Daire, faded into the happy atmosphere around us.

'If I know Sears, he won't be planning a romantic dinner,' I said.

But I was wrong . . .

Chapter Sixteen

Enviable Green Hair

It was Verde and Emer's fault that I'd worked myself up into a frenzy of nervous anticipation. They were the ones who'd put doubts in my head about passionate advances and lustful liaisons. Sears was due to pick me up at my hotel room, but my imagination had been working overtime, churning over the reasons why he'd invited me to have dinner with him. What if they were right? What if . . .?

There was a knock on the door.

Smiling to fool myself, if not him, that I was completely hunky–dory about our dinner arrangement, I opened it to find Sears standing there with a beautiful bouquet of flowers. All the flowers were blue, something I'd never seen before. There were delphiniums, cornflowers, Veronica blues, forget–me–nots and love–in–a–mist. The fragrance was lovely.

I was genuinely taken aback. 'These are wonderful, Sears.'

'I thought it was a safe bet that you liked flowers. Any woman who would run down a main street in Dublin still clutching two bunches of flowers has to love them.'

'You're never going to let me forget that, are you?' I said, inviting him in, and putting the flowers in a vase of water.

'Never,' he countered happily, and had a casual saunter around the room.

I put the flowers on a table near the window. But when I turned around he was closer to me that I realized and I brushed against him as I reached for my handbag on the bed. He smelled delicious as usual and was dressed in a very classic dark suit, white shirt and blue silk tie. He seemed somewhat nervous, which was strange for a man of his perpetual confidence.

He helped me on with my jacket, which I wore over the doozie of a dress I'd been saving for extreme emergencies. It was a blue cocktail dress, glistening with faux aquamarine gem detail. I wore my hair up, using diamante clips to secure it.

'Very different, very you,' Sears said, appraising me.

'I wasn't sure what you had planned for tonight.'

He was still too close to talk to without breathing in his scent, and admiring the intense color of his eyes and blonde hair. What the hell was wrong with him?

Or was it me? Was Sears acting like a man who'd asked me out on a dinner date and was I the one who was acting distant?

'I . . .' he paused, glanced down at the floor and then looked into my face. Whatever he was going to say remained unsaid. He swallowed the secret that had almost escaped from his lips and smiled instead. 'I thought we could have dinner at a restaurant near the cathedral. The view of the city is breathtaking, and the menu too tempting for words. Then I thought perhaps you'd like to have a night at the theater.'

Alarm bells were ringing in my head. Flowers, dinner, theater? What was going on?

'Don't be suspicious, Blue. It's just a night out. I thought we both deserved it. We're on the other side of the world in one of the most romantic cities on earth. It would seem foolish not to enjoy a night out together, don't you think?'

'It sounds very tempting,' I said honestly.

'Then be tempted.' He smiled and held my gaze for longer than was good for me. He was such a stunning looking man.

'Come on, let's go while the night is young,' he said.

Outside, the rain had stopped, the air was clear and the sky was like dark blue crystal. A few puddles where the rain had gathered merely added to the

262

reflections of the colorful nightlife. I could feel the energy from the city, and as I looked at Sears opening the car door for me, I thought — yes! I will have this evening out with Sears and enjoy every minute of it.

We drove off in his silver bullet on wheels, and I pushed my suspicions to the back of my thoughts. I could always be suspicious tomorrow. Tonight I was going to let my hair down.

Sears had booked a candlelit table at the exclusive restaurant. We had a view of the cathedral silhouetted against the night sky and the backdrop of the city.

The meal and the company of Sears were a real treat. We'd promised not to talk shop during dinner but sometimes strayed into topics of conversation that bordered on work, or futurehunting — and Morgan.

'I heard what happened last night at Murphy's fashion promotion,' he said.

'I think everyone's heard about Verde's dress,' I said, thinking this was what he was talking about.

He leaned across the table. 'It's not Verde I'm interested in.'

My heart jumped, whether from surprise or excitement. I shouldn't have been so surprised, and yet you have to understand that Sears, in the untouchable category I kept him in, never quite came out and made a pass at me. Tonight he was pulling out all the stops.

'I heard about you dancing with Morgan. Apparently the performance was one for the archives.'

In more ways than one, I thought. Murphy had secured himself a copy of it. By all accounts it was doing the rounds. Without even trying, Morgan and I had created another scandal–mongering fiasco. It was just like old times.

'Morgan was determined to get me to dance properly with him, but as you've witnessed my dancing prowess you'll understand how futile this was.'

'I thought you danced fine with Murphy the first evening the four of us were dining together,' he said, trying not to smirk.

'Liar,' I said, laughing. 'Morgan should've learned from that performance that I'm just not a dancer.'

'In your heart you are,' he said kindly.

'What about you? Where do men like you learn to dance so well? You never seem to put a foot wrong — on the dance floor or off it. Is there some secret hideout where you're taught how to dance, choose the right wine, always look effortlessly immaculate —'

'Almost get us drowned at sea,' he added, smiling.

'Ah, well, that would be included in the adventure category. Life with you would never be boring.' Oops! It was out before I could stop myself. I sounded as if I was talking about some sort of permanence with him. Luckily I was saved by the arrival of dessert — a fluffy confection of strawberries, raspberries, oatmeal and cream.

Unfortunately Sears waited until the waiter had gone and I'd taken my first dreamy mouthful of dessert before taking me completely off guard. 'We could have an excellent life together you and me.'

I looked at him.

'If it weren't for the shadow of Morgan,' he added, and then gazed out the window at the tall, imposing stature of the medieval cathedral. Its silhouette cast a dark shadow in the evening light. 'That's what Morgan Daire seems like to me. Until you let go of the past, the history you had together will never let you be part of the future you could have.'

He was right, but I wouldn't admit it.

We were quiet for a moment and then Sears said, 'You can't blame a man for trying.'

'I don't blame you for anything. I blame myself for everything.'

'Don't ever do that,' he said. 'I had to take a chance tonight before I left —'

'You're leaving?'

'Yes. I'm flying back to New York.'

'When? Why? Surely you don't need to go.' I could hear the mild panic in my voice. The thought of him leaving gave me a horrible feeling of emptiness. I didn't want him to go, but why would I want him to stay if I was only interested in Morgan? I couldn't think straight.

'I fly out before the crack of dawn. Morgan is merging with Randolph's company, so I need to watch my own business' back. I have to return to protect my corner. But I'm coming back to Dublin for the extravaganza.'

We looked at each other for a long moment across the flickering flames of the candlelight. Was he really coming back for the sailing challenge? I wasn't sure.

'I wish you wouldn't go,' I said finally.

He spoke softly. 'I wish you would come with me.'

I laughed nervously. 'I couldn't even if I wanted to. I couldn't just fly off and leave everything in Dublin.'

'You did before,' he reminded me.

It was weird. I'd truly forgotten about this, of all things, when I'd made this my excuse.

'The last time you'd been on your own. This time you'd be with me, and we'd have a future to fly home to.'

It was a brilliant sales pitch. One that nearly worked. But I couldn't go. That silhouette was still haunting me. Until I'd settled the past one way or another I was trapped in a web of my own making.

'Come with me,' he urged me, leaning over the table and squeezing my hand. 'You know I've always cared about you.'

'I can't,' I said, looking at the candle as I said it, feeling him withdraw his hand from mine. Not in a bad way, but in an inevitable way. He knew I'd say no, that I wouldn't fly off home with him. I really didn't blame him at all for trying. It was probably the most flattering gesture I'd had in years, perhaps ever.

He cleared his throat and brightened his manner. 'Let's not mope. It doesn't suit you or me. I've still got tickets for the theater. Let's go and enjoy the night.'

He was making such an effort that I decided to do the same. And so we did go to the theater. As we sat there together I kept wondering if this was the last night I'd see him in a long time. He'd said he'd be back for the extravaganza, but I'd had strange goodbyes like this before. In fact, I'd never had a true goodbye ever. People had always faded from my life, drifting on half promises that we'd see each other again but never did.

At the end of the evening he drove me to my hotel, and at my request he parked the car out of view of the reception. I didn't want anyone seeing what was possibly my last farewell to Sears.

He opened the car door and helped me out like the gentleman he always was. We stood together in the cool breeze that hinted at the possibility of more rain to come. I shivered, and he pulled my jacket around me, leaning close, close enough to kiss me, but in the end he didn't. I didn't blame him. For how was he to know my reaction, especially as I seemed quite prepared to stand there and wave him off.

'Try and keep out of trouble until I get back,' he said, smiling. His heartbreakingly handsome face was trying not to let its guard down. But his eyes betrayed how he really felt. It was the first time I'd ever seen those sapphires appear less than crystal clear. It was the saddest I'd ever seen him.

With a final smile and squeeze of my shoulders, he jumped into his car and sped off.

In that instant the most horrible feeling washed over me. Had I made a mistake?

I ran a few steps after him, letting my jacket blow off and fall to the dampened ground. 'Sears!' I shouted. 'Sears!'

But it was too late. My voice was buffeted by the wind, lost in the night like a passing stranger. His car disappeared from view, quickly swallowed up by the river of traffic.

I could've phoned him, but I didn't.

Had I made a mistake? Yes, I believed I had. Though I'd probably never know how deep the wrong path was that I'd cut for myself that night.

'Sears has gone?' Verde said, when I told her at work the next morning.

Emer overheard. 'He can't have gone. Not like that. What did you do to him?'

'I didn't do anything to him,' I said.

'Did he say why he was leaving?' Verde said.

I explained about him going back to protect his business.

'That's crazy,' Verde said. 'There's got to be more to it than that.' She eyed me suspiciously. 'Did he make a play for you?'

Two sets of eyes urged me to answer truthfully.

'Yes he did, and I turned him down.'

Emer slapped her hand on her forehead. 'Oh that he'd give me an offer like that. I'd have been on that plane and away with him.'

Verde's voice was low, and in one word summed up the problem. 'Morgan.'

I nodded.

No accusations were thrown at me, but I knew they thought I was wasting too much of my life on Morgan.

'I'll make us some coffee,' Emer said. 'At least Sears will be back for the extravaganza.'

As she walked through to the hallway to make the coffee, a postman arrived with a parcel.

'Special post for Bluebell Byrne,' he said, handing a pen to Emer.

Emer signed for it. 'Parcel for you,' she called through to me.

I hurried through and turned the box over to see the name of the sender. It was from Sears. I opened it and found all his notes and marketing work on fashion in Dublin. He'd given me all of his work — everything.

'Is there a note?' Verde said, trying to see into the box.

An envelope was lying on top with one word written on it — *Blue*. I opened it and read aloud the message. '*Find the future in Dublin, Blue. I know you can do it.*' It was signed, *Sears*.

'Does that mean he's not coming back?' Emer said, sounding bitterly disappointed.

'I guess it does,' I said, feeling as if my time in Dublin would now be less than it might have been.

The next two weeks were a blur of pandemonium. I do not use this word lightly. The flurry of activity from our Temple Bar niche would've generated enough power to illuminate a small town. Verde and Emer seemed to be perpetually up to their asses in work, organizing the fashion shows and coordinating everything with Morgan.

I hadn't seen Morgan since we danced together that fateful night. I could argue with myself that he was too busy dealing with the preparations in Dun Laoghaire for the sailing challenge, and the marquees, catering and accommodation for everyone involved in the fashion shows. Or I could pander to my paranoia and say that he was deliberately avoiding me.

I hadn't heard a peep from Sears either. Both of them had disappeared into the distant horizon. So I'd made myself extra busy and concentrated on my futurehunting work. My office was testament to that fact. After two weeks of working like a woman possessed, I'd gathered enough information, sketches, sample materials, jewelry and accessories to turn my office into a goldmine of future design trends.

Sears had told me to find the future in Dublin. Well, I'd found enough new trends to have made my trip here worthwhile. Randolph was pleased. I also hoped to find some other trends from the fashion shows at the extravaganza when I could look at the overall presentation and themes emerging.

The first of the fashion shows started at one in the afternoon and featured ready to wear designs, jewelry, shoes, bags, scarves, and accessories. From the photographs we'd been given, some of the shoes were a dream. I'd also contacted the green gold jewelry designers and they were now presenting a selection of their rings, necklaces and bracelets at the show. I'd a feeling that the green gold was going to be a huge hit. Swimwear and sunglasses were also part of this mix. Photo shoots with the models on and beside the yachts had been scheduled, and all the major events were being videoed.

Morgan had outdone himself advertising the event and there was an enormous buzz surrounding it in the press. He'd even organized speedboats to sail up and down the Liffey, under all the bridges crossing the river. I'd stood on the Ha'penny Bridge looking down at them cutting through the water and waving at everyone. That promotion alone got more entries pouring into the sailing challenge. Octavien O'Flannigan's name was down for the speedboat race. Bizarrely enough, he wasn't the oldest competitor.

The gorgeous Garda had popped into our offices a couple of times asking for our advice on what to wear to the masquerade ball. We got Murphy to sort him out, and Emer helped me design a mask for him.

Murphy had kept his feelings for Verde on hold, though I wondered what would happen at the extravaganza when he saw her in her masquerade outfit. Verde had insisted we all have another makeover a few days before the event. Emer and Verde were looking great.

Tomorrow was the big day — the extravaganza. We'd planned to finish work earlier than usual so we could each get some beauty sleep. Verde was driving the three of us down to Dun Laoghaire very early. The sailing event started at eleven in the morning. I planned to wear my gray bitch–proof suit for most of the day, and then change into my evening dress for the ball. I reckoned I'd need my bitch–proof suit as the event would be teeming with models, divas and fashionistas. I'd kept it pristine and hadn't worn it since Mr O'Flannigan made it.

As for Magenta . . . Murphy confirmed she'd arrived. 'A beady eyed witch clutching a journalist's microphone was seen soaring over Dublin's O'Connell Bridge on her broomstick during the full moon,' he'd said. 'Her bitchy cackle could be heard from here to Dun Laoghaire. No mean feat!'

So the witch had landed. We'd deal with her when the time came. Verde was of the opinion that we should go for the jugular. Attack rather than defend ourselves. I was fine with that.

Not hearing from Morgan turned out to be a good thing for me because it gave me a break to be myself. I was feeling calmer and clearer about things. Or so I told myself. I'd sort of slipped into how I was in Manhattan when Morgan was thousands of miles away. He was only just down the coast, but he'd have been as well being on the other side of the planet.

This morning I'd been up early for a hair appointment with a Dublin salon specializing in coloring. Emer had recommended them. Her hair was always in lovely condition so I'd decided to go there. She'd recently had her hair lightened to sparkling amber.

My blonde tones were given a glistening boost. They'd mixed the nearest color blend to my champagne and arctic cognac highlights. I was delighted.

'I love your hair, Blue,' Verde said when I walked into the office.

'You really suit those blonde tones,' Emer agreed, and then tapped her watch to remind me about the parade.

The parade was a popular celebration and literally thousands of people had turned out for it all over the city center. There were decorated floats, bands, music, dancers, and men on stilts. I'd wanted to see the outfits and razzamatazz.

'It'll be starting at the top of Dame Street any minute,' Emer said. 'You'll need to run.'

Dressed in my red bitch–proof suit, I grabbed my bag and raced from Temple Bar towards Dame Street. I could hear the sounds of the parade filtering down the street, and the whole area was packed with people wearing fancy dress outfits and extraordinary hats.

I stood in awe at the feeling of excitement that surrounded me as the parade made its way down Dame Street. Everyone was so happy.

I hadn't seen what the men on stilts were doing, but people were giggling and laughing and trying to dodge the stilt walkers as they passed by. Unfortunately, I got caught amid the frivolity. Within seconds, one of the stilt men leaned down and sprayed a bright green foamy substance on to my freshly blonded hair. It was piled on top like a big, foamy meringue.

The stuff he'd sprayed was harmless, just for fun, and would supposedly wash out easily. Except if you'd just had a cocktail of light blonde colors put into your hair.

I froze — and then I ran, and made my way through the crowds that were becoming busier by the minute as everyone gathered to see the parade.

I didn't stop at the Temple Bar offices. I kept going, over the Ha'penny Bridge and on to my hotel. The reception staff were getting used to me making unusual entrances and didn't flinch as I raced past them and up to my room.

I flung my clothes off (luckily there wasn't a mark on my red suit), jumped in the shower and shampooed my hair as quickly as possible.

Of course the green foamy stuff ran through my hair, from top to tip, as I tried to wash the color out. I washed it several times and then got out of the shower to see the damage.

The image I saw looking back at me from the mirror was one I'll never forget. My blonde hair, all of it, was green. I should've been horribly upset and usually I would've been. After all, the extravaganza was tomorrow and I'd wanted to look great, but the thing I'll always remember is the way the color made me look better than I'd ever seen myself.

I'll be honest, I thought perhaps I was suffering from some sort of delayed shock because I was so happy with my new green hair. As ridiculous as it seems, that's how I felt.

My hair didn't look like it had been colored a bright, brash green. Oh no, it looked like I really had *green* hair. And that's what sold me on it. Because I'd washed it, I'd toned it down to such a gorgeous shade — like the color of a clear, green peridot gemstone. It was that wonderful green that glistens in the light. My hair shimmered from the blonde highlights, though those highlights were now a lovely shade of peridot. It made my skin look flawless, younger, and lifted my features from reasonably pretty to — wow!

In hindsight it was a portent of things to come at the extravaganza. But for now, I was completely delighted to be Blue Byrne with green hair.

I dried myself off and went back to the office. Verde laughed. Emer gasped. Then we all agreed it looked spectacular.

Verde circled me to admire my hair. 'I never thought I'd say this, but I'm green with envy. Your hair is sensational.'

Emer kept blinking, as if trying to understand why it looked so good. 'No offense, Blue, I loved your blonde hair but that green is out of this world.'

Verde was smiling. 'Wait until Morgan sees you. He's going to flip.'

Emer nodded. 'It'll look great with your masquerade mask.'

I hadn't thought of that. My mask matched the colors of my dress which was aquamarine, sea green and shimmering silver. 'People will think I've dyed my hair green for the masquerade ball.'

Verde shrugged. 'Let them think what they like. You're going to knock their eyes out. Oh yes, I want to see Morgan's face when he gets a load of you.'

Chapter Seventeen

Mayhem at the Extravaganza

'Have you seen Morgan?' Emer said, her amber colored hair shining in the bright Dun Laoghaire sunlight. She wore a chic taupe trouser suit and creamy blouse and looked the epitome of a personal assistant.

'Yes,' said Verde, cupping her hand above her brow to shield her eyes from the reflections of the sun glinting off the sea. 'He's over there on his yacht posing for photographs.'

Emer's eyes widened. 'No — have you *seen him*? He's hotter than hell. I swear that man improves with adversity.'

A smile curved up one corner of Verde's perfectly painted, rich rose lips. 'Either that or all the sailing practice and running around organizing has honed him to an even finer perfection.'

Emer was nodding but not taking her eyes off him. 'I've never really seen Morgan stripped to the waist, or as good as.'

His black shirt, worn casually over his manhood enhancing black jeans, was unbuttoned and blowing open in the warm, fresh breeze. The weather for the morning of the extravaganza was perfect for sailing and for spectators. Hundreds of people were already milling around Dun Laoghaire harbor, and the buzz and anticipation of the activities to come was palpable.

I looked over at Morgan, but Emer put her hand up. 'Avert your eyes, Blue. Or risk succumbing to his sexy, Irish charm.'

'I've survived his charms so far,' I said, but even I hadn't been prepared for how handsome he looked. I actually heard myself gasp. Had this been another era, my reaction would've been described as swooning, or better still, having an attack of the vapors. His appearance wasn't deliberate. In all the time I'd known him, he'd never been a mirror primper. Morgan could shower, shave and throw on a shirt and jeans in less time than it took me to put my hair up in a neat chignon.

This morning, he'd been climbing up the rigging of his yacht when some photo–journalists had asked to take pictures of him as the main host of the event. This was Morgan at his truest — the human equivalent of a male panther, always with that edge of danger in his own environment, looking just as he would've been whether there were crowds around him or if he was totally alone.

'Whatever he's been eating, or doing, I want some of that,' Verde said.

Not that she needed anything. She looked amazing. She was wearing a deep rose silk blouse, slinky black trousers and gold bracelets inlaid with fashionable pink and ruby colored gemstones. Her vibrant red hair was swept up, giving a lift to her features, and a touch of fearsome style. Pink and red may not seem like a good combination, but believe me Verde had got it damn right.

'Look at his torso. Honed to perfection,' said Emer.

I was still looking at him from afar.

'No, Blue, look away,' Emer said. 'I can look and dream, but you can look and remember — and that's the difference. It's bitter sweet for you and will do you no good whatsoever.'

'Life's got a shit sense of humor sometimes,' Verde philosophized.

As if to prove her right, a speedboat skimmed through the water's edge, causing a wave to splash in our direction. If we hadn't dived for cover behind an advertising stand, the three of us would've been soaked to the skin — and my gray bitch–proof suit would've been wasted again.

However, fate had a flip side, and it was lucky that we'd dived out of sight at that precise moment because who should shark past but Magenta with her television media team of four very obedient men. Like whipped dogs, these men were photographing everything she pointed out. They'd fuck up at their peril.

Magenta was wearing a business suit that was two shades lighter than her name. The fabric was all wrong for a warm day like this — too heavy and a bad clash with her short, shiny, chestnut hair. A long fringe covered the top of her huge sunglasses, giving her an unflattering appearance.

'I guess no one had the guts to tell her that look is all wrong for her,' I said.

While still hiding down behind the ad stand, Verde said, 'I can feel the bravery rising in me as we speak.'

We giggled among ourselves and then turned our attention back to Morgan, but he'd gone.

'Where the hell did he go?' I said, not even trying to disguise my annoyance.

'Looking for someone?' Morgan said over my shoulder.

Now I have to prepare you for what happened next. Because I'd been hiding in the shadow of the advertisement stand, and the three of us were huddled together, he hadn't seen my hair, not until I stood up.

The look on his face was priceless. I saw the color physically drain from him, and I'm certain he was fighting to regain his composure. He hadn't been ready to handle me and my verdant hairdo.

'Green hair,' he said incredulously, staring at me.

'It was accidental,' I said.

'I'll just bet it was,' he said, his tone changing from surprise to sarcasm.

'There was a parade in Dublin yesterday —' I began to explain.

'With hair like yours,' he cut in, 'I'm sure they put you at the front of it.'

I buttoned my lips, kicking myself for even trying to attempt an explanation. Then he came away with a remark that sent the three of us reeling.

His eyes raked across us, looking at our hair. It hadn't dawned on me the effect we'd unintentionally created with my green hair, Verde's red and Emer's amber hairdo.

'Going for the full traffic light effect, are we?' Morgan said, smirking.

'Mr Daire,' someone called to him. 'Can you verify this for us please?' A man was waving urgently, holding up some official looking sheets of paper.

Morgan nodded and hurried away, throwing a token remark over his shoulder. 'If we run out of markers for the finale, I'll give you a call, Blue.'

Emer muttered under her breath. 'Gobshite.'

The muscles in his back jolted underneath his black shirt, but he kept on walking.

Fuck him, I thought. He could fuck right off.

'Your hair looks wonderful,' Verde assured me. 'Don't let him rile you. He's just being extra Morganish this morning.'

'Did you see his reaction?' Emer said to me. 'The color drained from that chiseled face of his — and the pupils in his eyes were big and dark. That's a sure indication he liked what he saw. But he's a stubborn arsehole. Too proud to tell you.'

My blood was boiling. So it was advantageous timing that Magenta and her team approached us.

'Verde!' Magenta cried, tottering along the boardwalk in killer heels that were obviously doing their job. Her feet looked sore in the narrow, pointed toe shoes that owed everything to fashion and nothing to comfort. Magenta was tall, statuesque, the type of woman you'd want on your side in a tug of war. Some of her femininity had been lost at the expense of her imposing build. However, many men found her sexy. Yes, by some quirk of fate, Magenta was on the hot bod list of male lust for media totty.

'Here comes trouble,' Verde whispered.

Magenta opened her pursed red lips and let rip about our hair — Verde's and mine. This was her first mistake.

'Red hair and green hair?' Magenta said, ignoring Emer as she always did. 'Oh how horribly bizarre.'

'At least our hair isn't alive with extensions that look like they're straight out of a badger's ass,' I said.

I thought Emer was going to choke. Verde took it better. She'd been on the receiving end of my comments a few times. Magenta had yet to learn not to poke me with a verbal sharp stick. Our paths had crossed before but only at a safe distance.

'Well, well, Blue Byrne, the only woman who'd have hair that clashed with her name,' Magenta said snidely. 'Aren't you the stupid bitch who passed up the chance to marry a rich, sexy, handsome man not a million miles from where we are?'

'Murphy? No, he's not my type. We're just friends,' I said, deliberately misinterpreting her.

Magenta smiled tightly and directed her aim at Verde. 'I've heard Murphy's your type, Verde. Or are you just putting out in exchange for some free designer clothes?'

'Unlike you, Magenta, I don't need any help when it comes to clothes, financial or otherwise,' said Verde. 'If you'd like to change into whatever you're going to wear today, there are changing rooms in the modeling area.' Verde eyed her heavy suit. 'You can leave your traveling clothes there. Believe me, no one will steal them.'

'Or were you going to throw caution to the wind and actually wear that monstrosity of a suit all day?' I added.

I couldn't see Magenta's eyes behind her sunglasses, but I sure as hell could feel the glare. She raked up and down what I was wearing. Every part of my gray suit and white blouse was scrutinized.

I stood rock steady. Come on, find something vile to say. I dare you! But no, my bitch–proof suit beat her good. Mr O'Flannigan's handiwork and my design had stopped this monster in its tracks.

Like a vulture she retargeted her prey and was about to pick on Emer when I stepped forward, effectively placing myself as a shield between Emer and her. Oh no you don't I thought adamantly. Pick on someone who's not in the least bit intimidated by a power wielding bastard like you. Pick on me.

For a long moment not a word was said, and then Magenta finally shattered the silence.

'I don't like your attitude,' she seethed at me.

'I have no interest whatsoever in your opinion of me. Truly, wire me up to a lie detector and I'll repeat it again.'

She lifted her sunglasses and fixed me with a stare that would've withered leaves. 'Do me a favor. Don't address me unless you're spoken to.'

'Do us all a favor,' I said. 'Put those damn sunglasses back on. You're taking the good off the day.'

She dropped the sunglasses in an instant.

'Fuck you,' she shouted, and turned and tottered away.

'Nasty woman,' a man said, approaching us. It was the gorgeous Garda. He was talking to the three of us but seemed particularly interested in Emer.

'Magenta's an evil witch,' Emer said, probably tempering her language in front of the policeman even though he was dressed casually in his off duty clothes. And very handsome he looked too. Very fresh and clean. Very decent.

'I was hoping to buy you ladies a morning coffee,' he said cheerfully.

Emer and Verde linked their arms through his, one on either side. 'Not at all,' Verde said. 'We'll buy you one.'

Smiling in the aftermath of the bad taste left by Magenta, the four of us headed to one of the many open air coffee places dotted around the waterfront. En route, Morgan came striding towards us, or rather, towards me.

'I'll catch you up,' I said to them. 'Make mine anything strong with lots of sprinkles.'

'You got it,' the gorgeous Garda said, happily ensconced between Emer and Verde.

Morgan had buttoned his shirt, most of it anyway, but even that failed to lessen the effect he had on me. The vapors were rising just looking at his long, lithe body striding towards me.

Whenever I thought of Morgan, daydreaming or in the lingering memories that invariably crossed my mind from time to time, I always associated him with one thing in particular — the night. Perhaps it was the connotation that the night evoked — mystery, lust, secret liaisons and clandestine moments stolen in the sexy depths of the evening. We'd had many thrilling days together, but still I thought of him in tones of flickering firelight, starry skies and stormy nights snuggled up warm and sensual.

It was testament to Morgan's appeal that in the bright light of day, here in the sunshine of this warm, summer morning, that he was just as sexy, if not more so.

He was a handsome man, of that there was no doubt, but good looks aren't always enough, not for me anyway. There has to be something more, something deeper that only the heart can see. Maybe that's what had been missing from my time with Morgan. The night was only half the romance I could've had with him. The day had been missing. And now, I supposed it had been missing far too long for me to ever grasp it back.

'I apologize, Blue,' he said, stopping a couple of strides short of me. 'I'm in a foul mood this morning, and I shouldn't be. I've been looking forward to today for a while, but gremlins keep getting thrown into the works. Nothing's going according to plan. A million things to organize.'

'You'll want to get your yacht ready for the race too,' I said, noticing how most of the competitors in the opening race were milling around their yachts preparing to claim the first trophy.

'A million and one,' he added, almost smiling at me. Then he said. 'Your green hair, what happened?'

So I told him what happened at the parade.

'Always in the wrong place at the wrong time,' he said.

'The story of my life.'

'Perhaps you should rewrite it. Throw in a happy ending this time,' he suggested.

'Easier said than done.'

He nodded thoughtfully.

There was a moment between us, not long, but long enough for me to be forgiven for thinking that he still cared about me. The moment was broken when a commotion erupted behind us on the quayside.

A white limousine pulled up at the celebrities' marquee. Two star studded figures emerged into the sunlight, were photographed in a blaze of glory, and then disappeared into the main marquee.

As host, Morgan had to go and greet them.

'I have to get the mermaids ready anyway,' I said.

'Ah yes, the mermaids. Everyone's looking forward to seeing them. A very original opener to the event this year.'

'Mr Daire!' someone called from the quayside, and pointed in the direction of the main marquee.

'I'll catch you later,' he said.

I nodded, and watched him hurry away.

He turned quickly and called to me, 'You were always beautiful as a blonde, but I think your green hair is stunning.' Then he hurried on.

I was still smiling when my phone rang. It was Emer. 'The mermaids have fucked off!'

'What do you mean?'

'The models have changed their minds. They're not going ahead with the opening ceremony. They took one look at the platforms in the sea and said no way! We'll need to think of something else — and fast.'

'The mermaids were going to generate enormous publicity,' I said. This was true. With an event like this you can never tell what's going to spark people's interest. Verde had come up with the idea of having two top models jump into the sea to open the extravaganza. It seemed like a good idea, but even we were amazed how many people said they were turning up early to see it.

'Hang on. Verde wants to speak to you.'

Verde sounded very harassed. 'We're in the shit, unless . . .'

'Unless what?' I said.

'Unless we find two other good looking women to make the dive dressed as mermaids.'

Oh no, I thought, my heart sinking.

'We could do it, Blue. You and me. We've dived off higher things than those platforms.'

'No we haven't.'

'Okay, so I was lying, but we can do it. You know we can.'

I sighed. 'We'd have to dress as mermaids. Those outfits are skimpy. You'd have to show your ass in public.'

'I've showed a lot more than my ass in public recently. Besides, I'll get Emer to cause a distraction. Take the focus off us, and off my ass, until we're up on the platforms.

'Okay,' I said, hardly believing I was agreeing to this.

Is there any more to this outfit or is this it?' I said, looking at the flimsy mermaid's costume that barely covered my assets.

'Fluff the scales up a bit on your tits. Make them look bigger,' said Emer.

Verde and I fluffed our colorful scales which were no more than wispy pieces of stiffened chiffon strategically arranged on flesh colored nylon. One of the swimwear designers had made the outfits. They were stunning turquoise, green, lilac, shimmering gold and silver creations with long trailing tendrils representing the tails. Our legs were on show — and how, with the high cut thighs exposing our asses to full advantage.

We looked at ourselves in the large mirror of our private changing room in the modeling marquee. All the marquees were spectacularly decked out with huge screens, inside and outside, so that everyone could see the fashion shows and entertainment.

'Daring but gorgeous,' Verde said, summing us up.

'You both look sensational,' Emer said. 'And you'll dive a hell of a lot better than those models.' Then she said to me. 'Your green hair looks brilliant with your outfit, Blue. You look like a real mermaid.'

'Have you thought how to cause a distraction while we're climbing up the ladders to the platforms?'

Verde said to Emer. 'I hate the thought of my ass being on show.'

'No, not yet, but inspiration will strike at any minute,' Emer assured her.

Emer was trying on her bronze evening dress while we were in the changing room. She'd had a problem with her panties and was attempting to sort it out.

'I think I'll have to go commando tonight when I wear this dress,' Emer confessed. 'Every pair of knickers shows a visible panty line underneath the clingy metallic fabric. Even my skimpiest thongs have ties at the sides that show through. But wearing no knickers will be okay. No one's going to see up this dress. It's not as if I'll be doing the can–can at the ball tonight.'

I planned to try my evening dress on later. Right now I was wondering what color my hair would turn out after a dip in the sea, but I was prepared to take a chance, especially when Magenta peered into the changing room.

'So it's true!' she said, gasping exaggeratedly. 'I heard the models backed out. Verde, really, you couldn't organize a tea party. I knew the mermaid thing was just hype for publicity.'

Emer stood between us and Magenta, obscuring her view of our mermaid outfits. 'Everything's going according to plan. It was a surprise you see. We had to put up a smoke screen to hide the fact that Verde and Blue were making the dive.'

Magenta blinked. I think it was the speed and detail of Emer's lie that took her aback. 'Really?'

'Yes,' Emer said. 'It was planned all along. The models were just a ruse. We wanted to spring the surprise divers on the audience. We thought who better to do it than two of the female organizers. A show of good faith and participation in the event.'

'You're not seriously going to dive into the Irish Sea?' Magenta said incredulously.

'Just watch us,' I said, brushing past Magenta.

'Come and get a front row view,' Verde added.

'Yes,' Emer said, 'and if you'd like to have a go yourself, Magenta, you're more than welcome, though I'm not sure we've got a mermaid's tail big enough to fit your arse.'

Leaving Emer to cause a suitable distraction, off we went, dressed as mermaids with high heeled shoes. We'd worn our hair loose which seemed to suit the mermaid look.

Crowds had gathered at the quayside to see the opening ceremony. The compere was making the announcements.

Word had already got around about Verde and me. I heard a man muttering to another, 'Yes, two

American chicks are making the dive. One of them has green hair.'

'Not real green hair,' said another man.

'Looks real enough to me,' the first man argued. 'I saw it in the sunlight.'

'They're from *New York*,' another man said, as if this explained everything.

'Do some women in America have green hair?' yet another man said, blinking. 'I didn't know that.'

Murphy came running up the quay, all wild hair and white designer shirt flapping.

'The pair of you are kidding, aren't you?' he shouted as he ran towards us.

'We're fucked if we don't do it,' Verde summarized.

'Have you seen how high those platforms are? And can either of you swim?'

'They're American, of course they can swim,' a bystander commented and then hurried on.

'We're excellent swimmers,' I assured Murphy. 'And we've got men in scuba gear ready to haul us out if it all goes pear shaped.'

Murphy's eyes were sparking dangerously. 'Does Morgan know? Is that bastard okay about this?'

Morgan was securing the rigging on the sails of his yacht, getting ready for the off after we'd done our dive. I could see him in the background.

'We haven't told him yet,' Verde said. 'By the time he notices, we'll be splashing into the sea.'

Murphy kept ruffling his hair.

A fanfare started to play.

'It's showtime!' Verde said, forcing a face of bravado.

We waved to a very worried looking Murphy on the quayside as a speedboat took us out to the platforms.

'Dive on the count of three,' I said to Verde as they dropped her off at the bottom of her platform.

She nodded. 'And, Blue — thanks.'

I smiled, and on we went.

I saw Verde begin to climb the ladder, having left her high heels in the speedboat. And so had I.

They dropped me at the bottom of my platform.

The wind was stronger than I imagined and the railings of the ladder were wet and slippery. I told myself I'd be fine once I was actually up and standing on top of the platform. But jeez! When I got there and stood with nothing but the sea all around me, looking down at the waves bobbing along the surface, I wondered what the hell I'd got myself into.

I looked over at Verde. She gave me the thumbs up, but I could see by the expression on her face that the situation was unnerving her too. But we couldn't chicken out now.

We were going to have to jump.

Then I remembered what the fortune teller had said. Water and danger had been waiting for us. We could've avoided the danger, but we'd chosen not to. He'd been right.

I searched for Morgan's yacht, hoping he'd realized what was going on. The yachts were all gearing up for the first race which was scheduled to start ten minutes after our death defying plunge. No wonder the models had backed out. The wind was getting stronger, blowing through the skimpy tendrils of our mermaid outfits.

Verde and I then gave a spectacle wave. Lifting our arms up in the air we twirled defiantly around on the top of the platforms. Verde ran her hands through her hair, letting the wind blow through it. I heard the large crowds cheering us in the distance.

And then we stood, each in a diver's stance, feet together, right on the edge of the platforms. I looked ahead. The sky and sea merged at the far horizon. I wanted to look round at Morgan's yacht but I knew I risked losing my balance and concentration. Focus, I told myself. Focus, and just dive . . .

'One . . . two . . . *three*!' I shouted, sensing that Verde would do as we'd agreed. And she did. We dived in perfect unison, executing a somersault, which we'd also agreed earlier, and hit the water feet first, our bodies straight as arrows, slicing into the sea.

I went down further than I thought, and when I opened my eyes, the depth of the Irish Sea was quite terrifying. I turned my hands, pointing them upwards, and felt myself float up to where the water was a lighter green, and bobbed to the surface.

Verde emerged almost at the same time. We couldn't have timed it better if we'd practiced for a month. Both of us punched the air with glee and cheered ourselves and each other.

I swam towards her, but then I heard a speedboat closing in. It wasn't the scuba divers. It was Morgan, and he had Murphy with him. Murphy was standing up in the boat, tearing his shirt off — and his trousers!

Morgan cut the boat's engine a safe distance away and they both dived into the sea, powering towards us. Murphy was as good a swimmer as he was a dancer. They reached us in minutes.

'Are you crazy?' Morgan shouted, grabbing hold of me.

I couldn't stop laughing.

'It's not funny! You could've been hurt,' he raged.

Meanwhile, Verde was getting a similar telling off from Murphy, and I could hear her laughing too.

As a sea plane circled overhead, waiting for us to clear the area, the guys got us into the speedboat. We sat in the back, one on either side of Murphy, while

Morgan stood up at the front, rage still pouring through him, his clothes soaked to the skin.

The speedboat's engine roared into action and we cut through the water, arriving at the quayside within minutes. It was packed with people. Most were spectators. Those taking part in the first challenge were already on their yachts, getting ready to set sail.

Fireworks were soaring into the clear, turquoise sky, announcing the opening of the extravaganza. However, fireworks of a whole other sort were causing the air to sizzle with raucous gossip and media frenzy.

Something scandalous had happened in one of the marquees. I could hear the news being relayed around us.

I couldn't make out the full story, but they were muttering about an incident that had caused shock waves throughout the proceedings — and Emer had something to do with it.

Chapter Eighteen

The Edge of Viciousness

Murphy picked up his shirt and trousers and got out of the speedboat, reaching down to give Verde a helping hand.

Amid all the chaos and everything, I tried to avert my eyes from Murphy's ahem — package. Not that I was intentionally looking, but the sea had made his white pants slightly clingy. I couldn't help but notice and neither could Verde. We exchanged a glance. Murphy was still in the rescue zone frame of mind and had no idea what he was showing off.

Realizing that Verde and I were okay, Murphy said he'd go and get dried off and would see us shortly. He passed Emer on the boardwalk. She was racing towards us with her head partially covered with a hooded jacket.

She seemed distraught.

And there were photo–journalists following her.

A man whispered something to Murphy.

'She did what?' Murphy said and started laughing. I hadn't heard him laughing like that since the night he'd seen Morgan dancing the foxtrot with me.

Obviously something had happened, but what?

Morgan secured the speedboat, growled that he would talk to me later about the mermaid fiasco, and raced towards his yacht. He had no time to change into dry clothing. He'd have to sail with his black shirt and jeans dripping wet.

While the chaos and chatter whirled around me, I was deep in my own thoughts, watching Morgan's powerful body running along the quay and then jumping on to the deck of his yacht. Every other contender had people milling around their boats, wishing them good luck, helping to back them up in their challenge.

In stark contrast, Morgan stood alone on the deck, a strong but solitary figure, getting ready to haul up the anchor himself. There was no one to wave him off. No wife or girlfriend to blow kisses, or cheer him with banners and flags that matched each yachtsman's sailing colors, as was tradition. I didn't imagine it was because he was unpopular. It was because he seemed so capable of dealing with everything himself that others felt their help diminished in his shadow.

For the first time in years, perhaps ever, I felt sorry for him. This arrogant, confident, rich man looked so alone surrounded by crowds of people. Not one of them there to wave him off.

And so I ran, leaving Verde and Emer on the boardwalk, running barefoot as fast as I could, along the warm, sun bleached wooden boards, to reach Morgan's yacht. He'd come to rescue me twice from the sea. He had to feel something for me, and not just pity or obligation. He'd been so angry at me for making the high dive. Was I fooling myself to think it was because he'd have been devastated if anything bad had happened to me? I didn't think any deeper than that. I just ran in my skimpy mermaid's costume, my hair soaked by the sea.

Morgan's back was towards me. He was facing the sea, looking straight ahead, getting set to sail the moment the starters flare fired into the air. He wouldn't see me, I realized, but still I kept on running.

Look round, I urged him. Come on, Morgan. Just once, look round and see me.

The starters flare soared into the sky and a flurry of yachts with their colorful sails filled with the sea breeze were off.

Morgan's dark sailed yacht sliced through the water. He was among the front runners from the start.

In my mind I was waving and wishing him luck.

And then suddenly he turned around and looked right at me.

I jumped up and waved.

He raised one hand from the wheel and waved back at me. The look on his face was extraordinary. I guess he never thought I'd do this. And probably, neither did I. But I was glad I had. No matter what the future held for us, it was the right thing to do.

I smiled and waved again and then walked back to the others.

Everyone was pointing at a sea plane that had landed in the water, just short of the racing bay. I kept walking until I reached Verde, Emer and Murphy, cupping my hands to shield my eyes against the sun, watching a man climbing out of the plane and getting picked up by a speedboat. The boat roared towards a yacht — a yacht I recognized. I hadn't even noticed it was anchored at the event. There were so many other boats of all colors.

'Is that who I think it is?' Verde said incredulously.

I felt the warmth rise inside me. 'Yes, it's Sears!'

Even Emer paused from her distraught chatter. 'What's he doing? I thought he'd gone for good.'

'He's back for the racing challenge!' I said excitedly, thinking no one was more pleased to see him than me.

The closer the speedboat came, the more I could see the blonde hair blowing in the breeze. His white shirt sleeves were rolled up and his tan colored trousers gave him that classic look that always suited him so well.

His face was filled with determination. He'd obviously arranged for the yacht to be ready for him. Okay, so he was late, and maybe he'd never catch up with the others, but he seemed undaunted and climbed up the rope ladder on the side of the yacht with practiced ease.

Within minutes he'd set sail, turning the yacht around, sailing like the wind. He did have a certain style, there was no doubt. Even if I'd never known him, if I'd seen him do this as a stranger, I would still have thought — that man's in a class of his own when it comes to sailing. The top yachtsman in him adjusted the sails, and then he held the wheel, gaining on the others at a terrific speed.

I don't think he saw us standing in the crowd, but inside we were cheering him on. Morgan had always been the champion at these events, and yes, I did want Morgan to do well. But something inside me, if I was being honest, wanted Sears to do the same.

'Jeez! Look at the speed of him,' Murphy said.

Verde's voice was full of admiration. 'Doesn't Sears look magnificent.'

I caught a jealous glint in Murphy's eyes, and then he blinked, and playfully grabbed hold of Verde, telling her that she needed to get some clothes on before she drove him to distraction.

'I've never ravished a mermaid before, but ooh I could be tempted,' he joked.

If ever I saw a girlish look on her face, it was then. The woman had happily slipped back into her younger years, and gazed up at him and smiled.

While the yachts fought it out, I asked Emer what had happened, and why was she wearing a hooded jacket?

As if someone had pressed a button, she started to reel it all off at speed.

'Well, I'm mortified! Totally distraught,' she began. 'Create a distraction, Verde said. I didn't know what to be up to. A distraction? I nearly didn't do it. Then I thought of you two diving into the sea dressed as mermaids wearing next to nothing, and I felt bad. You two were definitely getting the rough end of the pineapple. Verde hates her arse being highlighted, and it certainly would be climbing up that blasted ladder.' She took a deep breath. 'So with no time to spare, I went behind the main stage area to where a camera was filming the big event. Only a few models were wafting around. And then I resorted to a tried and true method of gaining folks attention. Albeit scandalous.'

'What did you do?' I said.

'Flashed her arse for Ireland,' Murphy cut in.

'She flashed more than her arse,' a stranger commented, laughing.

Emer hid her face in her hands. 'Half of Dun Laoghaire's seen my twinkle.'

'There's an International news team here,' Verde reminded her.

None of us wanted to calculate how many people had now been privy to Emer's twinkle.

Not wanting to go into the nitty–gritty but needing some finer details, I said, 'No offense, Emer, but if you flashed your ass, how come people saw your twinkle?'

'It was awful, rotten, bad fuckin' luck,' she said. 'I was still wearing that bloody bronze evening dress. I'd no time to change out of it, and as you know, I was knickerless underneath it. When I flashed my arse for Ireland, as Murphy so delicately put it, I had to lift my dress up to show it off. But I didn't see the other camera *facing* me. Facing my . . . twinkle.'

'So your ass and your twinkle were both on view?' Verde said succinctly.

'Yes. If I'd been wearing knickers they'd have hidden the front view, but as I was bare naked from the waist down, well . . .'

'Surely no one knows it was you, if all they saw was a random ass,' I said.

Emer was nodding and grinding her teeth. 'That would've been true. And that's why I flashed my backside. Who would ever have recognized me? I thought a female arse wiggling on the big screens outside was sure to cause a diversion. But of course, Magenta had to put a spoke in the works.'

'Magenta saw you?' Verde said.

'Yes, and she's told everyone who'll listen, especially the local press,' Emer raged.

'Change your hairstyle and no one will know you,' Verde said. 'The hairs on your head not your lady garden. Though you may want them pruned while you're there. Have another makeover as a treat, and a Brazilian. It's on me.'

'Listen, the hairs on my twinkle aren't that long. I don't exactly have to pleat them in the morning before I put my knickers on. All this pious hot wax shite gets on my wick. I'm not having a Brazilian, a pecan or even a pistachio.'

'Can we quote you on that?' said a news reporter.

Emer's hackles were up. 'I'm warning you. I'm on the edge of viciousness, so fuck off.'

Sweeping Emer along between us, we walked through the news reporters, shielding her from the glare. Security stopped any unauthorized men at the entrance to the modeling marquee, so we hid out in there. We told Murphy we'd see him later and went into our changing room to redraw the battle lines.

The first thing to bite the dust was the bronze dress. Emer was still going to the ball tonight, but that dress was a flag to her identity as the twinkle flasher, so another evening dress had to be found. We reckoned we could wangle one out of the many designers at the show, though Murphy would probably insist on Emer wearing one of his designs.

'Murphy's got quite a build on him,' Verde mused while restyling her hair after a quick shower. We'd both used the communal modeling shower to rinse the sea water off our hair.

'He looks a lot stronger with his clothes off,' I said, putting on a turquoise silk dress, and planning to wear my bitch–proof suit later.

'Hmm, he certainly does,' Verde said.

Emer was putting her hair up into a chignon to change her image and disguise her identity. 'Was Murphy hiding a candle in his pants? That monster would light any woman's fire.'

Verde let out a raucous laugh. 'He was giving a better display than the fireworks.'

Emer smiled. 'Now if we could just give Sears a reason to strip down to his essentials . . .'

We were giggling and laughing when there was a knock on the changing room door. It was the gorgeous Garda.

'Don't open the door,' Emer whispered anxiously to me.

'Are you decent?' he called through to us.

'Just a moment,' I said.

'He's seen my twinkle. I can't face him,' Emer cried.

I took her by the shoulders. 'Yes you can. I'll sort this, okay. Just smile and agree with everything I say.'

I opened the door.

'Hello, ladies,' he said. 'I was slightly worried about you. There are all sorts of nasty rumors flying around.' He tapped the side of his nose. 'I suspect that hatchet faced woman is the instigator.'

'She is. She's vile,' I confirmed.

'Emer's been so upset,' said Verde.

'Oh don't you fret, Emer. I've got my eye on that troublemaker. Any more harassment and she'll have me to deal with.'

Emer brightened considerably. We all did. Magenta was in the gorgeous Garda's sights. Oh yes!

'All this fresh sea air has given me an appetite,' said Verde. 'We're going to have a light lunch. Won't you join us?'

'I'd love to,' he said.

Outside in the sunshine the crowd was anticipating the return of the yachts. We found a table at an open air cafe bar with a view of the bay and watched the end of the race while having something to eat.

'Do you know any of the competitors?' the Garda asked us.

'Yes, two of them,' I said. 'Morgan Daire and Sears Pearson.'

'Sears is the man who arrived on the sea plane,' said Emer.

'Ah, right, well the last I heard he'd caught the others up in jig time,' he said. 'It was neck and neck between the two of them.'

'Morgan and Sears?' I said.

He nodded. 'And can I just say how impressed I was by the dive you ladies did. You're just full of surprises.'

The crowd's cheering increased as the first of the yachts raced towards the finishing point. The dark sails of Morgan's yacht were stretched to their limit. To his right was Sears, his white and turquoise yacht curving around into the home straight.

They were still neck and neck.

'Sears has done well to catch up with Morgan,' I said, not knowing who I wanted to win. I'd waved Morgan off, wishing him well, and thought it would be great if he won. But he always won. I hadn't imagined that Sears would turn up at the eleventh hour to take part in the challenge. To arrive as he did on that sea plane is something I'll always remember. The other yachts had such a good head start. The fact that Sears had caught up with them and was now challenging Morgan for the title was extraordinary. In a way, it was almost fairer if Sears won. But I was still torn.

And so was the crowd.

There were cheers for Morgan, the local man, the reigning champion. Equally, there were roars of encouragement for Sears, for his sheer guts and ability.

'This is just too exciting,' Emer squealed.

The gorgeous Garda took the opportunity to put a calming arm around her shoulder. She didn't attempt to remove it.

Murphy hurried over to us. There were no prizes for guessing who he was voting for. 'Come on, Sears! Beat Morgan. Beat him, just this once!'

And he did — by a whisker.

The crowd went wild. No one seemed disappointed. It was a nail biting start to the sailing challenge. Sears had won this race, but there were further races to come. It was going to be quite a day.

I was spitting fire by the time we walked round to where the winner's yachts were anchored. Magenta and her news team, along with various other media, were interviewing Sears and Morgan. That bitch was practically draping herself over Morgan. Though thankfully he appeared to be uncomfortable with her closeness and kept stepping back, putting some distance between them.

'Magenta's making a play for Morgan,' Verde whispered to me.

'Bitch!' I muttered.

She also lavished attention on Sears, but he dealt with her differently. I don't know what he whispered in her ear but she stepped right away from him, glaring daggers. Sears had her measure. He knew her from Manhattan and didn't want anything to do with her.

She'd changed out of her heavy monstrosity into a creamy trouser suit that did her a lot of favors. Grrr!

'You agree that the best man won?' Magenta prompted Morgan.

'He did, but I hope he doesn't win everything worth fighting for,' he said, looking over at me.

Had I interpreted this correctly? Was Morgan going to fight for me? Or was I reading things into situations that just weren't there?

'Oh look,' a news reporter called to his photographer, recognizing us by our hair. 'The two mermaids!' He waved at us and dashed over thrusting a journalist's microphone in our faces. 'Is it true you're not professional high divers? What was going through your mind as you prepared to jump off the platforms? Where did you practice?' And all sorts of other questions.

'We didn't have time to think about it,' I explained. 'We wanted to surprise everyone and just did the dive.'

Verde filled them in on the details while I sidled off to talk to Morgan and hopefully prise Magenta off him.

'Ah, here's Blue, the daredevil mermaid extraordinaire,' Magenta said, snidely. 'The sea water hasn't washed any of that ridiculous green dye out of your hair. It's as vile as it was before you hit the water.'

I fixed her with a determined stare. 'The only green you need to concern yourself about is the jealousy that's killing you because Verde and I pulled off the dive. Something you could never have done.'

Several media reporters suddenly enveloped Morgan, wanting comments on the race. Magenta and I were sidelined for a few angry moments.

'Jealous of you and Verde Valmont? Never!' Magenta protested fiercely. 'And as for that PA of yours, Emer —'

'You shut your big mouth about Emer,' I said.

Magenta spread her arms wide. 'Everyone saw her. I'll only be reporting on what happened. Giving every detail of course.'

'No one saw her face.'

Magenta nodded. 'All the more reason I should put a name to the owner of the phantom ass. It'll make an interesting news snippet.'

'If you print or feature one word of this, I swear I'll get even with you.'

Magenta used her height against me and slyly pushed me against a railing at the water's edge. 'Don't fuck with me, Blue Byrne. Or I'll beat seven shades of shit out of you.'

Well, that was fighting talk in my book. I wasn't about to get into a blow for blow punch up with Magenta in full view of thousands, but being a rotten dancer with no sense of rhythm paid off yet again. One of the things I'd excelled at in my jiu–jitsu martial arts class was pressure point defense and attack techniques. Subtle, effective and fucking horrible if you were on the receiving end.

'I'm warning you, Magenta, keep your hands off me or I will retaliate and defend myself.'

'Don't make me laugh. Stupid little bitch,' she spat, and then made a furtive move to squash me into the railings and give me a sly kick in the shins.

Stepping this close to me was her mistake. I applied a very effective pressure point defense technique, involving only one hand, to Magenta's nose area. The strength in her faded almost instantly. Her eyes stared down at me in disbelief that a little bitch like me could screw with her.

She backed off sharpish! Her face was drained of color, and she had a wary look in her eyes.

'Keep the fuck away from me,' I warned her. 'And keep away from Morgan Daire.'

Her eyes sparked at the mention of his name, and I almost wished I hadn't said.

She smiled to herself and stepped away, melting back into the media crowd. Our confrontation hadn't even been noticed. Not by anyone.

Sears smiled over at me. I smiled back, feeling better just seeing him. There were too many people between us for me to talk to him, but I mouthed my congratulations. '*Well done, Sears. Good to see you back.*'

He nodded, pleased to see me too, and gave me a thumbs up for my green hair.

Oh that I wasn't being torn apart by feelings for both Sears and Morgan. But right now, if I'd had to say where my feelings lay, and had done for many years, it was still with Morgan. I couldn't help myself, and maybe, deep down, I didn't want to. I'd harbored a hope that Morgan and I would somehow get back together again, to have a chance to be what we could've been all those years ago.

Morgan saw me smiling warmly at Sears and looked away, his face suddenly dark, as if a shadow had crossed it. As he turned away from me, Magenta made another play for him. This time, he took the bait, or partially did, and accepted her offer to have lunch and do a full interview about the extravaganza.

There was nothing I could do. Or was there?

I hurried after them. 'Morgan, I need to ask a favor of you. Not for me, for someone else.'

He stopped immediately. 'A favor?'

'Yes. It's for Emer. Will you take her out on your yacht? Even for a quick trip? She's always wanted to sail on a posh yacht, but she thinks no one will ever invite her.'

Magenta opened her mouth and let rip with what she thought about Emer. Morgan frowned. 'How dare you stand there and undermine that young woman's character. You were invited to this event as a guest.'

Magenta reeled back. 'But I —'

Morgan ignored her and turned to me. 'Where is Emer?'

I pointed towards the opposite side of the boardwalk. 'Over there, with Verde and Murphy.'

He put his hand gently on my back and escorted me away with him, leaving Magenta to fume.

'What about the interview?' she yelled.

'Forget it!' he shouted, not even looking round at her.

The gorgeous Garda had disappeared again, leaving only Verde and Murphy chatting to Emer.

I could see the curious expressions on their faces as we approached.

'Emer,' Morgan said. 'I hear you've always wanted to sail on a yacht. I'm about to take mine out again. I want to do a run round the harbor area to eh . . . sort the sails. Would you like to come along?'

Emer perked up like I wouldn't have believed. 'Really? Oh yes. That would be grand.'

I think she assumed Verde and I would be going with her, and so it was an even better surprise to find out that it was only going to be her and Morgan. I heard him say he'd organize a proper trip for her at a later date. In the meantime, out she went on Morgan's yacht.

Verde and I watched her from the quayside, while Murphy went off to start organizing his fashion show. Soon, Verde and I would be busy making sure the shows ran according to plan. For now, we stood in the sunshine, waving to Emer.

'What's happening with you and Morgan?' Verde said.

I shrugged my shoulders.

'Don't make the same mistake you did the last time,' she advised.

'I won't.'

Sears came striding towards us, smiling, holding the first trophy of the event.

'Congratulations,' Verde said, kissing him on both cheeks.

I hesitated.

'No kiss from you, Blue? Whatever have I done?' he said.

'Nothing. I'm glad you came back,' I said, giving him a kiss and a big hug.

Over his shoulder I saw Morgan. He didn't see me or Sears. He was too busy sailing his beautiful, dark sailed yacht in the sparkling emerald sea.

I let go of Sears, thinking that I had made a decision. If Morgan offered me the chance to turn the clock back, I'd take it, but would he? Maybe too many years had passed for either of us to take another chance.

Chapter Nineteen

The Masquerade Ball

While the yachtsmen and speed boat racers fought it out in the sea, a fiercer challenge was gathering pace as the fashions got underway. Egos, divas, faux pas and runway chaos ensured there wasn't a quiet moment behind the scenes or in front of the audience at the fashion shows.

It had started out well, it had. All the designers and models were civil and polite to each other. I gave it an hour until the hissy fits kicked in. And I was being generous. The first screaming diva moment happened soon after the initial models set foot on the runways. Temperaments like tinder aside, the shows settled into a fast flowing array of top quality designs and innovative ideas.

Verde, Emer and I were kept busy, helping to make sure the shows' schedules ran tightly. Two of the designers were personal friends of celebrities in attendance and had persuaded them to model some of the clothes. This certainly got a lot of media attention and was an enjoyable impromptu addition to the shows.

Standing near the changing rooms, I ran a finger down the schedule to find out when Morgan was revealing his new designs. According to the list, he was on within the next half hour, followed by Murphy.

'Morgan's rescheduled his show,' Emer said, coming rushing over to me. 'There's been a fuck up and a fiasco backstage.'

Murphy joined us. 'I've been asked to bring my show forward, so I said yes, I'm fine with that. I'm now on before Morgan reveals his new designs.'

'Are you okay with that?' I said to Murphy.

'Yes, it's grand. The only thing I'll need is someone to introduce me and say a few words of encouragement. The DJ who was going to do it isn't here. Not his fault. He thought the show was on later and we can't find him anywhere. The last we heard he was trying his hand at windsurfing, which is sure to be a farce. On dry land that man's coordination leaves a lot to be desired. He's about as steady as a flag pole in a hurricane. He's got the gift of the gab though and makes an excellent DJ.' Murphy paused and then smiled at me. 'Are there any volunteers to be my wing man — Blue?'

'I'm not wing man material,' I said.

'Nonsense. You've got a great voice. Just hold the microphone and chatter into it about how wonderful I am and that my new collection is fantastic.'

'You can do it, Blue,' Emer encouraged me. 'You've done presentations for Randolph. And you look stunning in your lovely gray suit. I know every critical, fashion divas eyes will be on you, scrutinizing you, but don't let that rattle you.'

Murphy was smiling eagerly at me.

'Okay, I'll do it,' I said.

Murphy gave me a big kiss on my cheek.

'I'll go and get ready,' he said and then dashed off.

What had I let myself in for? My mind was a blank. What was I going to say? And then inspiration sauntered past me.

Magenta was on the prowl for her next victim, and judging by the triumphant look on her face she'd targeted me. She scrutinized my gray suit again as she approached and still found nothing derisive to say about it. The suit was working well as a shield. Not a word was exchanged between us, and she sashayed past leaving me alone.

She'd probably wanted to criticize Murphy for choosing me as his spokesperson, but seeing her made me determined to go up on that stage and tell the truth. Murphy and his designs were great, though I'd use far more eloquent words like spectacular, amazing and extraordinary. If I could remember them and didn't freeze when faced with hundreds of beady eyes ready to rip me to pieces.

Realizing the time, I made a mad dash for the changing room where I brushed my hair and adorned it with sparkly clips. I looked in the mirror. My bitch–proof suit teamed with green hair worked well, especially at a fashion show as it gave me a quirky edge.

Someone popped their head round the changing room door. 'You're on next.'

I smoothed my skirt down and hurried to the side of the stage.

Peering out into the audience I could see Verde and Emer at the back watching everything that was going on. The place was packed. Murphy's show was eagerly anticipated. The heat from the lights could've toasted marshmallows and the atmosphere was electric.

A manic stage hand, wearing communication headphones and more wires than a telephone exchange, came charging towards me. 'I've found her,' he said into the microphone attached to his headpiece.

'I'm sorry,' the stage hand said to me in a mildly panicky voice. 'Murphy's models will be entering from this part of the stage. It's all been rehearsed. To change it now would be tantamount to pandemonium. The DJ was aiming to make a big entrance down there.' He pointed to the end of the runway. 'He was planning on milking his moment in the spotlight for all it was worth. And good luck to him, I say. So if you could hurry up and get down into the audience, climb up the little steps at the end of the runway, and walk right along the modeling runway up on to the front of the stage to make your announcement that would be great. We'll smuggle you down the side. Come on.'

'But I —'

He grabbed me by the elbow. 'Hurry up. The show's rolling. Love the hair by the way. Snazzy.'

I was unceremoniously hustled through the throngs to the little steps and given a push to hurry me up them. A giant spotlight lit me up in an instant and suddenly all eyes were on me. If only that spotlight could've beamed me up — me and my green hair would've taken their chances with the alien spaceship.

The surface of the runway was a glistening perfection. Morgan had hired the best set ups available. I'm sure I heard Emer cheer, but it was the other voices and comments that unsettled me as I walked along.

'Who is she . . .?'

'Oh, she's that DJ, you know the one . . .'

'Isn't she the mermaid who dived into the sea . . .?'

'She's Murphy's muse . . .'

'She's a futurehunter out of her depth,' Magenta said.

'I think she's that celebrity off of the underwater game show . . .'

'She's one of those daredevil *Americans* . . .'

'Morgan Daire pulled her out of the sea a couple of weeks ago. She was with a blonde man on his yacht, sailing in a squall . . .'

'I made that suit she's wearing . . .'

Mr O'Flannigan? I mouthed to him. He was holding up a trophy and grinning at me with his half mustache.

'Love her gray suit . . .'

'Faultless . . . '

'Who designed it . . .?

'Adore her style . . .

'And her green hair . . .'

Finally I reached the stage and turned around to face them. I'd survived the gauntlet and my suit had come up trumps. Phew! Now all I had to do was announce Murphy. Then I saw myself on the huge screen, which meant I was on all the big screens inside and outside! My bitch–proof suit was emblazoned across twenty–foot high screens amid the fashionistas! And still, I didn't hear one snippy remark about it.

My throat was dry, but I took the microphone and said, 'I came to Dublin in search of the future. I was looking for fashions that would lead the way ahead. Fashions that were new and exciting. Murphy's latest designs will be part of that future. His designs make any woman look spectacular, which is what fashion, for me, is all about. So if you want to look great, look for Murphy's fantastic new designer collection which will be available soon.'

I felt I'd babbled, but hoped I'd said enough, and then I put the microphone down and stepped aside while the first flow of models took to the runway.

Murphy grabbed hold of me and pulled me to the side of the stage as the models poured past.

'Thanks a million, Blue. That was brilliant.' He almost hugged the breath from me before letting me run off backstage and into the changing room.

'Did you hear what happened to Murphy's DJ?' Emer said, dashing into the room followed by Verde.

'Well done, Blue,' Verde said. 'You look superb.'

'Yes, you look an absolute treat,' Emer said, and then rambled on about the DJ. 'The speed boat race was thrown into chaos because of him when he lost control of his windsurfing thingymajig and got carried right into the path of the speed boats. Morgan was leading, and was sure to have won, but they all had to scatter to avoid hitting the eejit. Suffice to say, the boats were all over the place, and while Morgan went and dragged the DJ out of the water, your bespoke tailor, Octavien O'Flannigan, sailed through on his speedboat and won the day.'

'I saw him with his trophy,' I said.

'Apparently Morgan could've called for the race to be restarted,' Verde said. 'But he let the old boy take the glory, which was very nice of him.'

'It was,' I said, and planned to congratulate Mr O'Flannigan later.

Having got myself a drink of water for my dry throat, we went back out to see the rest of Murphy's show, which was a brilliant success.

'Morgan's up next,' Verde said to me.

I was quite excited. 'This should be great. Have you any idea what he's showing?'

'No, like everything else he does, it's a deep, mysterious secret,' said Verde.

'Not for long,' Emer said. 'The music's changed. It'll be starting soon.'

We hurried through to where the models were getting ready. Cocktail dresses and other evening wear seemed to be what Morgan was presenting. And very stylish it was, with a theme of pale grays right through to barely black chiffon.

Verde nudged me and motioned that Morgan was over in the far corner making adjustments to the jewelry and accessories. He'd changed out of his black shirt and jeans into a dark suit and tamed his sea blown hair.

He must've sensed me watching him because he suddenly looked over at me. I'm not sure what the expression in his eyes was, I can only say what I felt — passion. Passion that burned deep. Then he looked away and busied himself with the designs.

We were making our way through the crowded audience to find a place where we could see Morgan's show, when we encountered Magenta.

At first all I saw was her mouth opening and yapping, but I couldn't make out what she was saying above the music and chatter of the people. Even more people were pouring in. The gorgeous Garda, although off duty, was directing uniformed officers to keep an eye on crowd control.

Like tuning in a radio, I picked up what Magenta was saying to Verde. 'I detest fancy dress events, but I have this sneaking feeling that you and Blue rearranged the dinner dance just for me. So it would be churlish of me not to attend the masquerade ball.'

Verde's expression showed a multitude of disappointment.

'In fact, I'm looking forward to the ball,' Magenta added, rubbing salt into our wounded efforts to thwart her.

'Remember to wear a mask — a big one, to hide that conceited face of yours,' Emer said to her.

Magenta lunged at Emer. 'Why you little shit!'

'Right!' a man's voice intervened sharply. 'I'm going to have to ask you to leave, madam.'

We looked round. It was the gorgeous Garda.

Magenta's eyes raked him up and down. 'Who the fuck are you?'

'A Garda officer. A police officer —'

'Yeah, right!' Magenta snarled. 'You're a fuckin' male model. Do you think I was born yesterday?'

'Not with those crows' feet around your beady eyes,' Verde muttered.

'More like vulture's talons,' said Emer.

Magenta screamed like only a diva of her caliber could and made a grab for Emer's throat, clearly disbelieving that the gorgeous Garda was in fact a police officer.

Well, the speed with which he defended Emer from harm was impressive. However, Magenta's rage flared up even more, and she took a wild punch at his jaw.

In the crowd, I wasn't able to step in and help him, but he tilted his head aside to prevent getting the full whack of the blow. It merely brushed his jaw, doing little if any damage.

But punching a police officer was a serious offense, and the last we saw of Magenta, the gorgeous Garda had her in an arm lock, and accompanied by two other officers, was marching her outside and into a police car. She was driven away and sadly missed Morgan's show.

The gorgeous Garda came back over to us. 'Are you okay?' he said, again taking the chance to comfort Emer with a strong arm around her shoulder.

We thanked him and assured him we were fine. Inside we were cheering like crazy that Magenta was now on her way to the main police station in Dublin.

The music suddenly changed again to an upbeat pace as Morgan's show began. Several models wearing evening dresses took to the runway. The audience clapped their appreciation.

'They're very stylish,' Verde said, almost cautiously. 'But I think Murphy's have more pizzazz. He definitely has the edge.'

Emer nodded. 'Murphy's designs were the cream on the bun. I like Morgan's dresses, but I prefer Murphy's.'

'I think those dresses lack a bit of love,' the gorgeous Garda said. Then as Morgan came on stage to take his bow of acknowledgment, he added, 'He looks like a loveless man to me. There's a sadness to him.'

Sadness or not, the fashion buyers in the audience were set to snap up Morgan's collection, and Murphy's of course. Each had their own niche market. But I couldn't help dwelling on what the Garda had observed, and I supposed that in his line of work he had to sum people up at a glance.

The other shows flowed by in a colorful stream of excitement and entertainment. Overall, the fashion shows were very popular. As the last model strutted along the runway, Verde and I were able to relax and think about getting ready for the night's ball.

'If it's all right with you two, I'd like to go for an ice cream sundae with the gorgeous Garda,' Emer whispered.

We said we'd see her later.

'It's strange that Emer's fortune teller predicted she'd marry a policeman,' Verde said thoughtfully.

'Hmm. I wonder if she'll hold out for an architect?'

'We'll have to wait and see, won't we?'

I nodded, wondering too about the fortune teller we'd encountered and the things he'd predicted for us.

It seemed like no time at all until the final yacht race of the extravaganza. Sears and Morgan had tied as winners in a second yacht race. Sears didn't take part in any of the speedboat races, and Morgan reigned supreme in those categories — except of course for Mr O'Flannigan whose name would be etched into the list of winners. The final yacht race would decide whether Sears really could out race Morgan to win the overall sailing challenge.

Verde and I were sitting at a cafe near the boardwalk having a cool drink. The air was warm and balmy, one of those perfect summer nights.

The early evening sun made the sea look like silver, sparkling in the approaching twilight. Everyone was eager to see who was leading the race.

'Here they come!' someone standing on the harbor wall shouted. 'Sears Pearson is in the lead.'

Sears was only just in the lead. Morgan was gaining fast as they sailed into the home straight. Against the warmth of the sky, the white hull of Sears' yacht took on a fiery orange glow, while the dark sails of Morgan's yacht became a shadow on the glistening sea.

Verde and I stood up to see the finish of the race. Over a thousand people had gathered to see who would claim the championship trophy. Suddenly, I sensed an increase in the wind, as the tides changed and the evening took another step towards the twilight. I saw the sails on Morgan's boat fill with air, as if taking a deep breath to make that final effort to cross the finishing line first. Sears' sails stayed steadfast, set on their course, holding tight against Morgan's challenge.

I was honestly proud of both of them, and although I'd have been happy for Sears to win, I wanted the day to belong to Morgan.

By now I could see them clearly. Morgan was adjusting the sails and gaining on Sears who had a firm grip of the wheel of his yacht.

'It's going to be close,' I said to Verde.

We stood together, hardly blinking as both yachts approached the finishing line, and then Morgan appeared to surge ahead through the water and pip Sears at the post.

'Did Morgan win?' Verde said.

'I think so.'

But it was up to the officials who'd photographed it to announce the winner.

As we waited, everyone was talking about how exciting the challenge had been. It had been a great day, filled with camaraderie and chaos.

The announcement rang clear in the evening air. 'The winner of the final race was Morgan Daire.'

I jumped up and down. 'Yes!' I shouted.

Morgan and Sears had by now brought their yachts in and anchored them at the quayside. Verde and I went to congratulate them, but couldn't get near them for the crowds of excited well wishers. We stood back and viewed the moment, one I would always remember, as Morgan and Sears shook hands. The winner's trophy was presented to Morgan and the runner up cup was given to Sears.

Verde smiled, linked her arm through mine and we headed back up to the marquees. 'Come on,' she said, 'let's get ready for the ball.'

I turned and looked over my shoulder. Morgan was looking at me. I smiled and nodded, sensing the night ahead was going to be extra special.

Verde's violet and purple chiffon dress was a hazy perfection in the light of the changing room. The gold stardust cast across the fabric added a magical feel, and matched the gold and silver stars on her masquerade mask. The winged edges made her eyes look incredible.

My shimmering aqua and deep sea green dress was hanging up. I was fixing my hair into a fantasy style, upswept with lots of sparkling clips, and refreshing my makeup before getting dressed.

Emer held up the bronze dress. 'This dress stands out from the crowd. People will recognize me as the twinkle flasher. They'll all know it was me.'

'You can wear mine,' I said. We'd been so busy we hadn't arranged another dress for Emer.

Emer was surprised. 'I can't, it's yours, what would you wear?'

'Do you have Morgan's phone number?' I said to Verde.

She called him on her mobile and handed the phone to me.

'We've got a dress shortage' I said. 'Can you help?'

'How many dresses do you need?' Morgan asked.

'One, for me.'

'Come round to the other changing rooms. I've got something I think will suit you,' he said.

So round I went, telling Emer to put the blue and green fantasy one on, and the mask that went with it. I took her mask, the gold, bronze and copper one, with me.

Morgan was waiting for me at the door of the changing rooms holding up one of the evening dresses from his collection. It was in shades of gray, beautiful and dramatic, scattered with tiny sparkles.

'This one should fit you. Try it on.'

'It's stunning,' I said. And really it was. I've always loved gray. My gray bitch–proof suit is proof of that. I think gray goes well with blonde hair, and even though my hair was green, at heart I was still a blonde.

He gave me the dress, and as I took it, my hand brushed against his, and it was as if an electric charge had sparked between us. I moved past him into the changing room and closed the door over, not locking it. Through a gap I could see him pacing around like a caged panther.

'Does it fit?' he called to me.

I stepped out wearing the dress and the mask, whose glistening gold edged design suited my gray eyes better than the blue one. I gave him a twirl.

Morgan nodded in approval.

'Can I do a Cinderella and hand it back at the end of the ball?' I said.

He shook his head. 'The evening won't end at midnight,' he said in a seductive whisper. 'It doesn't have to end at all.'

I hesitated. Was he offering a night of passion? Or was he making the first step towards us getting back together again? I guess he misread the hesitation in me and pulled back from revealing his feelings.

'Keep the dress, Blue. I'd like you to have it.'

I went to explain, but an event manager had come looking for him.

'Morgan, a few of the celebrities in the VIP area would like to meet you for a drink before the ball.'

The heavy sigh indicated his lack of enthusiasm, but as host he was obliged. 'If you'll excuse me,' he said. 'I'm pleased you like the dress. It looks better on you than on any model I've seen.'

'Thank you for everything,' I said, not sure where I stood with him. Not sure at all.

'Perhaps you'll promise me a dance?' he added.

'It's a promise.'

Then he strode off with the manager.

I went back to our changing room and got an astounding gasp from Verde and Emer. They loved the dress.

'Did he make a pass at you?' Emer asked.

'No, we didn't have time. He had to dash off to meet some celebrities before the ball.'

'I can't be arsed with the celebrities,' Emer said. 'I think the likes of Morgan, Sears and the gorgeous Garda are better looking than any of the celebrities I've seen today.'

'And Murphy,' Verde added in his defense.

Emer and I smiled at each other.

Verde put her hands on her waist. 'What?' she said defiantly.

'Listen to yourself, Verde,' said Emer. 'You sound like a woman who's smitten.'

'I'm not smitten,' Verde protested. 'I've never ever been smitten and I've no intention of starting now.'

'Murphy's candle impersonation could smite many a woman,' said Emer.

'And who would've thought he'd be quite so hot with his clothes off,' I said. 'Not that I was looking.'

Verde laughed, and within a moment all three of us were giggling.

While we were in a happy mood I asked them to pose for photographs. 'I promised I'd send Harry some snaps of my masquerade outfit.'

We took numerous photos with the camera I'd brought with me. I processed them within minutes on my laptop and e–mailed a selection to Harry.

'E–mail them to me as well. I'd like a copy,' Verde said.

After sending them to Verde and Emer, I put the laptop away, and we were ready for the ball.

The main marquee where the ball was being held looked spectacular. I stepped back to admire it. Flickering candelabras and flame effect lighting illuminated the ballroom. It was decorated with large gold, silver and sparkling fantasy masks that I absolutely loved. Dining tables were situated around the dance floor and an enormously elaborate buffet stretched along one side. For those who wanted a full dinner, another marquee was set for dining and drinks. Around five hundred guests were expected to arrive, and as Verde, Emer and I were on time, rather than fashionably late, we headed for the buffet to get something to eat.

We took our food and sat down at a table and Emer read out a dance card which was lying on the table listing the various dances that were scheduled for the evening.

'It gives little diagrams of how to do these traditional dances,' Emer began. 'I'll definitely give it a go. My gorgeous Garda says he loves to dance.'

So now he'd become Emer's gorgeous Garda, I thought, smiling to myself.

Verde studied the dances. 'I'm sure Murphy will try a few of these with me.'

'Try what with you?' Murphy said, arriving with a distinct flourish, all cream linen and lace shirt with long cuffs, and styling that looked like something from an historical novel. His dark wine velvet trousers were worn with a jacket of the same color and his mask was a black and burgundy masterpiece of design.

Verde flashed the dance instructions at him.

He took them from her, pulled her to her feet, and while holding the instructions in one hand, and Verde in the other, began to learn the steps.

I must've blinked or been so engrossed in laughing at Murphy's antics, that when I looked around, the marquee was suddenly busy with people. More were pouring in through the main entrance, with everyone decked out in their masquerade masks. I couldn't see one killjoy who wasn't wearing a mask. In a sea of people, black, white and red evening dresses were the most popular colors and dark suits for the men.

One man stood out from the crowd — Sears. He wore a beautiful cream dinner jacket and dark trousers. I'd describe it as a gentleman's look from the cocktail era. His blonde hair was smoothed back into a classic short back and sides, and his mask was various tones of silver. He walked towards us.

'You look beautiful, Blue,' were the first words he said.

He also acknowledged how lovely Emer and Verde were.

'I saw the footage of your mermaid escapade,' Sears said, smiling at me. 'I'm completely impressed. I actually saw you and Verde on top of the platforms when the sea plane flew over you. I didn't recognize you, not dressed as mermaids, or with green hair. The last time I saw you in Dublin, you weren't quite so exotic looking.'

'Speaking of exotic looking, can I ask you a hypothetical question?'

'Sure,' he said.

'If we were in bed,' I began.

Sears let out a gasp and a laugh.

'It's only a hypothetical question,' I said, feeling the color rise in my cheeks. 'And I woke up in the morning with a large spot on my nose, what would you do?'

'Is that the question?' he said, laughing.

'Yes.'

'Okay, if you had this blip on your nose, I would tease you endlessly all day. I'd even stick a puffed cereal grain on my nose and gazump you in the pimple stakes.'

What a wonderful answer I thought.

'Was that the right answer? Or is there a bonus question?'

I smiled at him. 'No, that was a great answer. Thanks.'

During our conversation, the gorgeous Garda had joined our company and was standing easily with Emer. I couldn't help but think that without really trying they'd become a couple.

Murphy was laughing and flirting with Verde. Perhaps that's why Morgan didn't approach us. I saw him looking over at me, and then he noticed Sears. I suppose we seemed to be three couples, and there was no room for him in our company. I sensed this was the reason he kept his distance. If I'd been on my own, I think he'd have spent his time with me. Shit timing for me as usual.

It was only later that we met when I was alone. He approached me and hesitated, and for the first time ever I saw a nervousness in him. His evening suit was black, worn with a white shirt, black tie, and black and gold mask that emphasized his green eyes to devastating effect. According to Verde, he'd designed the mask himself.

'Everything okay?' I said.

'Yes.'

A long pause.

I smiled. 'Did your celebrity meeting go all right?'

'It did.'

What the hell was up with him? To fill the gap I thought I'd ask him the hypothetical question I'd given Sears.

'If I woke up beside you in bed in the morning —'

'That's what I wanted to talk to you about,' he cut in, speaking anxiously.

About the spot on my nose? I think we'd got our wires crossed.

He continued. 'I'd like to invite you, and your friends, Verde and Murphy and Emer and the policeman, to stay at my house tonight. Save traveling back to Dublin. There are plenty of spare rooms.'

I was so taken aback I was speechless, but then the hard lesson of hesitation hit me and I said, 'That's very good of you to offer.' I was playing for time. Time to think. Sears' name wasn't on the invitation list. That made us three couples. His mansion had about eight rooms, so even if the others just wanted a late night drink at Morgan's house and then to sleep by themselves, there was plenty of room at this particular inn. Not including the skylight extension on the roof where you could lie in bed and look up at the stars on a clear night.

'Is that a yes?' Morgan asked.

'I'll certainly ask them. I'm pretty sure they'll be happy to stay at your house.'

'What about you?'

'Me? Well, it's been quite day. It would be lovely not to have to travel back to Dublin tonight.'

We were quiet for a moment, and watched everyone dancing.

'Verde and Murphy dance well together,' I said.

'They do,' Morgan agreed.

'Who'd have thought that Verde and Murphy would get together,' I said.

'Murphy's good for Vee–Vee.'

But was she good for him? I wondered.

'I can't see Verde waltzing up the aisle with Murphy,' I said.

'Stranger things have happened,' said Morgan.

This was true. I was living proof of it.

'Though it could just be a wild fling,' Morgan said.

'Yes, Verde's not the type to settle down. It could be a summer affair.'

'As long as it doesn't rip both their lives apart when she goes back home to New York,' Morgan said, with an underlying hint in his voice.

We watched the couples on the dance floor and then he held out his hand to me. 'You promised me a dance.'

'I did. But you know I'm no good at dancing.'

He silenced me with a look that said it didn't matter. The dance floor was filled with people unfamiliar with the dance steps suggested, while others did their own thing.

'I don't feel like I stand out as the worst dancer tonight,' I said, managing the steps quite well. Or at least, faltering the same as everyone else.

'It was worth the effort then.' The green eyes behind the black and gold mask looked at me, as if implying something.

And then I realized. He'd organized these dances to make me feel better.

'You did this for me?'

He nodded, smiled and pulled me into the center of the dance floor where we stood out for all the right reasons.

Chapter Twenty

A Storm Was Brewing

It was past midnight, and I was still having a ball, literally. I'd danced with Morgan, though as host he had to keep circulating with the other guests, but this let me enjoy dancing with Murphy and even the gorgeous Garda. Everyone had loved the masquerade ball and they were still wearing their glamorous masks.

Sears came up to me near the end of the evening and wanted to dance with me. The pace of the music had slowed to a smooth, romantic waltz, and there was more room on the dance floor as people started to trickle away, heading home to wherever they'd come from. I'd agreed to go to Morgan's house later, and so had the others. That left Sears out in the cold. He didn't mention it. He didn't have to.

'I thought I'd claim this dance with you before saying goodbye, again,' Sears said, holding me close to him.

I pulled back and stared at his face, searching the eyes behind the silver mask. 'You're kidding?'

'No. I only came back for the sailing challenge. I'm flying back to New York first thing in the morning.'

I felt distraught. And I felt sad for Sears. Leaving always made me sad.

'Oh don't look so sad, Blue. I'll see you at the end of the summer when you leave Dublin. We'll have dinner in Manhattan and take in a show.'

'Don't forget about me, okay?' I said.

'Never. I'll always be here for you no matter what.'

Then we danced, and danced . . .

'It's starting to rain,' someone called out as the party came to a close.

I looked up at the top of the marquee. I could hear the rain begin to batter down and people gasped as a flash of lightning lit up the entrance of the marquee.

'A dangerous night,' Sears said, still holding on to me.

Morgan and the others came rushing over.

'Let's make a run for the car before this storm gets any worse,' Morgan said, prying me expertly out of Sears' grasp.

Sears squeezed my hand and let go of me.

Morgan and Sears gave each other an acknowledging nod.

'I expect to challenge you again next year,' Morgan said to him.

'I expect no less,' Sears replied.

Verde, Murphy, Emer, the gorgeous Garda and Morgan and me hurried outside. Morgan swept me up in his arms and carried me across the wet ground, which I thought was very chivalrous, and practical, because my beautiful gray dress would've been ruined if it had trailed through the puddles.

Taking Morgan's lead, Murphy and the Garda did the same with Verde and Emer. All I could hear behind me were giggles and squeals of silliness and glee. I think too much champagne had been consumed. Not by me. I'd only had a couple of glasses. Morgan hadn't had anything to drink so that he could drive and keep his wits about him during the extravaganza.

It was a short drive to Morgan's house. The driveway was lit by antique lamps and the house was in virtual darkness. Soon we were all inside, having made a mad dash from the car to the front door. Morgan lit the log fire in the lounge, and flicked on the table lamps to create a lovely, warm glow.

'Anyone want coffee?' Morgan offered us.

We all took him up on it. I offered to help but he wouldn't hear of it. He told us to relax in the lounge while he went through to the kitchen.

'Sears is going back to New York,' I whispered to Verde.

She blinked. 'When?'

'He flies out tomorrow. He only came back to challenge Morgan at the sailing.'

'Well, never mind. I'm sure we'll see him when we get back home,' Verde said. 'We seem to have become part of each others lives no matter what.'

I was thinking about this when there was a knock at the front door.

Murphy pulled back the curtains and peered out. 'It's Sears. Will I go and let him in?' he called through to Morgan.

'Yes,' Morgan shouted, sounding slightly irate.

I went with Murphy to the front door.

Sears was standing there.

'You left this in the marquee, along with some clothes,' Sears said to me. He took something from underneath his dinner jacket. It was my laptop computer. He'd been protecting it from the rain.

'I'm sure the clothes would've been fine,' Sears said. 'I've got them in the car, but I thought you wouldn't like to loose your laptop.'

I gasped at the thought that I'd been so careless. 'Thank you,' I said.

'You're welcome to come in and join us,' Morgan said, not sounding in the least bit welcoming.

I think it was probably to spite Morgan's attitude that Sears said, 'Is that coffee I smell? I've been having soft drinks all evening so I can drive back up to Dublin, but a coffee in this weather would be very welcome. I won't stay long.'

And he didn't. He stayed long enough for me to access my e-mail messages.

Verde asked if I'd send a quick mail to Randolph. She was supposed to let Randolph know how the fashion shows at the extravaganza had turned out. When I checked my e-mail I found two messages had arrived.

The first was from Harry. He loved the photographs of us dressed for the ball. He had a bit of news for me too. Although he was an established number cruncher working in the city, he'd decided to make a career change, to do something he'd always wanted. He was going to train to be an architect. It was going to take him three years to study and then he'd find a placement with an architects firm. I replied telling him I knew he'd be brilliant.

The second e-mail was marked urgent. It was from Randolph. It said, *Blue, contact me. Use the webcam.* So I did.

Within minutes I was having a webcam meeting with Randolph on my laptop in Morgan's lounge while we had coffee.

'Blue, I've got people interested in some of those fashion ideas you've been sending me. We're having a meeting about a big money deal on Monday morning about these new designs and outlines of yours. I want you to get back for the meeting.'

'Monday morning?' I cried. 'I'll have to fly out —'

'First thing in the morning,' Randolph said. 'Emer will arrange the flight details. Leave everything to her. Pack your bags. You've done a sterling job in Dublin. You've worked hard. Damn hard, and it's paid off. You won't need to be over there any longer. See you tomorrow. Wear that gray suit of yours. It's a deal making suit. I like it.'

He closed the webcam.

Dublin was over? It couldn't be. Was I really going to be back in Manhattan within the next forty-eight hours?

'Are you okay?' Murphy said.

I shook my head.

'You don't have to dance to Randolph's tune,' Murphy said.

'But it's my job. I've worked hard, very hard to get to this position. Remember, this isn't a holiday. Randolph is paying me to be here, picking up the tab for the hotel and everything.'

I thought Murphy was going to say something funny, make a joke of it, encourage me to tell the silver fox to go and take a run and jump in the river Liffey. But he didn't. We both knew this was business, my career. I couldn't just give it up and be left with nothing. Yes, I could find another job, but I liked my work. And what about Verde and Emer? If I quit I'd never be working with them again. Within the blink of an eye everything could be taken away from me. I had no family as back up, only a few close friends, like Harry.

'What are you going to do?' Morgan said.

'I need time to think.'

Verde came over beside me. 'Listen, go back to Manhattan for the meeting, just do it and then come back to Dublin. I'll wangle something out of the silver fox.' I think we all knew she was spitting in the wind. I was needed in New York to do these deals with Randolph. That was the whole point of coming here.

Apart from the crackling log fire, there was an awful silence in the room. No one had a good solution to the dilemma, unless I was prepared to tell Randolph to get stuffed, which I wasn't. Business was business. And Verde and Emer's jobs relied on Randolph's company making lucrative deals. Deals like the one sitting waiting in Manhattan. More than my livelihood depended on me doing my job.

Emer, who was usually one to voice her thoughts, was quiet. She sat beside the gorgeous Garda looking quite pale.

I looked at Morgan who seemed to be seething at the situation and distraught at the same time. 'I could have a word with Randolph,' he said.

I shook my head. No amount of arm twisting was going to get these deals done. I couldn't imagine Azuree or Marina DeMar, who was still hanging on to her job by her fingernails, cutting the mustard. And Verde wasn't the true futurehunter, I was. She didn't know the marketing trends of the new fabrics or anything about the green gold jewelry.

I turned to Sears. 'Can you give me a lift back to Dublin?'

Sears nodded. 'Certainly. I'll get your things from the car. You'll want to change out of your ball gown.' He went out to his car to get my suit.

He hurried back and handed me my gray bitch–proof suit. That's when fate thumbed its nose at me. The clock above Morgan's fireplace chimed that it was one in the morning. An hour past the Cinderella time line.

I ran upstairs into one of the spare rooms because I couldn't bring myself to use Morgan's bedroom. I changed out of my lovely dress and into my gray suit. I wanted to be in Sears' car and driving up to Dublin rather than drag this awful situation out in Morgan's house. It was better to hurry up and get out.

'I'll get you a window seat on the plane and ask them to have extra chocolate biscuits for you,' Emer said, her voice sounding shaky.

I nodded. If I'd opened my mouth I would've cried. Or sworn like a demon. Neither of which would've been pretty.

Verde gave me a hug and whispered, 'Don't let the silver fox get to you. Phone me when you arrive in New York.'

'I will,' I said.

The gorgeous Garda shook my hand and assured me he'd keep a watchful eye over Emer and Verde and keep them out of trouble.

Murphy was sniffling. It was such a shame. 'I'll come out and see you, Blue. Manhattan won't know what's hit it.'

The last goodbye was for Morgan. He walked with Sears and me to the front door. I'd left my ball gown upstairs. I already had too many clothes to pack. And if the dress was anything like the other things I'd taken back with me from Dublin before, it would spend its time wrapped in tissue paper and polythene at the back of my wardrobe.

The muscles in Morgan's jaw were throbbing, clenching back the rage. He was rich, powerful in his own right, and yet he couldn't stop me leaving.

'Be good to the girls,' I said, meaning Verde and Emer.

'I shall,' he said, his voice as low as the thunder growling in the distance.

'We'd better go before the storm gets worse,' Sears said.

I thought that Morgan may have taken this chance to kiss me, to kiss me goodbye, but no, he didn't.

'Be good to yourself,' I said, and then ran out into the rain with Sears.

The silver bullet crunched through the wet gravel and turned on to the main street. I looked back at Morgan's house, at the warm glow of the lights from the front room.

And then we were heading towards the city, hoping to beat the storm that was charging in with its ominous dark clouds over the sea.

Sears turned the radio on to hear the latest update on the weather.

A local radio announcer was reading the news.

'*A raucous troublemaker was arrested by a plain clothes garda for fighting like a hell cat at a lovely fashion show in Dun Laoghaire today. The ferocious floozy was driven to police headquarters in Dublin, promptly cautioned, and then taken to Dublin airport where she was escorted on to the first flight back home to Australia.*

Vicious to the last, and protesting vehemently that she came from America — a likely story — she was put on a plane to Sydney. We can only say, good riddance.

'And now for the weather forecast. If you're up at this unearthly hour and looking out your window, you'll see that the weather is extra stormy, so get your sturdy umbrellas and wellies at the ready folks.'

Sears drove me to the offices in Temple Bar. He parked outside and offered to go in with me while I collected my belongings. I thanked him and said I'd rather be by myself.

'We could be on the same flight,' Sears said. 'Though I'll probably be on the one before yours. I only just managed to get a seat.'

'I'll see you in Manhattan sometime,' I said, forcing myself not to cry as I got out of the car. I had the strangest feeling I wouldn't see him again in a long, long time.

He nodded, unsure, as if he felt the same as me.

Then I smiled at him and made a dash for the entrance to the offices. The rain was pouring down all around me, but the entrance offered shelter.

I heard his car start up, and then the car door opened. He ran towards me just as I'd unlocked the entrance door.

He stood there in the rain, his creamy dinner jacket getting soaked in seconds, his blonde hair dripping wet, and put his arms on either side of the entrance, towering over me, making me listen to one last thing he had to say before we parted.

'I'll always be there for you,' he said, his voice deep and serious. 'I think your future is with me. You and me, Blue. Just not yet. The timing isn't right.'

I frowned. My head was so full of other thoughts. I tried to understand what he was saying.

His eyes held me in their gaze. 'I've never been so sure of anything. Be safe, and take good care of yourself.'

Then he hurried to his car and drove off at speed, but this time I didn't shout his name. I just let him go, and watched the tail lights of the silver car fade into the rainy night.

Temple Bar was empty except for a few stray, hardy souls defying the weather. The storm was getting stronger, whipping the rain along the cobbled street.

I shivered and went inside.

I packed up everything I needed into two large bags that looked like they would keep my things dry while I walked across the Ha'penny Bridge to the hotel.

I didn't have a coat with me, but then I remembered about the umbrellas and rain wear Verde and I had bought. I put my red rain jacket on and took both umbrellas to keep me and my belongings dry.

Within minutes I was back outside, facing the elements, grappling with the red and yellow umbrellas and struggling with the bags.

As I approached the bridge, I dropped one of the bags. The handle was slippery in the wet, and when I bent down to pick it up I saw the tall figure of a man, wearing a long dark coat, at the far side of the bridge. I blinked away the rain but couldn't see him clearly.

He was walking towards me, his coat open, flapping like a cape in the stormy night. It looked like he'd thrown it on and not buttoned it against the rain.

I hesitated. Strange man, dark night, no one else around. Warning bells sounded. And then I felt the anger rage inside me. I was going across that bridge no matter what! Whoever he was, he'd have a fight on his hands if he tried to cause me any hassle. Everything I'd worked hard for was in these bags and I'd be damned if some brute was going to take them.

Who the hell was he anyway? Anyone out in this weather with their coat flapping in the wind was crazy. Definitely a shifty character.

I was mentally preparing what I'd do to him with my two umbrellas (another handy lesson learned from the martial arts class) when I suddenly saw that is was Morgan. What was he doing here?

I walked towards him and we met near the middle of the bridge.

'Let me carry those for you,' he said, taking the bags from me.

For a second I thought I was hallucinating. The stress and the storm and the sad goodbyes had taken their toll. But no, he really was there.

Morgan looked around us. 'Here we are on this bridge again.'

'History repeats itself,' I said sadly.

'If you want history to repeat itself I'll stand aside and let you go, but if you'd rather make a future with me and leave the past behind, tell me now.'

'We can't change the past,' I said.

'No, but we can change how we think about it, how we feel about it. These past two weeks have been torture. I've been torn apart since the night you came back to Dublin. I don't know what I thought would happen. I didn't imagine that you'd be as beautiful as the day you left.'

'I'm not the same person. You said so yourself.'

'I'm glad about that. I need a woman who'll keep me right, who'll challenge me. And you do that.'

He stepped nearer. 'There's never been anyone else to take your place, Blue. There never will. Stay. I'll speak to Randolph. I'll pay for his clients to fly here for the meeting. It'll let them see the fashions for themselves in the real environment. I think they'll jump at the chance of an all expenses paid trip to Dublin.'

'You'd do that?' I said.

'For you, yes, I would.'

'If I were to say yes, where do we go from here?'

'Short term — out of this blasted rain, into my car and home to Dun Laoghaire. Long term . . .' He paused. 'We'd forget the past, and I'd buy you a new ring. Something you'd love forever.'

'Or . . .?' I said.

'Or you can go back to Manhattan, and I'll never mention this to you ever again.'

It was my turn to step nearer to him. 'The first option seems like a good deal to me.'

Morgan pulled me close, held me tight and I thought that he would crush me. And he kept his deal. He swept me up, took me to his car and drove me home to Dun Laoghaire.

Epilogue

Dublin

Randolph's business clients were indeed pleased to have an all expenses paid trip to Dublin.

For the meeting, I wore my gray bitch–proof suit. He was right, it was a deal making suit.

Randolph came with them. Now he's thinking of visiting Dublin more often. He says it's handy for business meetings in London and Europe — and is even further away from Honolulu. Verde says we'll need bigger offices in Temple Bar, but Randolph wants to share her office whenever he's here. He likes the view. You can imagine how delighted she is about that.

Harry's flying over next weekend. I couldn't have my engagement party without Harry.

Emer is almost as excited as me about the party, and Emer and Verde are helping to organise the celebration. Verde insists there will be a theme — and is creating a special Irish cocktail for the night.

Morgan and I are planning to divide our time between Dublin and Manhattan — the prime of both worlds.

So now I'm designing my bitch–proof wedding dress. I think I'll need it. Marrying Morgan Daire, all eyes will be on me. I'm thinking not dazzling white, but not deep cream either, an almost white . . .